THE TEXAS TATTLER

All the news that's barely fit to print!

FORTUNE HEIR ALIVE!

Telling Clue Sheds Light on Baby's Whereabouts

Texas's most talked-about family was rejuvenated with hope last week with the sudden appearance of enlightening evidence in the dramatic kidnapping case of beloved Bryan Fortune. On the one-year anniversary of the baby-snatching, a plain white envelope was delivered to the palatial Double Crown Ranch, which included a second shocking ransom note and a photograph of a grinning Bryan next to a recent issue of the *San Antonio Star*.

Though the kidnapper(s) failed to comply with the FBI's baby-for-money trade, top-notch law enforcement officials are encouraged and combing the area for signs of the cooing heir. Red Rock's Sheriff Wyatt Grayhawk predicts, "The villains are probably closer than we think."

And talk about closer than you might think.... Lovely marriage planner Hannah Cassidy, daughter of Lily Cassidy—soon-to-be wife of mogul Ryan Fortune—was spotted in a candlelit cuddlefest with ferocious divorce attorney Parker Malone. And just when *The Tattler* had all but voted this ultra-eligible bachelor most likely to go down the aisle...kicking and screaming! Looks as if this wedding-hostess-with-the-mostest has her toughest assignment yet....

About the Author

SANDRA STEFFEN

Her fans tell Sandra how much they enjoy her fictional characters, especially her male fictional characters. That's not so surprising, because although this award-winning, bestselling author believes every character is a challenge, she has the most fun with the men she creates, whether they're doctors or cowboys, toddlers or teenagers. Perhaps that's because she's surrounded by so many men—her husband, their four sons, her dad, brothers, in-laws. She feels blessed to be surrounded by just as many warm, intelligent and funny women.

Growing up the fourth child of ten in a family of ambitious and opinionated people, she developed a keen appreciation for laughter and argument, for stubborn people who aren't afraid of other intelligent people. Sandra lives in Michigan with her husband, three of their sons and a blue-eyed mutt who thinks her name is No-Molly-No. Sandra's book *Child of Her Dreams* won the 1994 National Readers' Choice Award. Several of her titles have appeared on the national bestseller lists.

Lone Star Wedding

SANDRA STEFFEN

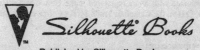

Silhouette Books

Published by Silhouette Books

America's Publisher of Contemporary Romance

Special thanks and acknowledgment are given
to Sandra Steffen for her contribution
to The Fortunes of Texas series.

 SILHOUETTE BOOKS

ISBN 0-373-65038-8

LONE STAR WEDDING

Copyright © 1999 by Harlequin Books S.A.

This edition published by arrangement with Harlequin Books S.A.

® and TM are trademarks of Harlequin Books S.A., used under license. Trademarks indicated with ® are registered in the United States Patent and Trademark Office, the Canadian Trade Marks Office and in other countries.

Visit us at www.romance.net

Printed in U.S.A.

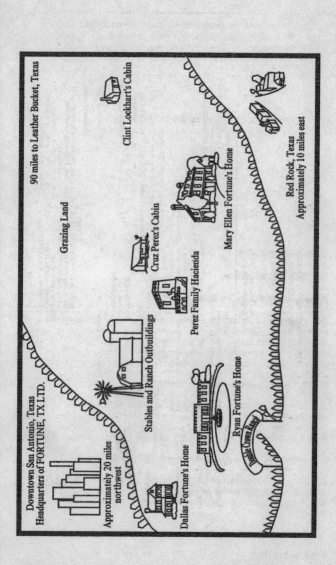

Downtown San Antonio, Texas
Headquarters of FORTUNE, TX LTD.

90 miles to Leather Bucket, Texas

Clint Lockhart's Cabin

Grazing Land

Approximately 20 miles
northwest

Cruz Perez's Cabin

Stables and Ranch Outbuildings

Perez Family Hacienda

Dallas Fortune's Home

Mary Ellen Fortune's Home

Ryan Fortune's Home

Red Rock, Texas
Approximately 10 miles east

THE FORTUNES OF TEXAS

KINGSTON FORTUNE (d)

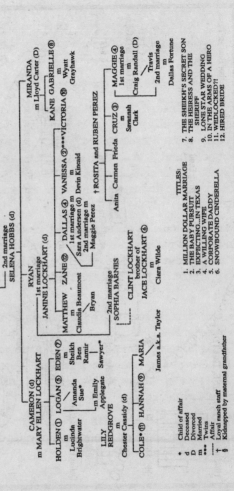

1st marriage
PATIENCE TALBOT (d)
Teddy §

2nd marriage
SELENA HOBBS (d)

CAMERON (d)
m MARY ELLEN LOCKHART

RYAN
1st marriage
JANINE LOCKHART (d)

2nd marriage
SOPHIA BARNES

MIRANDA
m Lloyd Carter (D)

HOLDEN ① LOGAN ⑤ EDEN ⑦
m   m
Lucinda   Amanda
Brightwater   Sue*
              m Emily
              Applegate
              Sawyer*

m Sheikh
Ben
Ramir

LILY
REDGROVE

m
Chester Cassidy (d)

COLE* ⑪ HANNAH ⑨ MARIA
m
James a.k.a. Taylor

MATTHEW ZANE ⑫ DALLAS ④ VANESSA ② ***VICTORIA ⑩ KANE GABRIELLE ⑧
m   m
Claudia Beaumont   1st marriage m   m   Wyatt
Bryan   Sara Andersen (d) Devin Kincaid   Grayhawk
                    2nd marriage m
                    Maggie Perez

† ROSITA and RUBEN PEREZ

Anita Carmen Frieda CRUZ ③
                       m
                       Savannah
                       Clark

MAGGIE ④
1st marriage
m
Craig Randall (D)
        Travis
2nd marriage
m
Dallas Fortune

CLINT LOCKHART
brother of
JACE LOCKHART ⑥
m
Clara Wilde

TITLES:

1. MILLION DOLLAR MARRIAGE
2. THE BABY PURSUIT
3. EXPECTING...IN TEXAS
4. A WILLING WIFE
5. CORPORATE DADDY
6. SNOWBOUND CINDERELLA
7. THE SHEIKH'S SECRET SON
8. THE HEIRESS AND THE SHERIFF
9. LONE STAR WEDDING
10. IN THE ARMS OF A HERO
11. WED...LOCKED?!
12. HIRED BRIDE

* Child of affair
d Deceased
D Divorced
m Married
*** Twins
† Affair
⌐ Loyal ranch staff
§ Kidnapped by maternal grandfather

THE FORTUNES OF TEXAS™

 Meet the Fortunes of Texas

Hannah Cassidy: She never expected to be enamored with Parker Malone, the man who was trying to stop her mother's upcoming nuptials to mogul Ryan Fortune. And although the daughter of the bride had no intention of changing her mom's mind about marriage, she had every intention of changing Parker's....

Parker Malone: As a divorce lawyer, he didn't believe in love and marriage. As a man, he couldn't resist sweet Hannah's charms. Still, the lovely wedding planner couldn't convince Parker to surrender his heart...could she?

Sophia Barnes Fortune: The soon-to-be ex-wife of billionaire Ryan Fortune was just weeks away from signing a fifty-million-dollar divorce settlement. But she was having second thoughts about settling for such a *paltry* sum when what she *really* wanted was the *entire* Fortune empire.

Victoria Fortune: A woman in danger, she found shelter in the arms of a handsome bodyguard. Could she trust him with her heart?

For Melissa Jeglinski
I was your first author at Silhouette and you were my
first editor there. This is our twentieth book together,
and I'm still thanking my lucky stars for your insight,
skill, understanding and humor.

One

Hannah Cassidy hitched the strap of her big leather purse onto her shoulder and hurried down the sidewalk toward her friend's restaurant. The traffic on the street was heavy; the honking horns, hiss of brakes, and the pounding of a teenager's car stereo were typical for a late Saturday afternoon in downtown San Antonio. Hannah's jacket clung to her back and a sheen of perspiration dampened her forehead. She didn't mind the heat. It was July, and like her father used to say, the only thing hotter than July in San Antonio was August.

She'd just come from a former classmate's bridal shower, and she had to admit she was still smarting a little. All any of her friends talked about these days was settling down and biological clocks. She was only twenty-seven. What was the hurry? Oh, she'd grown adept at smiling demurely when her friends offered advice concerning her single status, but even she'd had to stretch to find her smile when she'd opened the consolation prize this afternoon. They'd thought it was hilarious.

Hannah hadn't bothered defending the stand she'd taken when it came to settling for less than honest love. Couldn't they see that she liked her life? Her business, The Perfect Occasion, was challenging and rewarding and was even starting to show a profit. Her mother and brother were happy, and lately she'd felt a strange sense of anticipation, as if excitement was just around the corner.

So what if she spent more Saturday nights working than she spent dating? She was good at what she did, and she was earning a reputation for her ability to dream up wonderful, unusual themes for everything from birthday and retirement parties to graduations and weddings. Traditional weddings would always be in style, but lately she'd seen a trend toward weddings with a theme. Her newest client wanted a mobster-style wedding and Hannah wanted to talk to her closest friend about reserving The Pink Flamingo for the evening of the big event.

She ducked around the building that housed Adrienne's restaurant, and slipped through a bright-pink side door. The air inside the small, trendy restaurant was decidedly cooler, but the pace was no less hectic than it had been on the street out front. Waiters and waitresses in black trousers and fuchsia-colored shirts bustled from the kitchen to the dining room, heavy trays balanced high on their hands.

Hannah's best friend, Adrienne Blakely, was nowhere in sight, not in her usual place behind the dais in the lobby, or in the dining room, or in the office near the back door. Hannah poked her head inside the kitchen last. The chef and his assistant, a spiky-haired, forty-year-old woman named Desiree who was dicing vegetables, glanced up at the same time.

"Have either of you seen Adrienne?" Hannah asked.

Gerard raised his eyes expressively, but it was the woman brandishing the knife who said, "Last I knew, she was sweet-talking a customer who burned her tongue on Gerard's soup."

"How many times must I tell you it's called fricassee?"

"Freakin' whatever," Desiree insisted. "I'm telling you, one of these days somebody's gonna figure out how to sue God for making the sky blue."

A waitress bustled in with another order. "Is that true? Somebody's suing God Almighty?"

Hannah laughed out loud. She'd never been able to figure out where Adrienne found her employees. As unusual as The Pink Flamingo itself, they never failed to make Hannah smile.

Leaving poor Gerard to explain, Hannah hurried from the room. Her footsteps slowed when she entered the dining room. There was still no sign of Adrienne, but that giddy feeling was back, stronger than ever. Excitement was just around the corner, so close she could almost taste it.

A movement to her left drew her attention. A tall, dark-haired man in an expensive-looking suit pushed his chair out just as a waiter she hadn't met rounded the corner. Hannah could see the collision coming, and hurried forward, arms flailing. "Look out!"

Parker Malone glanced at his watch and reached for his briefcase all in one motion. The Pink Flamingo wasn't the type of establishment he normally frequented, but his client had insisted on this trendy uptown restaurant with its brightly colored napkins and plastic pink flamingo on every table. Parker preferred more subdued settings, but the dinner meeting had gone well, all things considered. His client left. Next, Parker had an appointment across town with his father, the legendary J. D. Malone, and J.D. didn't like to be kept waiting.

Parker was planning the most direct route to his father's house when he felt a slight jab against his shoulder. His stop was automatic, his sudden jump backward a reflex action. A dark-haired woman and a pimply faced kid both stopped abruptly. Unfortunately the objects in their hands didn't. A tray and a purse toppled to the floor. Everything else went flying. Parker bit back an expletive the same instant a coffee cup bounced off his elbow. He spun around, steaming coffee arcing like a miniature tidal wave, heading straight for the woman's arm.

She jumped, winced, and made a grab for her jacket. Parker's hands were already there, whisking the jacket off her as if it were a cloth off a magician's table. He was vaguely aware of something cold that had splattered the back of his hand, but his attention was trained on the skin he'd bared. The hot coffee had left red splotches on an upper arm that was otherwise golden brown. Her shoulders were slightly bony; her collarbone looked fragile. His gaze strayed slightly lower. She definitely wasn't skinny everywhere. His perusal had made it as far as her chin when he felt a small object beneath the sole of his shoe. He glanced down, then lowered to his haunches and took the small square packet into his hand.

The floor was littered with all kinds of women's paraphernalia: combs, lipstick, one earring, keys, a pen, a pack of gum, and at least a dozen packages similar to the one in his hand. He'd known women who carried one or two, but a dozen or more? He was speechless, no small feat for an attorney with the reputation for having a razor-sharp tongue.

"I'll take that. I just came from a shower, and this was the consolation prize." The woman's voice, deep and sultry, stirred his senses; the flutter of her fingertips on his palm all it took to kick his libido into high gear. He didn't know what the hell she meant by consolation prize, but her mention of showers evoked a potent image of long limbs, full breasts, steaming water and sultry sighs.

"Here, le'me help." The waiter poked his way between Parker and the woman. "Are these what I think they are? Oh, my God, pink, yellow and blue? Cool."

Parker glared at the kid. "It's bad enough that you're

inept, but you're in the goddamn way. I have a meeting across town in twenty minutes and I didn't plan to wear chocolate mousse on my Italian tie. This is the stuff lawsuits are made of.''

The woman gasped, her gray-eyed gaze meeting Parker's for the first time. ''I really hope you won't do that. I think I have something that will help diffuse the situation. Let's find a quiet corner and get you taken care of.''

She began scooping the remaining pastel-colored packets back into her purse. With the exception of the blood thundering through his ears, Parker couldn't seem to move.

''This won't take long,'' she said, rising to her feet. ''I assure you that you won't be more than a few minutes late for your appointment. If you'll just follow me.''

Parker rose to his feet very slowly. Regardless of how long *it* took, he was going to be late.

Hell, J.D. could wait.

She strolled toward a narrow hallway, and he followed, aware of the sway of her hips beneath that beige skirt. Upon closer inspection he noticed that the only thing nondescript about the skirt was the color. The fabric and fit were noteworthy, to say the least. She'd tucked the matching jacket over her arm. Funny, he didn't remember handing it to her. They passed a series of doors marked Employees Only and finally entered what appeared to be a small storage room. She switched on a light, but didn't close the door. Parker thought that was interesting but refrained from comment.

Until a couple of minutes ago he'd thought he'd heard it all, seen it all, and experienced most of it, but this situation had all the makings of one for the record books. Assuming a watch-and-listen attitude, he stood back and waited to see what she would do.

Her head was tipped forward, her gigantic purse held at

waist level. "I know it's here somewhere," she said, rummaging through the bag. "I just had it in my hand."

"Do you—" he had to clear his throat to finish "—do this often?"

She shrugged, the action drawing his attention to the front of a flesh-colored silk tank he'd uncovered when he'd peeled her jacket off her shoulders. "No, but I enjoy helping out now and then." Still digging through her purse, she continued. "My best friend owns this place. You know how hard it is to get a business off the ground. A lawsuit could ruin her. You don't want to sue, do you? I mean, the courts are already crammed with petty lawsuits, aren't they? If I can just find that silly little package I can get you taken care of and you can be on your way."

The single bulb overhead cast a golden glow over her dark hair, casting a shadow on her cheeks every time she blinked. Who in the hell was she? *What* in the hell was she? She didn't look like a hooker, that was for damn sure. Prostitutes didn't wear beige suits. And he'd never seen a hooker with dewy-looking skin or hair so many shades of dark brown it had to be natural.

"A-ha." Smiling, she lifted a square foil package to her mouth and placed it between her teeth.

Parker sucked in a deep breath. Okay. She didn't fit any preconceived notions he had, but with that little package opening between her teeth, several of his fantasies swirled through his mind then dove to a place straight south of there.

If he didn't say something pretty soon, he was going to lose his ability to speak.

"Lady." His gaze got caught on her mouth and he almost chucked his conscience. She reached for the package with one hand and looked up at him, her eyes large, her lips lifted in a half smile he found stimulating as hell.

He straightened his back, squared his shoulders, and took a small backward step. "Look, it's a tempting offer, but I don't have sex with women I don't know. I haven't in years."

Hannah froze. Sex? Was that what he'd said?

A gong went off inside her skull, understanding dawning with all the subtlety of a hurricane. The consolation prizes, her assurance that she would alleviate the situation. He'd seen, he'd heard, and he thought she was a common...an ordinary...a woman who...

She knew her mouth was gaping. Clamping it shut, she took a backward step. He'd said it was a tempting offer. Of all the egotistical...

She could still hardly believe the insinuation. Why, she was no more a...

A...

How dare he...

Why, she ought to...

With utmost control and precision, she pulled the premoistened towelette from the little package in her fingers and shoved it into his hand. "You'd better get your mind out of the gutter, mister. And while you're at it, clean your own stinking tie."

She spun on her heel and left him standing there, his eyes wide, his mouth set in a grim line, a crinkled, premoistened towelette in his outstretched hand.

Hannah rushed headlong through the restaurant and out the side door. She hadn't found Adrienne, but her instincts had been right. Excitement *had* been just around the corner. Excitement and embarrassment, that is. And nestled tightly between the two had been an incredible awareness of the man's height, the breadth of his shoulders, his chiseled features softened slightly by a small cleft in his chin.

For a moment when she'd first seen that little indentation, she'd wanted to place her finger there, ever so gently.

She'd never felt so instantaneously attracted to a man. It had almost been lyrical. She'd practically heard violins.

And he'd thought she was a hooker.

Reaching her boutique in record time, Hannah unlocked the door that led to her apartment and quickly took the stairs. Feeling slightly off-kilter, she opened some windows and thanked her lucky stars that she never had to see that man again.

"What I want to know is why y'all didn't get his phone number?"

Adrienne Blakely lifted the lid on a container she'd brought with her from the restaurant, sniffed, and replaced the lid, only to move on to the next container. A former Miss Atlanta runner-up, Adrienne was drop-dead gorgeous, loved bright colors, and had maintained her Georgia accent despite the fact that she hadn't been "home" in nearly ten years. "And why in hades aren't you using the air-conditioning?"

Hannah scribbled a note on the wedding planner on her lap then popped a cocktail shrimp into her mouth. A fan stirred the hair at her nape. She'd changed into shorts and a tank top hours ago. Her feet were bare, her face clean-scrubbed. Returning to her notes, she said, "You know I like to dress light when I'm home."

The two women were upstairs in Hannah's apartment, and as they often had these past three years since they'd met, they were spending a companionable evening together eating the leftovers Adrienne had brought with her after closing The Pink Flamingo for the night.

Stretching out on Hannah's sofa, Adrienne fluffed a pillow and placed it beneath her head. "And the other portion of my question?"

"I told you," Hannah said, shaking her head because Adrienne never let a question go, no matter how relaxed she appeared. "The man's a shark."

"So?"

"What do you mean, 'so'?"

"So y'all stay out of the ocean. That doesn't mean you have to stay out of his bed."

"I'm not getting into his bed."

"Whyever not? Just because I've decided never to have sex again is no reason you shouldn't."

"He mistook me for a prostitute. That's hardly a good basis for a relationship."

"Who said anything about a relationship? I was thinking more along the lines of head-reeling, toe-curling, mind-boggling sex."

"Get real."

"I am real. One hundred percent." Adrienne glanced at her chest. "It's what cost me the crown. My mother reminded me of it a little while ago over the phone. Now, if I would have been born with a chest like yours, I would have been a shoe-in, but I didn't develop large breasts naturally, and I just couldn't put silicone in my body, not even for a title and a shiny tiara. My mother still hasn't forgiven me."

"I thought you said it was the congeniality contest that got you."

"Oh, that."

Hannah smiled. Adrienne joked about that fated beauty contest from time to time, but she'd once confided in Hannah that the real reason she'd lost was much more scandalous and heart-breaking. Rather than reminding Adrienne of painful memories, she said, "Besides, if you had a chest like mine, you'd have to wear a bra."

Adrienne wrinkled up her nose. "That wouldn't be any fun. But we digress. I thought he was sort of cute."

"Sort of cute? The man was a god in a suit and an imported silk tie, which you'll probably be sued for, by the way." Adrienne waved the notion away, and Hannah added, "And even if I was interested, I don't know his name."

"Parker."

Hannah looked up from the wing chair where she'd been curled up for the past hour, and slowly lowered her feet to the floor. "What did you say?"

"His name is Parker." The trendy Southern blonde had Hannah's undivided attention now, but Adrienne continued to stare at the chipped purple nail polish on her big toe. "Parker Malone."

"How do you know that?"

"He told me."

"You've met him?"

"Somebody had to save my newest waiter from the interrogation your john was giving him."

"J—John?"

Adrienne laughed at the stricken expression on Hannah's face. "You know I love to kid. Did you really dump a whole box of pastel-colored condoms at his feet then politely tell him to follow you? My, but you do know how to make an impression. No wonder he was so interested."

"He wasn't interested."

"He wanted to know your name. Actually, I think he would have appreciated any information he could have weaseled out of us. Your phone number, your driver's license number, your social security number, your birth date, address, star sign, shoe size, whatever."

"You didn't tell him!" Hannah was on her feet, and Adrienne raised noisily to a sitting position.

"Relax," she said, pushing her short blond hair behind her ears. "Jason doesn't know you yet, and I'm not intimidated by the Parker Malones in this world."

Hannah fell back into her chair. "How did you get so much backbone?"

"I was raised in the South, remember? Y'all don't think those finishing schools only teach girls how to drink tea with their pinkies in the air, do you? What are you working on, anyway?"

"Plans for my mother's wedding."

Adrienne paused in the middle of picking up their used paper plates to glance at the lists Hannah was making. "I still can't believe your mother is going to marry one of the Fortunes of Texas. My mother would die to marry me off to a rich man. I'm thirty-three. I think she's giving up hope. But Ryan Fortune is rich, and his ranch, the Double Crown, is one of the biggest, most prestigious and profitable ranches in the entire state. It's just so romantic that your mother loved him when they were both practically children, and now they're finally being reunited. Have y'all decided what you're going to wear to the engagement party next weekend?"

"Mother refuses to call it an engagement party. It's just a get-together." Hannah motioned to a tiny closet in the alcove between the living room and her bedroom. "I picked up a dress the other day."

"Tell me it isn't beige." At the expression on Hannah's face, Adrienne said, "Sugar pie, you should wear something bright pink or purple, or better yet, red." She spoke into the closet, causing the words to sound muffled. "Something that'll make y'all shine."

"It's my mother's big night, Adrienne. She's the one I want to shine."

Adrienne swung around so suddenly the long dress in her hand swished. Her eyebrows formed two identical blond arches, her lips shaped around a long whistle. Holding a filmy, wispy dress the color of walnut shells up to Hannah, she said, "It may not be pink or red, but lordy, I do believe you're gonna be doing a little shining of your own. What a shame you're going alone. Whoever could you call? Perhaps some tall, dashing man with an adorable little cleft in his chin?"

Leave it to Adrienne to have noticed that.

Hannah stared past the other woman, picturing the stranger's strong face. Now that she knew his name, their brief encounter seemed even more intimate. It didn't change the fact that he'd assumed she was a woman who made her living on her back. It stung her pride, and her pride was important to her.

She took the dress from Adrienne and hung it in the closet. "He's pompous, he's arrogant, he's shrewd and he has a sharp tongue. A man like that wouldn't think twice about using a woman like me and then tossing me aside."

Hands full of containers, Adrienne headed for the door. "From what you've told me about that little episode in the storage room, he didn't take you up on what he thought you were offering. He must have at least one scruple."

"Maybe you should call him."

"He wasn't after *my* phone number, sweetie. I still say you should give it the old college try."

With a wink the Southern belles of old would have never gotten away with, Adrienne left. It didn't take long for Hannah to notice the flat, gray object on the table where she always dumped the mail. She padded over and reached out with one finger, sliding the card closer as if it might bite her.

Malone, Malone & Associates, P.C. Attorneys At Law

Adrienne was about as subtle as her bright pink capri pants.

There was a business address, a business phone number. Hannah turned the card over. On the back was another telephone number, this one written in black ink in a distinctive, masculine scrawl.

She knew his name. She knew his phone number. Now what? she wondered.

Now nothing, she told herself. Her encounter with Parker Malone was over. It didn't matter that he'd been the most ruggedly attractive man she'd ever seen in a suit. He'd embarrassed her. Worse, he'd jumped to conclusions, the most degradingly possible kind.

Striding to an antique desk, she bent to drop the card into the wicker basket filled with wadded-up notes and paper plates. She stared at the card for a long time, then opened a drawer and dropped it inside.

Hannah accepted a glass of white wine from a pleasant, friendly woman who spoke with a Mexican accent. Taking a small sip, Hannah glanced around. She'd seen Ryan Fortune several times since he'd come back into her mother's life. The first time she'd visited his home, she'd been in awe of its size. She'd heard someone say the house had eight bedrooms. It was grand, and at the same time warm and lovely. The ceiling in the great room was high and beamed. An old stone fireplace dominated an entire wall. Handwoven blankets hung on the other three walls, pottery made by local artists from the same type of clay on which the house sat leant warmth and interest to shelves, corners and on the top of a painted armoire that probably hid a television and stereo system from view.

The house was large, opulent and cordial, as was its owner. Hannah had liked both on sight. Ryan Fortune had promised her mother the party would be a small, friendly gathering. Hannah was beginning to realize that to a man of Ryan's wealth and social standing, sixty-five to seventy people constituted a small group.

Hannah stood with her mother near the entryway leading to the dining room. Following the course of her mother's gaze to the group of men on the other side of the room, one of whom was Lily's future husband, Hannah smiled. Lily Redgrove Cassidy was lovely, and perhaps even more exotic-looking at fifty-three than she'd been at seventeen. Her firstborn and only son, Cole, stood across the room with Ryan and two men whose backs were to Hannah and her mother.

"He'll be back in a moment, Mom."

Lily glanced around sharply at Hannah. "I know that, dear."

"Then what is it?" Hannah asked, trying to understand the reason for her mother's obvious discomfiture. "Maria isn't coming, is that it? Is that why you're chewing on your bottom lip?"

Smoothing an errant strand of hair back into the intricate knot on the back of her head, Lily said, "I'm disappointed that your sister isn't here, but that's not it."

"Then, what is it?"

Lily squeezed her middle child's hand. "You know me so well. Am I really so transparent?"

"You're beautiful, and you know it. I can tell when something's bothering you, that's all. What could possibly be marring this happy occasion?"

"I've learned that Ryan's attorney is dead-set against

Ryan and I making our engagement public. Ryan won't listen, but what if he's right? He started divorce proceedings long before he and I found one another again, but what if my presence in his life makes it even more difficult for him to finally break free of Sophia?''

Hannah shook her head sadly. Her own brother was an attorney, so she didn't dislike all lawyers, but at that moment she very much disliked the attorney who had put the worry in her mother's brown eyes. ''Ryan Fortune has been to hell and back with that woman he married when he was too blind with grief to see her for what she was. He deserves happiness, Mom, and so do you. I'm proud of him for wanting to proclaim his love for you to the world. Maybe Ryan should tell his attorney to take a flying leap the next time he sees him.''

''Oh, his attorney is here tonight, dear.''

''He is?''

Laughter erupted on the other side of the room. Ryan slapped the man closest to him on the back, then held up a glass, his eyes meeting Lily's. ''I'd like to propose a toast.''

Little by little, conversations throughout the room ceased and everyone looked toward Ryan. It was common knowledge that Ryan had gotten his height and build from his father, the late Kingston Fortune, but his dark hair and eyes came from his mother, Selena. Ryan's personality, drive and conviction were all his own. ''To my future wife.''

Suddenly all eyes turned to Lily. Lily Redgrove Cassidy stood out in every crowd, but the smile she cast at her future husband made her appear radiant in a way Hannah had never seen. A smile tugged at Hannah's mouth, as well. She raised her glass, her gaze darting over people all around the room. There were plenty of Fortunes present, of course, but the rest of the guests were a mixture of people who wore power and prestige as if it were their right, and others who had worked for Ryan Fortune for years and had earned a permanent place in the Fortune household as well as in all the Fortunes' hearts.

Pleased that all these people were welcoming her mother into their circle, Hannah smiled warmly at her brother, who winked, eliciting a broader smile from her. Her glass was almost to her lips when her gaze meandered to the man standing to Cole's right. Her eyes widened, her head turning automatically for a more direct look.

Disbelief had her lowering her glass. She might have glanced right past the piercing blue eyes that were staring directly at her, the chiseled jaw, prominent cheekbones and slightly arrogant tilt of the man's head, but she couldn't have overlooked the shadow in the tiny cleft in Parker Malone's chin even if she'd tried.

Two

Hannah couldn't believe her eyes. Unless Parker Malone had an identical twin, he was staring at her across this very room. Surely every ounce of blood had drained out of her face. It stood to reason, since her heart seemed to have stopped beating.

She managed to turn her attention to her mother and arrange her features into what she hoped passed for a normal, nonplussed expression. Hannah believed in fate and in chance. She even believed in luck, good and bad. But what in the world were the chances that the same man who had mistaken *her* for a hooker not only knew the man who was going to marry her mother but knew him well enough to be invited to an intimate party honoring his intended engagement to her mother? If the odds of that weren't slim enough to constitute bad luck, they were close.

"Do you know the dark-haired man on Ryan's left, Mom?"

Still smiling, Lily answered, barely breaking eye contact with Ryan across the room. "That's Parker Malone."

So much for Hannah's identical twin theory. "Is he a friend of the Fortunes?"

"Their families go way back, but Parker is Ryan's divorce attorney."

Malone, Malone & Associates. Ryan's divorce attorney, who was adamantly opposed to Ryan's wish to make his engagement to Lily public. And the first man Hannah had been completely attracted to in a long, long time. Three separate identities all rolled into one. Hannah couldn't believe her run of lu—

"Luck," Ryan said.

Hannah started, because Ryan said the word in the exact moment she'd been thinking it.

"It was a fluke, really," he added, "that has reunited Lily and me. Therefore, I'd like to propose another toast. To the divine wheel of fortune that brought Lily back into my life. To chance and circumstance and a marvelous coincidence that changed my life."

Hannah's gaze was inexplicably drawn to Parker once again. He lifted his glass to her in a private toast and graced her with a smile that was stark and white and so intimate she had to remind herself to breathe.

While Ryan made his way toward Lily, people throughout the room drank to his health and future and patted him on the back as he passed. Hannah admired the way her mother held her ground, raised her chin, as regal as a queen, and waited for Ryan to stroll gallantly across the room. She was old-fashioned that way, wanting the man to come to her. The Cassidys had never had the Fortunes' money, but they equaled them in pride.

Although Ryan accepted congratulations on his way by, his attention on Lily was steadfast. The degree of his devotion to her mother brought a lump to Hannah's throat. It was the kind of love she was waiting for.

Ryan kissed Lily's lips, and then Hannah's cheek. "Thanks for coming, Hannah," he said.

"You're welcome."

"I mean it," he said. "It means so much to me to have both you and Cole here. I understand Maria isn't as pleased about Lily's and my upcoming wedding as you and Cole.

I only hope that in time, she will come to realize how deeply I care for your mother."

Lily and Hannah shared a long look and a heartfelt sigh. Maria was every bit as beautiful as Lily, but there was a hard edge to Maria that simply didn't exist in her mother and sister. Although Lily had spoken with Maria by telephone a month ago, neither she nor Hannah had been successful in connecting on a meaningful level with the youngest Cassidy in a very long time.

"I don't like to admit it," Lily said, looking earnestly into Ryan's eyes, "but I'm afraid Maria is ashamed of her meager roots."

Ryan placed his hand on Lily's cheek as if he couldn't get enough of touching her. "Families are complicated. God knows, mine is." His gaze strayed over Lily's head where his son, Matthew stood, all alone.

Hannah had heard rumors that Matthew and his wife, Claudia, had separated. Her heart went out to the couple, whose lives had become twisted in tragedy and haunted by unanswered questions since their newborn son had been kidnapped and another child returned in his place. Matthew and Claudia were both here, but not together, the events of the past year etched in each of their faces.

Ryan shook his head. "My family history is riddled with enough twists and turns to fill several books. My son, Zane, thinks I should write them down. Maybe I will. In my old age. Suddenly, at fifty-three, I feel like a very young man."

He took Lily's hand and turned to the guests. Raising his voice above the laughter and noise, he motioned to the wide double doors Rosita Perez, his devoted friend and long-serving housekeeper, had just opened. "Some of the finest musicians in San Antonio have been tuning their instruments for the better part of the past hour," he said good-naturedly. "Let's all go outside where we can appreciate their music as well as the stars on such a beautiful summer night."

Hannah was swept forward with Lily and Ryan and the throng of guests heading outdoors. She found herself in the courtyard, surrounded by people she didn't know. Ryan had been right about the beautiful summer evening. Night had tamed the scorching temperature, turning it gentle, touching it with mystery. Lily had once told Hannah that Ryan's mother, and later, his first wife, had been avid gardeners. The courtyard and the grounds were testimony to the love and care they'd given the lawns and gardens surrounding the sprawling adobe-styled house. Masses of large, purple sage plants looked almost black beneath the pale glow of artificial lights. Roses covered arbors, and flowering vines climbed the sandstone walls that surrounded Ryan's home.

The orchestra was playing, and several people moved onto the dance floor. Hannah had gotten separated from her mother and Ryan. Making small talk with an older couple nearby, it occurred to her that she and Cole were the only guests present who were connected more closely to Lily than to Ryan. She made a mental note to remind the ushers, when the time came, to seat guests on either side of the church, so as to better balance the guests, rather than in the traditional manner of the bride's guests on the left, the groom's on the right.

"It's a small world."

Hannah recognized the deep voice spoken a few feet behind her. She took a calming breath, then turned to face Parker Malone. "Sometimes it seems that way."

There was something deliberate in the step he took in her direction, something just as deliberate in his smile. He'd removed his navy jacket, loosened his tie and rolled up the sleeves of his white dress shirt. By all rights, he should have looked less intimidating. Her heart pounded an erratic rhythm because he didn't look less anything. She cleared her throat, pretending not to be affected.

"I'm Parker Malone."

Since it would have been impolite to refuse it, she took his outstretched hand, but only briefly. "I know."

Parker waited to see if she would add anything, for instance, her name. She didn't say a word. Evidently she knew her etiquette, but she only took civility so far. He'd always been under the assumption that women were uncomfortable with long stretches of silence. Hell, now that he thought about it, most of the women he knew never shut up long enough to find out. There was something different about this woman. He'd tried to dismiss memories of their brief meeting, but he'd had very little success putting her out of his mind. That wasn't so surprising. He'd always believed that first impressions were the most potent, and his first impression of Hannah Cassidy had been a fantasy in the making.

"Are you enjoying the party, Hannah?"

She acknowledged his use of her name with the barest lift of her eyebrows. Parker would have preferred a proper introduction even though he'd grilled Ryan regarding all the Cassidys weeks ago.

"Yes, I am."

It might have been her intention to instill her voice with an overlying coldness, but Parker earned a very good living by paying attention to the most subtle nuances and inflections in his clients' voices. She wasn't as cold as she wanted him to believe. A smug feeling of satisfaction settled over him. No matter what she pretended, she was aware of him. He'd venture a little further to say she was attracted to him, too.

"Nice night."

She glanced at the guests, the orchestra, and the lawns far beyond the patio, and slowly nodded.

"Hannah?"

She turned her head very slowly, and looked up at him. There was a softness in her eyes, and a directness he liked very much. "Ryan was right about that orchestra. They're very good. Would you care to dance?"

She hesitated, as if surprised by his question. "As a matter of fact," she said, the sound of her voice as dusky as secrets whispered in the dark, "I would love to."

Parker felt the way he did when he was nearing the end of an intense game of chess. Victory was close. Check.

She smiled sweetly at him. And he reacted in the most basic and masculine way.

He reached for her hand, but she'd backed up. Increasing the distance between them, she lowered her voice and said, "Perhaps if you combed the numbers on a public rest room wall, you could find someone to accommodate you."

He watched through narrowed eyes as she stopped a dozen feet away to speak to her brother, Cole. She didn't glance back at Parker, but when she dragged her brother onto the dance floor, Parker got her message loud and clear. She wanted to dance. Just not with him.

Checkmate.

Parker considered himself a reasonable man, but he still saw red. He wasn't accustomed to having his overtures rejected, dammit. Although he had to admit her technique had been noteworthy.

Everything about Hannah Cassidy was noteworthy.

He'd noticed her when she'd first arrived. Every hair on his body had raised slightly, as if he was standing too close to an electric fence. He'd been on sensory overload ever since. It wasn't the color of her dress that made such an impression, but the lack of color. It was a pale shade of brown, so close to the color of her skin that at first glance it almost appeared as if she wasn't wearing anything at all. Almost. Every man in the universe knew just how provocative *almost* could be.

The dress was semi-transparent from the knees down, and if you looked close, in a three-inch band around her waist. It left her shoulders bare, but wasn't low cut in the front or in the back. It was the kind of dress a woman who neither felt compelled to flaunt her body nor hide it wore. That such a woman existed was an intriguing concept, one Parker would have to ponder later. Hannah wore no necklace or rings. He'd checked her left hand twice. Her hair appeared darker beneath the twinkle of hundreds of tiny lights, a few tresses curling down her neck and in front of her ears, the rest secured high in the back with a single brown comb.

He didn't know much about her. He sure hadn't had any luck garnering information from the waiter who'd dumped chocolate mousse on his tie, or from the eccentric blonde who owned The Pink Flamingo, although he was certain *she* had been withholding information. Still, Parker hadn't had to ask who Hannah was tonight. He'd known the moment he'd seen her standing next to Lily Cassidy. Although the eyes and color preferences were different, the resemblance between mother and daughter was unmistakable.

He was still watching Hannah when his father materialized out of a nearby crowd. Ice cubes clinked in the bottom of the older man's empty glass. "Ryan Fortune is as stubborn as a mule, but his bourbon is the best money can buy."

J. D. Malone was an inch shorter than his son and kept his weight within fifteen pounds of what it had been when he was young. Women enjoyed him. Men either feared him or revered him. Few actually liked him. Most of the time, the jury was out as to where Parker stood in regard to his father. "I take it you haven't had any luck talking sense into Ryan concerning his affair with Lily Cassidy. The man's not thinking with his head. I never trust the opposition, and I trust Sophia Fortune less than most. That woman isn't going to let go of Ryan's fortune without one hell of a fight. His infatuation with the Cassidy woman is a serious mistake."

Parker shook his head. "Infatuation? Ryan wants her the way a man in the desert wants water."

J.D.'s tone hardened. "That's lust. If he can't control his sexual urges he should find himself a call girl, at least until his divorce is final. I wouldn't expect a man like him to shop on street corners. There are agencies these days that operate out of penthouses. Hell, as far as I'm concerned, it's the only way to go. You get what you pay for, I always say."

Parker wouldn't want to be the one to suggest such a thing to Ryan Fortune. He wouldn't recommend J.D. do it, either. His father had never preached honor when it came to sex. His sex talk had consisted of taking precautions and using discretion. No wonder Parker had jumped to the wrong conclusion in that damned storage room last week.

J.D. returned to the group of men he'd been talking to. Parker stayed in the shadows, scowling.

The song finally ended. He noticed it didn't take long for one of Ryan's nephews to ask Hannah to dance and for her to accept. Sipping seltzer water over ice, Parker stood apart from the crowd, biding his time. Fifteen more minutes and he would be able to leave.

Time was almost up when he noticed a pale-brown blur

out of the corner of his eye. He turned his head just in time to see Hannah slip away from her latest suitor and stroll along one of the curving walkways in the distance. Placing his empty glass on a passing waiter's tray, Parker glanced at his watch. Might as well put his time to good use.

Trying to catch her breath after all that dancing, Hannah smiled as she passed the teenage girls sitting on a weathered bench near the rose arbor. She strolled slowly along the path, her step light, the heels of her shoes clicking softly over the flagstone walk.

The garden was lovely, scented with honeysuckle and roses moist with dew. The paths were lit, but not nearly as brightly as the courtyard near the house. Here, shadows beckoned guests to enjoy the quietude of a leisurely stroll. If her mother's wedding could have taken place anytime other than winter, Hannah would have loved to see it set right here. A few months ago she'd planned a wedding that had taken place in an arboretum where the lush ground cover had been mowed, creating a cloudlike carpet of delicate purple blooms.

Winter weddings were lovely, too, and would be the perfect time to accent in her mother's favorite color, red. Hannah was so lost in her thoughts she didn't notice the muted sound of a man's footsteps behind her until they were very close. She glanced casually over her shoulder, and came to an abrupt stop.

"I didn't mean to startle you," Parker Malone said quietly.

She rallied quickly, impatient to be on her way. "I startle easily."

"I called your name," he said. "But I think the saying goes something like you seemed to be miles away."

"I have a lot on my mind. Now, if you'll excuse me."

They both stepped in the same direction, paused, then tried going the other way. Hannah said, "What are you doing, Parker?"

He ran a hand through his hair. "I have to kill a little more time before I can make a departure that's socially acceptable. I thought I'd take a walk."

"That's a good idea. I'll leave you to your walk." This time she darted around him, only to sigh in resignation when he fell into step beside her.

"I find myself in unfamiliar territory," he said quietly.

The grounds were magnificent, but something told her that Parker Malone was accustomed to the finer things in life. "Unfamiliar, how?" she said, curious in spite of herself.

"I seem to be in the middle of a situation that calls for an apology."

She felt his eyes on her, but she continued to look straight ahead.

"I'm afraid I've never been good at saying I'm sorry." His voice had dropped in volume, losing its steely edge.

"At least you're honest."

"I'm sorry."

She glanced up at him then, and they shared a small smile, because the way he'd said it, he could have been apologizing for being honest.

"I jumped to the wrong conclusion about you the first time we met. I would have apologized sooner, but I didn't know your name, let alone your telephone number. So I left my card with your friend and waited for you to contact me. Evidently she didn't see fit to pass it on to you."

"Adrienne gave me your card, Parker." Hannah fell silent, letting the implications soak in. She'd chosen not to call him. End of story. He didn't need to know she'd taken his business card out of the drawer three times last week.

Strains of music wafted from the courtyard. Night insects hummed and squeaked as if the musicians were playing just for them. No one else had ventured this far away from the party. Hannah was aware of how secluded this section of the garden was, and how alone she and Parker were. "Well," she said, "I think I'll turn back."

"Hannah, wait." His hand felt warm on her bare arm, so her shiver must have been the result of something else.

"Look," she said. "Cole just told me you've already confronted him with your view on marriage in general, our mother's and Ryan's in particular. If you followed me because you want to enlist my help in talking her into signing that prenuptial agreement you drew up, you can forget it."

The pressure on her arm changed slightly. "I followed you because there's something I've been wanting to do all night."

Suddenly he was directly in front of her, his face angling toward hers, blurring in front of her eyes. "I followed you to do this."

His mouth covered hers before she had the presence of mind to resist. She must have closed her eyes, because suddenly she had to rely on her other senses. Her lips parted, and a rush of feeling flooded over her. Their breath mingled, their lips clung. His hand went around to the small of her back, pulling her closer, until their bodies touched ever so lightly.

Her hands found their way to him, one inching up to his shoulder, the other spreading wide over his chest. He made a sound deep in his throat, and his heart raced beneath her palm.

Parker had always had a good imagination. God knew, it had been working overtime this past week, but imagery couldn't hold a candle to the jolt of excitement that had begun to pulse through him the moment his lips touched Hannah's.

She sighed, her long, lean body going fluid against his. Her three-inch heels made her the perfect height for kissing. Her waist fit his hands, the flare of her hips enticing him to explore. A few moments ago the garden had seemed idyllically private. Suddenly it wasn't nearly private enough.

Music played from the other side of the courtyard. A bed of tall ornamental grasses blocked them from view of the others. Another shudder went through him, want and need melding, burrowing deep inside him.

"I don't want to stop." His voice was a rasp in the semi-darkness. "But we have to, at least for now."

Hannah came to her senses slowly. She glanced nervously around, relieved to find them alone, the shadow of an old sweet gum tree on one side, tall grasses swaying in the breeze on the other. She placed her hands on her cheeks and took a backward step.

"That shouldn't have happened."

"I disagree."

No doubt. She had to think, and it wasn't easy to do with him standing there looking at her. "In a sense, you're the enemy."

"If you'd care to explain, I'm all ears."

He wasn't really, she thought. He was all shoulders and planes and angles and...

He slid a hand into the pocket of his dress slacks, the action drawing attention to a place she really shouldn't be looking. She glanced up at his face, only to find herself staring at the cleft in his chin. For heaven's sake, did everything about him have to be riveting?

Taking control of her senses, she said, "I've overheard

bits and pieces of several conversations tonight, and the general consensus around here seems to be that you don't want Ryan to see my mother. Something tells me it isn't a moral issue with you.''

"At least you're not blinded by my brains and good looks.''

He was very good at deprecating humor. If this had been a laughing matter she would have smiled. "At least it hasn't gone to your head.''

"That isn't what's gone to my head, Hannah.''

She had absolutely nothing to say to that. Thankfully, footsteps sounded on the garden path, and she was saved from having to try to reply.

"Hannah, there you are.'' It was her mother. "Oh, hello, Parker. Am I interrupting something?''

"Yes,'' Parker said.

"No,'' Hannah said at the same time.

"I see.''

"Parker and I have been talking. I was just telling him that neither Cole nor I will try to influence you when it comes to your relationship with Ryan. I didn't have a chance to tell him how I feel about prenuptial agreements. Perhaps you'd like to enlighten him.''

"Parker's just doing his job, dear.''

It was hard to tell who was more surprised, Hannah or Parker, but it was Hannah who said, "You're defending him?''

Lily looked at Parker, but spoke to her daughter. "I believe Parker has Ryan's best interests at heart. Ryan trusts him, and Ryan doesn't trust just anybody.''

Parker found himself at a rare loss for words. He was accustomed to receiving respect when he earned it, but there was compassion in Lily's expression, too. It left him feeling raw, as if something was missing from his life. It

made him uncomfortable. Almost as uncomfortable as unspent desire.

Hannah linked her arm through her mother's. Bidding
Parker good-night, the pair strolled away. Parker watched
until they rounded a curve and were out of sight.

He finished his walk alone, deep in thought. He had to
get hold of this situation. His fantasies had been playing
tricks on him. Now that he'd kissed Hannah Cassidy, he
could get her out of his system.

He glanced at his watch. Coincidentally, his fifteen
minutes were up.

Parker strode out the back door of the business complex
that housed Malone, Malone & Associates. Snagging his
key out of his pocket, he pointed it at the ground-hugging
Corvette parked between the Mercedes and the Cadillac.
The push of one button unlocked his door. The touch of
another started the engine. Pausing, he listened closely.
The timing was off. He'd better make an appointment to
have his mechanic take a look at it.

Footsteps sounded behind him. "Parker," his father
called. "You're just the man I wanted to see."

Parker stopped and slowly turned. Another minute and
he would have made his escape. His car wasn't the only
one whose timing was off.

"What is it, J.D.?"

"I'll make this brief. I just came from the Double
Crown Ranch."

Parker acknowledged the information with a slight nod.
"Any luck convincing Ryan to push that prenup?"

Tucking his briefcase beneath one arm, J.D. shook his
head. "He wants his divorce from Sophia, and he wants
it now. All he can think about is marrying the Cassidy
woman. He says he trusts her." J.D. made a disparaging

sound. "You've got your work cut out for you, son. I understand you've made contact with Lily Cassidy's daughter."

Parker's eyebrow rose a fraction of an inch, his only indication of surprise. "I suppose you could call it that."

"Think you can get close enough to her to make her see reason?"

Parker knew how J.D.'s mind worked. By "reason," he meant whatever suited him in his efforts to win the most money, the most assets, the lion's share for his client.

"I don't think so, J.D."

"You kissed her."

Parker didn't even try to hide his reaction to that one. Did the man have spies?

J.D. smoothed a hand down the length of his tie. "I happened to be on that garden path last week. She looked pretty...shall I say, pliable."

Parker clenched his jaw. "She's refusing my phone calls. The flowers I sent her were returned to me, wilted."

"So you're already on it."

J.D. turned to go. Accustomed to his father's dismissals, Parker quickly strode the remaining distance to his car door.

"Parker?"

He looked up, one foot already in the car.

J.D. was watching him, eyes narrowed, his gaze cool and steady. His father had an uncanny ability to assess a person, a situation, a half-truth or an out-and-out lie. As a kid, that look had made Parker feel like a germ under a microscope. It still did.

"Check your calendar and let me know when you have an evening free," J.D. said. "I'll have my cook broil some steaks. You look like you could use a cattleman's cut, medium rare."

Parker hadn't planned to smile. "I'll do that, Father."

J.D. smiled, too, but only briefly. And then he headed for the office. The father-son moment was over. It was business as usual.

An hour later Parker strummed his fingers on the steering wheel. His windows were down, but there wasn't much air moving in downtown San Antonio today. Consequently, the plush leather seats felt at least a hundred and five degrees.

Come on, come on. He was parked along Smith Street, two car lengths away from a storefront painted a subtle charming beige. Two women, probably a mother and her grown daughter, had left a few minutes ago, arms filled with books and bags, heads undoubtedly filled with wedding plans.

It was twelve o'clock on the dot when he got out of his car and headed for the building bearing the sign The Perfect Occasion. A wind chime jingled softly when he opened the door, and air that was slightly cooler greeted him.

Hannah glanced up, the ready smile on her face suddenly looking a little less steady. "Parker, what are you doing here?"

He strolled farther into the room, the epitome of nonchalance, a hand on one hip, the other fiddling with a clasp he picked up off her desk. "I just happened to be in the neighborhood, so I thought I'd stop in and say hello." He failed to mention that Ryan "just happened" to drop the name of Hannah's business in passing that very day. He paused. "Is your air-conditioning on the blink?"

"No, why?"

His gaze made a quick trip over her sleeveless dress.

She appeared cool and comfortable. "Never mind. I'm on my way to lunch. Care to join me?"

He could tell from her expression what her answer was going to be. Raising a hand, he said, "Would it sway your decision if I told you how much trouble I went to and how much time I spent juggling appointments so I could *just happen to be in the neighborhood* right now?"

"If you would have called first," Hannah said, straightening pamphlets lying on her desk, "I could have saved you the trouble."

"That's a marvelous idea. I should know. I've tried it. You won't take my calls." He waited until she looked up to grace her with his sexiest smile. "And I take it you don't like flowers."

Her hands stilled for a moment, then resumed their task.

"Come on, Hannah. I've been burning the candle at both ends for weeks. Even my father thinks it's taking a toll on me. From the looks of all the brochures and swatches of material and files in this room, you've been busy, too. I have to eat. You have to eat. We might as well eat together."

He gave her a second dose of his sexy smile.

"I can't, Parker."

Parker understood a simple no when he heard one. This wasn't a courtroom, and she wasn't a witness he could badger. She was a woman, and she'd made herself perfectly clear. He straightened and carefully returned the clasp to the edge of her desk. He did a quick inventory of the room. There were framed photographs on several shelves behind her; a yellow flowered sofa sat at a comfortable angle near a matching overstuffed chair. White lights were strung through the fronds of huge potted plants. Balloons bobbed from strings that were tied to an antique filing cabinet, a cardboard cut-out clown propped nearby.

It occurred to him that Hannah Cassidy made her living from planning more than weddings. Redistributing his weight to one foot, he said, "I'd like to hire you."

"What?"

She had a suspicious mind. He'd given her good reason for it. "I'm thinking about having a party."

"You're kidding." Her disbelief showed in the tone of her voice. Recovering slightly, she said, "What kind of party?"

"I don't know. I just thought of it."

"Parker, why are you really here?"

That was a good question. He worded his answer very carefully. "It isn't because I have a lot of idle time. It's just the opposite. Yesterday I was trying to talk an irate husband out of hiring a private investigator to follow his wife, whom he suspected was cheating. I was in the middle of trying to explain that in no-fault divorce states, there's no use. Suddenly your image crowded into my brain. You're interfering with my concentration."

Hannah didn't know what to say. Doggone it, she felt complimented. She had no business feeling that way. She and Parker were complete opposites. While she planned weddings down to the smallest detail, he took marriages apart, asset by asset.

"Look. I have an appointment across town with a very anxious bride to be." She opened a drawer and pulled out a price list and several brochures depicting the different themes she'd used in planning parties. Placing the pamphlets near the edge of her desk, she said, "You can look these over, if you'd like. If you truly want my help planning a party, let me know. Otherwise…"

He glanced at the brochures, the rest of her statement hanging in the air, unfinished. That "otherwise" spoke volumes. He could hire her services as a party planner, but she didn't plan to see him socially.

"I see," he said. "Maybe I'll do that."

"Goodbye, Parker."

Hannah watched him stride toward the door. It was in her own best interests to let him go. And she was letting him go. It was better this way. A clean break from what could have turned out to be a disastrous relationship.

She covered her lips with three fingers, remembering how it had felt to kiss him. If she let him go, how would she ever know what might have been?

She didn't need to know. It was for the best. For both of them.

She wondered if he'd really been burning the candle at both ends. Had there been shadows beneath his eyes?

"Parker?"

His fingers were already wrapped around the doorknob when he turned around. His eyes looked hooded. She couldn't read their expression from here. "You forgot your brochures."

He retraced his steps, taking the brochures from her out-stretched hand. Praying she didn't regret this, she took a breath for courage and said, "I can't have lunch with you, but I could free up my schedule for this evening. We could talk about this party you suddenly want to have then."

The eyes staring into hers filled with a curious intensity. "Dinner?" he asked.

She pushed her chair out and stood. "That would be too much like a date."

There was a good reason for that, Parker thought. "What else did you have in mind?"

"Do you own a bike?"

"A motorcycle?"

She shook her head. "A bicycle."

"Not since I was thirteen."

"That's what I thought. You probably don't have a pair of in-line skates in the back of your closet, either. Something tells me you get your exercise playing racquetball or walking on a treadmill. I prefer more spontaneous activities."

Parker had the strangest urge to defend himself.

"Maybe we could go for a walk," she said.

"You want to take a walk?"

She smiled. "That sounds lovely. Thanks, I'd love to."

Parker shook his head. She thought she was so smart. That was okay. He happened to like smart women. "I'll stop by around seven."

"You can if you want to, but I won't be back until seven-thirty." She was grinning openly now.

"Seven-thirty, it is."

"Oh, and Parker? I have one small stipulation."

Of course she did.

"You can't try to arm wrestle me into using my influence to change my mother's mind about going public with her engagement to Ryan."

Parker took a frank and admiring look at her. Her hair was down today, her dress a creamy beige that seemed to blend in with her surroundings. She had a great body, but he was beginning to realize that in front of him stood a woman who preferred to be recognized for having a great mind.

"If we arm wrestle," he said, his gaze delving hers, "it'll be to determine how far we go."

Leaving her to mull that over, he strode loftily out the door.

Three

"Look, Parker, there's a paddleboat."

Parker glanced at the contraption moored to the edge of the boardwalk that lined the San Antonio River. Yes, he supposed the apparatus floating on two plastic pontoons was in the paddleboat category. Why Hannah was hurrying toward it was beyond him. "Where are you going?"

She slowed down as she glanced over her shoulder, but he noticed she didn't stop completely. "I heard they were going to try these out again along with the newer, motor-powered ones they've been using these past several years. Let's take a boat ride. Hurry, before someone else beats us to it."

Following her around a table of women who were lingering over desserts and iced teas along Paseo del Rio, or River Walk, a dining and shopping district in downtown San Antonio, Parker wondered if he was the only one who noticed that people weren't exactly lining up to ride the leg-powered devices. He figured there was a good reason for that. It required energy, something that Hannah hadn't run out of since they'd set off on their "little" walk an hour and a half ago.

It turned out he and Hannah had two entirely different approaches to walking. He'd expected a leisurely stroll down Smith Street, and had assumed that taking a walk involved walking. Hannah took flight. He'd planned to find a quiet table in a coffeehouse somewhere. Hannah had informed him that she didn't drink coffee. It was the caffeine. It was bad for a person. When he got home, Parker was going to have to alert the press. *If* he had enough energy left to make it home.

She had more energy than she could contain.

She'd met him at the door wearing an airy brown skirt that rode low at the waist and stopped a few inches above her ankles. Once again, it wasn't the color that drew his attention, but the fit and style. Her shirt bared her arms and part of her shoulders. It wasn't tight, but it was cropped short at the waist. When she moved just right, he caught a glimpse of her navel. And the woman moved a great deal. If she ever found herself in need of another occupation, she could try her hand at modeling. Her mixture of wholesomeness and sensuality would undoubtedly sell everything from women's jeans to lingerie.

He was imagining her in lingerie right now. A serious mistake for any man who needed to keep his wits about him.

Hannah stepped onto the paddleboat. The seat was wide enough for two people. It occurred to her that Parker wasn't excited about climbing off the boardwalk and sitting on the other half of the seat. He appeared lost in thought, the same breeze that lifted the hair off her shoulders trifling with the collar of his knit shirt. "Are you coming?" she asked.

He slid his hands to his hips, peering first one way and then the other. "How far do you want to go?"

She stared up at him, remembering when he'd said they would have to arm wrestle to determine that. His gaze warmed at least ten degrees as it slid over her, letting her know he was thinking the same thing. Oh, no, he didn't. She wasn't touching that line.

"There's a little ice-cream store just beyond that curve

in the river.'' She pointed to a series of lights upriver, but wound up waving at another paddleboat coming their way.

"I don't recall seeing an ice-cream place in the area."

"It's been there forever. I thought you said you grew up in San Antonio."

"My family wasn't the type to go out for ice cream."

This was the first time he'd mentioned his family all evening. She'd met his father, the legendary J. D. Malone, at Lily and Ryan's party. She'd be hard pressed to say for sure whether she liked or disliked the man.

"My family didn't always have a lot of money for things like going to ice-cream parlors," she said. His eyes narrowed, and she threw up her hands. "My mother isn't after Ryan's money, if that's what you're thinking."

"I didn't say she was."

"You didn't have to. My brother's an attorney. I know how your minds work. My mother may have been poor as a child, but there's no disgrace in that. She and my father worked hard in the grocery store they owned back in Leather Bucket. There's no disgrace in working hard, either. After my father died, my mother went back to college. She's perfectly capable of earning her own living on what she makes as manager of special functions at the Willow Creek Hotel. She's marrying Ryan because she loves him."

In some far corner of her mind, Hannah was aware that Parker had taken the seat next to her, but she didn't consciously acknowledge his presence until her voice had trailed away and the only sound was that of the water falling over the paddlewheel at the back of their boat. She glanced up at him. He was looking at her in silence, making no attempt whatsoever to hide the fact that he was watching her.

"Sometimes I get a little carried away defending the people I love."

"I like a woman who gets carried away."

Hannah knew better than to comment. She was becoming well enough acquainted with him to realize that Parker Malone rarely spoke without thinking. There were layers to what he said, hidden meanings, underlying messages. Cole was like that to an extent. Maybe all attorneys were. Her brother was good at what he did, and Hannah was proud of him, but Parker took innuendo farther than anyone she'd ever known.

"Let's get this boat moving, shall we?" she asked, manning the steering lever between them.

At five feet seven, she'd always considered her legs long, but Parker's were longer. He might have complained a little about the distance they'd come, but he hadn't so much as broken a sweat from the exertion. His flat-front khakis and navy-blue shirt were the kinds of clothes hundreds of sharp, young executive types wore, but Parker's hugged muscles that were obviously accustomed to a good workout. She wondered what drove him. She wanted to know everything about him, but she was beginning to realize that information of a personal manner was seldom forthcoming.

She steered around a paddleboat that was drifting slowly down the river, a Just Married sign on the back, the man and woman lost in a long, searing kiss. Once they were out of hearing range, Hannah whispered, "When my sister and I were little, we used to sing 'first comes love, then comes marriage, then comes Johnny pushing a baby carriage' every time we saw a couple kissing like that."

Hannah's thoughts became introspective. There *were* fond memories of good times and shared secrets between her and Maria. A few.

"In five years," Parker was saying, his deep voice drawing her out of her musings, "they'll be fighting over who gets to keep the baby carriage."

Hannah shook her head. "You're a natural born romantic, Parker."

"I'm a realist."

"I don't have my thesaurus handy. Is that another word for pessimist?"

"If it isn't, it should be."

They'd reached the landing area in front of the trendy ice-cream store. Parker stepped out and moored the boat to a little pier, but Hannah made no move to climb onto the lighted dock. "You make divorce sound inevitable."

He brushed his hands on his thighs. "Fifty percent of all marriages in this country end in divorce. In other words, half of the people who have stars in their eyes when they come to you will be shooting daggers at each other by the time they come to me."

She took the hand he held out to her and stepped onto the dock. His cynicism was more difficult to accept. "What about the other fifty percent?"

"I didn't invent the statistics, Hannah. I'm only repeating them."

The river swirled by, lapping at the paddleboat, splashing softly against the pier. Hannah was very aware of the color of the sky in the deepening twilight, of the warmth of Parker's hand around hers, and the directness of his gaze. "Do you still want that ice cream?" he asked.

She shook her head. The ice-cream parlor had merely been a destination. Now, she wanted to make him understand. Better yet, she wanted to change his mind about his views on marriage. "All your statistics don't seem to be slowing people down," she said. "My day planner is full of names of couples who still believe in marriage. It seems as if I'm invited to a bridal shower every other week. I'd just come from one the first time we met. It was where I'd received that embarrassing little package of consolation prizes."

He released her hand. As if by unspoken agreement, they started back toward Smith Street. "I thought those little numbers were only passed around at bachelor parties."

"Men pass out condoms at bachelor parties?"

"It's been known to happen."

This was a subject that had always made her curious. "What else do men do at those things?"

"Telling you would require using obscenities."

She looked up at him in silent expectation.

"I don't talk dirty to a woman so early in a relationship."

"We're not having a relationship."

"If you'd agree to come home with me, that would change."

The deep cadence of his voice was as dusky as a whisper, as sensuous as a kiss placed ever so softly on her bare shoulder.

"Do you play chess, Hannah?"

Hmm. Her steps slowed and her breathing deepened. She was trying to follow the course the conversation was taking, really she was, but a young woman with dark hair and a skintight dress drew her attention. Why, it almost looked like Maria.

"Or are you more the arm-wrestling type?"

What would Maria be doing in San Antonio? She never came to the city anymore. Hannah's heart beat a little harder. She loved her younger sister, and she ached for a glimpse of her. She wanted so much more.

"Hannah?"

"Hmm?"

"Is everything all right?"

She glanced up at Parker, and then back at the sidewalk across the street. She'd lost the young woman in the glare of headlights. Hannah surveyed the entire area. There were other dark-haired women out and about, but the woman in the brightly colored dress was nowhere to be seen.

"I'm fine," she told Parker. "I thought I saw someone I knew."

She told herself it couldn't have been Maria. Surely there were a lot of women in San Antonio who bore the dark, exotic traits of their Apache and Mexican parentage. And Maria certainly wasn't the only girl in Texas who had a walk she claimed measured seven point five on the Richter scale.

"An old flame?"

She tried to recall how the conversation had gone from bachelor parties to old flames. They'd reached an intersection a few blocks away from The Pink Flamingo. Waiting for the crossing signal, she studied Parker's profile. His nose was straight, his chin was well defined and set at an angle that was the epitome of smugness. He glanced down, his gaze homing in on hers.

"Not an old flame. My sister. But it wasn't. Either of those things. An old flame, I mean, or Maria."

Hannah wondered when she'd become daft. While she was at it, she wondered when she'd been so drawn to a man she had no business being drawn to. She was so caught up in what was happening between her and Parker that she didn't notice the voluptuous redhead until she'd sauntered up to Parker, ran a long, bloodred fingernail along his cheek, and slipped something into his pocket. She wiggled her hips, winked, puckered up her painted lips and kissed the air near Parker's cheek.

With a quirk of her eyebrows, Hannah watched her saunter away. Oh, no, Maria most definitely did not have sole rights to provocative moves and gestures.

The Walk signal came on. Ignoring it, Hannah reached blithely into Parker's pocket, pulling out a skimpy pair of panties. "How sweet."

"That isn't what it looks like."

Hannah lifted her gaze to his. "This isn't a pair of silk, thong bikini panties?"

"Silk? Really?"

She batted his hand away. "It's white, but in this case I doubt it's virginal."

Parker regarded the item in Hannah's hand. She was right. Paula was definitely no virgin. "All right. It's what it looks like, but it isn't what you're thinking."

"Then, she isn't a friend of yours?"

"A client, actually. A former one. Paula's just trying to show her appreciation."

"For what, pray tell?"

The unusual combination of vitality and sarcasm in Hannah's expression made it difficult for Parker not to smile. His heartbeat sounded in his own ears as they started across the street, hurrying at the prodding of a car horn.

Reluctant to release her elbow even though they'd reached the other side, he said, "I won her ten thousand dollars a month, the summer place, the winter condo in Florida, and if I remember correctly, the family poodle."

"What did the husband get?"

"Let's just say he's never slipped a pair of his Jockey shorts into my pocket."

"I'm relieved to hear it. Tell me, Parker...never mind."

"What do you want to ask me?"

"It's none of my business."

"I'll be the judge of that."

They'd reached the sidewalk in front of The Perfect Occasion. She stared up at him, but she didn't finish her question. He answered as if she had. "No, I don't, Hannah."

Her eyes must have shown her surprise, because he said, "That's what you wanted to know, wasn't it? If I sleep with my female clients?"

Some would call her a fool for believing him, but her instincts told her he was telling the truth. After all, he might have jumped to the wrong conclusion when they'd first met, but he hadn't taken her up on what he'd thought she was proposing.

"Or were you wondering if I sleep with every woman who slips her underwear into my pocket? Why don't you try it and find out?"

"That isn't my style."

He seemed to be assessing her statement. "Your style of panties? Or your style of invitations?"

She fought a valiant battle not to smile. And lost. "Neither."

"Pity."

The streetlight cast a white glow over Parker, deepening the blue of his eyes, making his smile appear stark and white and oh, so inviting.

"I like what you're thinking."

She closed her gaping mouth. Could the man read her mind?

"I want to see you again. Say you'll have dinner with me tomorrow night."

She shook her head, fitting her key into the lock. "We're complete opposites."

He took the key from her hand and opened the door. The man had smooth down to an art form. "Opposites attract."

She chided herself for falling into that one. "This is a good place to end our walk, Parker."

"I can think of a better place."

She was on the first of two steps that led to another door, which ultimately led to her apartment above the boutique. "I'm not looking for a fling. I'm not into casual sex."

"There would be nothing casual about the sex we'd have."

Her breath came out in a rush. "You're presumptuous."

"I'm honest."

"So you've said."

"I honestly want you, Hannah. But I'll settle for getting to know you better. For now. Invite me upstairs."

He was standing so close she could feel his breath on her hair. Hannah loved summertime. She loved the heat, the intensity, the vibrancy of it; she didn't even mind the humidity, but suddenly, she felt too warm. She couldn't seem to come up with the word no, couldn't seem to think, couldn't seem to move.

Parker had no such problem. He tried another key, and opened the second door. "We can discuss the party, have a cup of—that's right, you don't drink coffee, it's the caffeine—decaf. I can invite you to dinner, you can say yes, and then you can kiss me."

Before she knew how it had happened, she was raising her face to his, and kissing him, exactly as he'd said. He hadn't coached her about touching him, so that must have been her own idea. What an idea it was. He felt like a dream, but he was solid, hard, real. His shirt bunched in her fingers; heat radiated outward from his chest, his arms, his shoulders, warming her hands everywhere she touched.

One minute they were standing on the stairs behind a closed door; the next thing she knew she was sprawled on top of him on the stairs, a tangle of arms and legs, hearts racing, breathing erratic, mouths joined. His hand inched between their bodies, covering her breast. She arched toward him, passion rising up in her, clouding her brain.

She couldn't control her gasp of pleasure at the feel of his mouth at her breast through the thin fabric of her shirt and the lace of her bra. She grasped his head, and whispered his name, only to groan slightly when the corner of the step jabbed into her back.

"Let's go upstairs." His voice was a husky murmur, at one with the tremor he'd started deep inside her. He rolled her on top of him, so that she straddled his legs. The level of intimacy in their positions was about to go through the roof.

She had to stop.

She wanted him to kiss her again. She wanted to feel his mouth on her naked skin.

"Hannah?"

Her head was spinning, but she heard herself say, "No, Parker."

He went very still.

"We don't even know each other," she whispered. "And we just can't do this. *I* just can't do this."

She felt the change that came over him. He stiffened. Not with anger, but with quiet acceptance. "I know I should apologize, but that felt too good, and I'm afraid I'm just not sorry."

He'd said he was honest. Tugging at the hem of her shirt, she stood. He climbed to his feet much more slowly. She noticed he didn't ask her to invite him upstairs again, but he wanted to. It was there in his eyes, in his deeply drawn breath and the grim set of his jaw.

"We never got around to discussing that party you mentioned this afternoon," she said conversationally.

He quirked an eyebrow in her direction.

She shrugged. "I was trying to take your mind off it."

To his credit, he didn't say, "It?" But he might as well have. Hannah made a valiant effort not to smile.

Parker's heart was still racing, his breathing was still deep. No wonder. He was still in the throes of a strong, swirling passion, and her "barely there" grin wasn't helping. It wasn't like him to lose control. Hell, he was thirty-one years old, not eighteen.

It was probably a good thing one of them had kept their wits about them. Probably. He bent one knee in an effort to ease the fit of his pants. It was going to take him a couple of minutes to get himself completely under control.

"I've always heard it's helpful to think about negative things."

Under other circumstances, there would have been something enchanting in her humor. "Unspent desire *is* negative," he said.

She smoothed a hand down her skirt, and sat again, patting the space next to her. As he lowered to a sitting position on the steps, she said, "Perhaps it would be better to think more along the lines of a cash flow problem, or maybe the inflation rate, or world hunger, maybe, or family difficulties."

He scowled.

Aha, she'd hit a nerve. "Tell me about your family."

"There's not a lot to tell."

"There's always a lot to tell when it comes to family. Everybody thinks their family is the only one with problems, but I think pretty much every family has its eccentricities."

He cleared his throat. "I wouldn't know where to begin."

"Come on, Parker, give it your best shot."

His sigh was long and loud. "I grew up in your basic bitter, all-American dysfunctional family. One father, one mother, one sister. There was a lot of yelling, a lot of doors slamming, a lot of accusations and recriminations. My parents divorced when I was eight. I lived with my father, my sister lived with our mother. And everyone nurtured the bitterness for all it was worth."

"Time hasn't helped?" she asked.

"My sister hasn't spoken to my father since my mother's funeral, five years ago. Even then, it wasn't pretty."

"What about you?" she asked. "Do you ever talk to your sister?"

She felt his shrug near her own shoulder. "Not often. She's stubborn. Won't accept my help. I guess you could say Beth and I aren't close."

"My sister and I aren't close, either."

"Ah, yes, the ever-elusive Maria."

Hannah's strained relationship with her only sister was her greatest sadness, greater even than the loss of her big, burly, gentle father ten years ago. For a moment she'd let her guard down, forgetting that Parker put as much thought and effort into obtaining divorces for his clients as she put into planning weddings for hers. His description of Maria reminded Hannah that she and Parker weren't on the same side when it came to her mother's marriage to Ryan. Parker was Ryan's divorce attorney. She was Lily's wedding planner.

"My parents were happily married, Parker. They were living proof that marriages can survive obstacles, heartaches, hard times, and that the two people involved can grow more deeply in love over time."

That's what she wanted. To love, honor and cherish the man she eventually married. Until death. Apparently, Parker didn't believe in love or in marriage. She remained pensive, deep in thought.

"Tell me," she said quietly sometime later. "Have you always felt this way about marriage? Or has your profession tainted your view?"

He slid his palm over the fabric covering his knee. "It has nothing to do with being tainted. People are born. For the next twenty or thirty years, they're single. They get married. Ultimately, they get divorced. Eventually, they die. Some people repeat a couple of those steps. Once was enough for me."

She turned her head fast, but the implication rendered her speechless. He'd been married? Once? When? Was he still married?

He caught her looking at his left hand. "I've been divorced for almost four years. But you're right," he said, glancing into her eyes, and then at her lips. "Talking about the negative side of life has done the trick."

He moved fast, but she still should have seen the kiss coming. His lips moved over hers swiftly, intensely, masterfully, but only briefly.

"Although *that*," he said while her mind was still spinning, "had the potential to reverse some of the progress. I'll call you tomorrow. We can discuss our plans for dinner then. Good night, Hannah."

She rose to her feet, then stood perfectly still. Her heart pounded an erratic rhythm. It came from trying to keep up with a man as sharp and witty as Parker. It came from trying to listen to every word he said, no matter how quickly he said it. It came from the fact that he'd been married. Once, he'd said, had been enough.

She sat back down on the step, landing with a heavy little thud about the same time the outer door closed behind him.

* * *

There was exhilaration in Parker's step as he left Hannah's building. He'd gotten the last word, and he'd gotten the last kiss. Hannah had been so surprised she'd failed to turn down his invitation to dinner. Earlier, she'd been the one with all the exuberant energy. She'd turned that energy on him, and frankly, he could hardly wait to give her the opportunity to do it again.

He'd rounded the corner and was heading for his car when he noticed a woman hiding in the shadows. Probably in her mid-twenties, she seemed nervous, jumpy. Guilty? He didn't get a good enough look at her face to make that kind of determination because she spun around the instant she noticed him, her feet carrying her away quickly.

She disappeared down a narrow alley, leaving behind a hazy impression of dark hair and a brightly colored, skin-tight dress that reminded him of a neon sign, garish and gaudy. In comparison, Hannah was all subtle nuances and sultry sighs, as inviting as deep evening shade.

Maria Cassidy placed a hand slightly above her flat stomach and breathed deeply. Holding very still, she listened for the sound of footsteps behind her. All was quiet.

That had been a close one, she thought, letting out a long breath. She'd nearly panicked when she'd seen Hannah coming toward her a little while ago. For a second there she'd been afraid her older sister had recognized her.

Maria's lips thinned. Hannah thought she was so smart. Boring, that's what she was. All her life, all she'd done was lecture Maria about the importance of studying and furthering her education. Hannah didn't know how to have fun. She didn't know how to dress, that was for sure. Maria couldn't begin to fathom what the man with the impressive biceps, long, lithe legs and interesting face saw in Hannah. Her sister usually only attracted computer geeks and nerds.

When she'd first seen Hannah and the man disappear behind closed doors, Maria had thought that maybe Hannah had changed. She should have known Miss High and Mighty wouldn't know how to keep a man busy for more than five minutes. She was probably still a virgin, for God's sake.

Not Maria. She'd always known what a woman's body was made for. She had breasts to die for. Men used to tell her that all the time. It had been a while since she'd heard it. Oh, how she missed it.

Lately her life had gotten out of control.

Why couldn't things just go her way for once? Nothing ever did. And she was so tired of working, so tired of living in that awful trailer in Leather Bucket. So tired of people who refused to take her seriously.

Just look at her. She was only twenty-three. She should have been having fun. She'd found the perfect way to get ahead and make those uppity Fortunes give the Cassidys their due. Her mother had refused to listen. So had Cole and Hannah. So Maria had taken things into her own hands. It had been a good plan. Brilliant. But then things had gone wrong. So wrong.

Now she was stuck in that dingy trailer in the dowdiest town in the country, working two menial jobs to make ends meet. And when she wasn't working, she was taking care of the baby. Life had been so much easier when she was a child.

She'd felt a tiny pang of homesickness when she'd first happened to glimpse Hannah. For a moment she'd wanted to go to her older sister the way she had when they were kids. Back then she used to give in to the loneliness and unhappiness that had dogged her whole life and knock on

Hannah's door. Good old boring Hannah was usually studying, but she always smiled at Maria, and invited her in. Sometimes, Hannah would brush Maria's hair for a long time. Maria would stare at her reflection in the mirror, mesmerized, smiling only when Hannah told her she was pretty.

"But remember, Maria," Hannah used to whisper. "Pretty is as pretty does."

Maria rolled her eyes all these years later. What did Hannah know?

Maria was the one who was going to have the last laugh. She was! Her plan to present the Fortunes with an off-spring had gone awry. She had spent months trying to get into one of the younger Fortune's bed in order to get pregnant. It had all been for nothing. She'd been forced to go to a sperm bank for what she'd needed. It hadn't been fun, but she hadn't done it for pleasure. She'd done it to ensure that at least one Cassidy got what she deserved: a portion of the Fortune dynasty.

At last it had seemed as if something had gone right. She'd know that a certain Fortune bachelor had donated to a sperm bank years before, and she had asked for just the right donor profile... All she'd had to do was have her baby, and wait for the right time to present the Fortunes with another heir.

The christening for Matthew and Claudia Fortune's son, Bryan, had looked like the perfect family affair to unveil her little surprise. She'd put her baby in the crib in the nursery, then joined the party, waiting for the perfect moment to present her son. But when she had returned to the nursery, *her* baby was gone. Kidnapped. She'd panicked. Who wouldn't? She didn't know what to do. She only knew that nobody would give a damn about her child, certainly no one would pay his ransom. So she did the only thing she could to protect her child. She picked up baby Bryan and crept away with him.

Now they had her baby, and she had theirs. And she was so confused and so utterly tired. Why, lately she'd become as boring as Hannah. That was why she'd decided to come into San Antonio tonight. She'd needed to get out, to have a little fun. She'd been a long time without a man.

Smoothing a hand down her narrow hips, she settled a demure smile into place and set off for the club down the street. It shouldn't take her long to find what she needed.

"Pretty is as pretty does," she whispered to herself.

She wet her lips and eased her hips into a traffic-stopping sway. Pushing through the nightclub's door, she glanced casually around. Music blasted, but she was more interested in the heads that turned as she entered.

All she'd thought about for weeks was her troubles. Tonight, she just wanted to have a little fun.

Tonight, Maria Cassidy felt very pretty, indeed.

"What was her name?" Hannah asked.

Parker's silence forced her to stop fiddling with the pink flamingo directly in front of her and look at him across the small table for two. He was wearing a gray suit and conservative tie. He had no business looking so utterly rugged and appealing.

"Her name *is* Jolene. Divorce doesn't change people irrevocably, Hannah."

A shudder went through Hannah. Ignoring her meal, she leaned forward, wishing there was some way to make Parker see that he was wrong. Divorce *did* change people. Oh, they usually recovered, but not without scars.

She'd been thinking about Parker ever since he'd left her sitting on the stairs after their walk last night. She'd thought about canceling their dinner date for tonight, but she hated to go back on her word, even if she *had* agreed to have dinner with him while she'd been speechless over the revelation that he'd been married.

He'd said once was enough. Since Hannah wasn't looking for anything less than forever, this could very well be the last time she saw him. First, she wanted to open his eyes to the possibility that he was wrong about divorce. She wanted him to realize that it wasn't something people did without heartache. Couldn't he see that most people mourned the end of a marriage? What he did for a living wasn't illegal. She wasn't so sure about unethical. She wished Parker didn't view it as a swift and final ending. Pain and loneliness didn't often end with the judge's decree.

So she'd kept her date for dinner, but she'd insisted upon meeting him here, at The Pink Flamingo. She wanted to be close to home. For some reason she felt that as long as she remained on her own turf, so to speak, there would be less risk to her heart.

Spearing a lettuce leaf, she said, "*Is* she pretty? Never mind. You don't have to answer that. Your wife would have had to be pretty, wouldn't she, Parker?"

"That depends. Was that a compliment or an insult?"

She shook her head, because it was neither. It was just a fact.

Parker Malone kissed like a dream, he had a quick wit and a sharp mind. He made her think, and he kept her on her toes. Tonight, she was being careful not to let him sweep her off them. Going back to her salad, she said, "Where is she now?"

"Last I knew she'd moved to Cleveland."

"Do you miss her?"

He lifted his glass of wine to his lips. "No."

"Did you love her?"

He shrugged. "I thought I did. Later I realized it wouldn't have mattered who the girl was. I'd finished college and had started practicing law. It was time for the next step. I took it. A few years later I took the next one and got a divorce."

"You're a cynical man, Parker."

"That's what she said."

Hannah wondered if Jolene had loved Parker. Probably. She'd read somewhere that women lived their lives through their hearts, and men lived theirs through their minds. What men thought, women felt.

"Adrienne has a theory as to why the divorce rate is so high today."

Parker swirled the wine in his glass. He didn't want to talk about divorce, or marriage, either, for that matter. Actually, he didn't feel like talking, period. He would have preferred to find a quiet corner, or a quiet room. His house came to mind, but hers would have sufficed. Hannah, on the other hand, didn't seem to be in any hurry to leave.

He took another sip of his wine, not quite certain what to make of her tonight. She'd worn her hair up. She probably had a reason for choosing the brown tweed pantsuit, but if she thought it detracted from her beauty, she was wrong. It covered, but it sure as hell didn't hide. When he'd left her yesterday evening, he'd been feeling extremely lofty. Very sure of himself and of her. Tonight it seemed he was back at square one.

"Sex."

He choked on his wine. Coughing into his hand, Parker said, "Did you say sex?"

She nodded sagely.

"Do you mean adultery?" he asked.

She shook her head, and lowered her voice to a whisper. "I should have been more specific. Adrienne is convinced that having sex before marriage is today's couples' down-fall.''

"Let me get this straight. The thirty-something blond bombshell and former beauty queen in the bright pink miniskirt who called me 'sugar' thinks people should wait until they're married to have sex?"

She nodded again, as if pleased that he was getting this. "I have to say I agree with her. And I'm not just saying that because I'm—"

She turned suddenly, smiling at the waiter who'd just appeared at their table. Parker's mind came to a screeching halt.

Hannah's lips were still shaped around a word that be-gan with "w." She wasn't just saying that because she was *what?*

Wise?

Winsome?

Waiting?

Was that it? She was waiting?

When Parker coughed this time, it wasn't from the wine.

Four

"Would either of you care for dessert?"

Parker ignored the interloping waiter and continued to stare at Hannah. She was smiling now, but her lips had been pursed slightly, dammit, and he wanted to know why. She'd said she happened to agree with Adrienne, who evidently believed there was a direct relationship between sex and the divorce rate in this country.

Had Hannah been about to say she was waiting or hadn't she?

Waiting for what? Christmas?

"Parker, you remember Jason, don't you?"

He glared at the kid who'd run into him a week or so ago.

The boy's Adam's apple wobbled nervously. "I'm sorry about the other day, sir. I'll pay for the tie, or the dry-cleaning bill. Or if you want, I'll have Adrienne deduct your dinner from my paycheck."

"That won't be necessary, Jason," Hannah said. "Will it, Parker?"

Parker's lips twisted. He didn't want the kid's money. Hell, he would have paid *him* to take a hike. Running a finger inside the collar of his shirt, Parker said, "Forget it. I have other ties. Did you want to order dessert, Hannah?"

Hannah nodded, and said, "Gerard's chocolate mousse is always a sure hit."

The boy gasped. Hannah smiled guilelessly. And Parker

conceded defeat. The woman was one step ahead of him all the way.

"You heard the lady," he said to the young waiter. "Bring us each a chocolate mousse. This time, I'll take mine in a bowl."

Jason hurried away before his blush had made it past his neck. Hannah was almost sure something had shifted deep inside of her. Parker was a sharp-tongued lawyer who could have read Jason the riot act, demanding retribution, making degrading, demoralizing comments. Instead he'd let the boy off the hook. He wasn't as ruthless as he wanted people to believe.

There was absolutely no reason she should suddenly want to touch him. And yet she leaned forward, and slowly placed her fingertips over the back of his hand.

Dishes clattered on the other side of the room, and people murmured in low voices at a nearby table. Parker remained perfectly quiet, his gaze trailing in the direction Jason had just taken. When he finally looked at her, his blue eyes had darkened and were filled with intensity. It was easy to get lost in the way he was looking at her, easy to see why his female clients felt inclined to tuck their underclothes into his pockets.

"If you're not careful," she said quietly, "people are going to discover that you have a soft spot in your heart."

Parker was aware of the sultry tone in Hannah's voice. And he could feel the gentle warmth in her touch. He tried to decide whether either of those things were provocative in nature. They certainly stimulated him.

"I'm not feeling particularly soft, Hannah."

Her smile changed slightly. "I'm not touching that—" she shook her head when he quirked one eyebrow in silent expectation "—line."

An innocent virgin, her? In this day and age? A twenty-seven-year-old woman with her build and sassy grin? No. Uh-uh. Absolutely not. Unexperienced virgins didn't laugh that way, move that way, touch and smile and react that way. Virgins were timid and unsure. Hannah seemed to know exactly what she was doing.

And Parker liked what she was doing very, very much.

"Ah, Hannah. You are planning another beautiful wedding, *sí?*"

"Yes, Consuela." Hannah glanced up at Parker first, and then down at the elderly woman who was taking a walk with her husband. "I'm working on three. Four, if you count my mother's. I'm also planning a party following a Bar Mitzvah, two engagement parties, and eight birthday celebrations."

"You should concentrate on the weddings," the woman said, her smile young-looking in her old, wrinkled face. "It is what you were born for, I think."

Hannah's exhilaration grew. "You know weddings are my favorite."

The old couple bid Parker and Hannah goodbye in Spanish, then ambled down the street, hand in hand. Inclining his head close to Hannah's ear, he said, "Do you know everybody in this neighborhood?"

They'd reached the back of her building. Going up on tiptoe, she plucked a leaf off a vine trailing up the stairs that led to her fire escape on the second floor. "I like people."

Parker folded his arms and leaned one hip against a wrought-iron post nearby. They'd left The Pink Flamingo via a side door, and had decided to take the back alley to Hannah's place. She lived less than a block away. The trip had taken nearly an hour.

It turned out that Hannah couldn't pass any of the people

who were sitting on stoops or fire escapes facing the alley without saying hello. Parker hadn't minded. A long time ago he'd learned that some of the best knowledge was easily obtained by simply listening. He'd certainly learned a lot about Hannah. Her neighbors loved her. Of course they did. She genuinely cared for them, asking after grandchildren, brothers and sisters, even an old man's long lost cousin in Mexico.

"Do you know all your neighbors' relatives by name?" he asked quietly.

"Don't you?"

"Except for Maxwell Lewis, who I met when I handled his divorce a few years ago, I only know my neighbors by the cars they drive."

She lowered her voice, being purposefully mysterious. "That wouldn't work on this street. Half the people who live in these buildings don't drive." Angling her head toward the old couple who had ambled away, she said, "Manuel and Consuela have been married for sixty-two years, and they still hold hands. Just goes to show that romance isn't exclusively for the young."

He waited until they were halfway up the stairs to say, "I'm not opposed to romance. I'd be happy to prove it to you."

"You're too kind."

Following her to the top, he said, "That's the first time I've ever been accused of that."

He sensed her small smile, but she seemed to know better than to reply. She unlocked a heavy steel door, which swung in on silent hinges. Together, they stepped into a small sitting room. She flipped a switch, and the room was bathed in soft light.

Glancing around, Parker wondered why he was amazed when the room was exactly what he should have expected.

Once again, it wasn't the colors that made it uniquely feminine, but the style. The off-white carpet was soft beneath his feet, the beige overstuffed sofa with its gracefully curved back and all those lace-covered pillows could have only been purchased by a woman.

"Would you like something to drink, Parker?" she asked, opening a window and turning on a ceiling fan. "I'm afraid my only concession to liquor is cooking sherry and Chianti, a gift from a former client. But I have lemonade in the refrigerator."

"Nothing for me," he said, watching as she strode to an antique writing desk and punched the button on her answering machine. She listened to the beginning of each message, then fast-forwarded to the next. Wondering who she was hoping to hear from, he wandered to a unit of shelves across the room.

Her reading material ranged from coffee-table books to recent bestsellers, to Kafka, which further proved that Hannah Cassidy was a study in contrasts. Beige and lace. Kafka and an entire book devoted to comics. Cooking sherry and Chianti. A brown tweed pantsuit and that body.

"How long have you lived here?" he asked.

"Four years."

"It suits you."

"Adrienne swears it needs a little pink. Preferably bright pink."

He thought she sounded preoccupied. "Bright pink isn't your style, is it, Hannah?"

Hannah turned slowly. Her messages droned in the background. She barely heard. Parker was standing across the small room, one hand in his pocket, his feet spread a comfortable distance apart, his head tilted slightly. The lamp in the corner cast shadows behind him, deepening the cleft in his chin. She couldn't see the color of his eyes from where she stood, but the sensual intent came through loud and clear.

Fumbling behind her, she turned off the answering machine. She'd just spoken to every neighbor she'd happened to see. How could she suddenly be at a loss for something to say to Parker?

There was something deliberate in the step he took in her direction, something just as deliberate in his smile. "What's your favorite color, Hannah? No. Let me guess. It's brown."

She smiled. She couldn't help it. He thought he was so intuitive. "Nobody's favorite color is brown, but you're close. Actually, I like anything in the brown family. Honey, beige, tan, cocoa, cinnamon, coffee, terra-cotta."

"Warm colors for a warm woman."

He walked closer, his stride as smooth as that last line.

She wasn't afraid of him. She knew on an instinctive level that he wouldn't take advantage of her. Still, to insure that he didn't get the wrong idea, she held up one hand in a halting gesture.

He took her hand in his. Before she could do more than gasp, she toppled into his arms.

He covered her lips with his as if he knew exactly what he was doing, and was enjoying it immensely. She could have fought the kiss, but the way he held her, as if she was delicate and special and a rare gift, was difficult to resist.

Impossible to resist.

She closed her eyes. Giving in to the delicious sensations pouring through her, she parted her lips and kissed him in return. She took a deep breath the moment his lips left hers. He smelled like summer and spice and man. Pressing one hand over his chest, she spread her fingers wide over his heart, inching upward to his neck. On some level she was conscious of the whisker stubble on his cheek, of the broad bones and taut skin along his jaw, of the narrow little dip in the center of his chin, but she was more conscious of the warmth that was weakening her knees, and the desire that was quickly spinning out of control.

His lips left hers. Covering her hand with his, he brought it to his mouth, pressing a kiss into her palm. Hannah's eyes opened dreamily, his features blurring slightly, the dark blue of his eyes turning hazy and deep.

"You're beautiful."

This close, her features had to be as blurry as his. It didn't matter. She wasn't beautiful, not the way her mother and Maria were, but that didn't matter, either. Because he was making her feel beautiful, and every woman alive knew that that mattered a great deal.

Lowering from her tiptoes, she said, "Are you sure I can't get you anything?"

"You can show me to the bedroom."

"I could." She made no move to do it, though.

"Hannah?"

She chanced a glance up at him, and slowly shook her head. "I'm trying to think of the right words to make you understand."

"I understand the attraction that's between us. You can't deny that you feel it, too."

Just like that, he kissed her again, without warning, devouring, cajoling, enticing. By the time he raised his mouth from hers, she was breathless all over again.

"You're a hard man to resist," she said softly.

"There's no need to resist." His voice was a husky murmur close to her ear.

"It's too soon, Parker."

"The timing is perfect."

A shiver of wanting strummed through her.

"You want this," he whispered.

She practically swooned at the feel of his lips along the sensitive skin below her ear. "That's beside the point."

"Honey, that is the point."

"Maybe," she whispered. "But…"

He paused, the sound of his deeply drawn breath loud in her ear. "I'm listening."

"I'm waiting."

There was that word again, Parker thought. "Define waiting."

She wet her lips, straightened her clothes, took a deep breath. And finally met his gaze. "I'm waiting. For the right man. For a commitment. For forever."

"You can't mean you're waiting for your wedding night."

She pulled a little face. "Nobody can say that with absolute certainty. I mean, people with the best of intentions have been known to get carried away. After all, sex is a heady, pleasurable sensation."

"I know how pleasurable sex is." He decided to try a different tack. "Look, I make a very good living from clients who prove over and over that marriage and forever are two completely different concepts."

"Maybe for some. I know what you're thinking, Parker. But there are still a few of us around."

The implication hit him between the eyes like a sledgehammer. He didn't know whether she was a virgin—he grimaced at the notion—or one of those born-again virgins he'd read about. Either way, it was insane.

He must have said it out loud, because she bristled. "You're welcome to your opinion. I'll stick to mine. Attraction is nice, but so often it fizzles. Love lasts."

"Love is overrated."

Hannah could have argued. But she refrained. Instead she took a frank look at Parker. After quiet deliberation she decided that only someone who had never been in love could say such a thing with so much quiet conviction.

She crossed her arms and redistributed her weight to one foot, and finally said, "And sex isn't overrated?"

She thought his derisive snort was uncalled for. *She* shouldn't have to defend herself, or her morals, or her standards. She wasn't judging him, and he had no right to judge her. The more she thought about it, the more it rankled.

Parker didn't know how he'd ended up at the door. He must have followed Hannah there. Her mention of sex had wiped his mind clean of every thought except one. "You *have* been with other men, haven't you?"

Her head came up and her shoulders went back. "Define 'been.'"

He knew he was out of line, but what the hell. He'd come this far. "Been with. Slept with. Made love with. Take your pick."

"Would you like names?"

He would, yes. "That won't be necessary."

"I'll tell you."

He was so intent upon what she had to say that he put up absolutely no resistance when she opened the door and propelled him through it.

"I'll tell you," she said again, licking her lips in a way that was provocative as hell. "When pigs fly. Watch that first step. It's a doozy."

The door slammed so fast he barely had time to get his nose out of the way.

He stood at the top of the fire escape, gritting his teeth. Street noises carried to his ears from the other side of the building, but not a sound came from inside Hannah's apartment.

She'd made herself extremely clear. She'd all but called him a name, for crying out loud. She was the one who'd said they were complete opposites. He should have listened. Next time he...

Swearing under his breath, Parker started down the steps. There wasn't going to be a next time. He didn't trifle with women who were waiting for a commitment. He knew all too well that commitments were made to be broken.

There absolutely, positively, wasn't going to be a next time. And that was that.

"Sophia's attorneys have finally responded to our last settlement offer, Ryan." Parker held up the thick sheaf of papers that had arrived from Sophia Fortune's attorneys late yesterday afternoon.

Her lawyers were cunning, he'd give them that much. Sending something of this significance so late on a Friday insured that Ryan's attorneys couldn't retaliate until Monday. Parker had used the tactic himself.

Being on the receiving end of the maneuver was a relatively new experience. Parker planned to use the weekend to plan his strategy and set up his next move.

"What does she want now?" Ryan pushed to his feet and paced to the window in his study.

"It's carefully worded in lawyer gibberish. But it boils down to more demands, more money, assets, stocks. Actually, it even says she would like to reconcile."

Ryan spoke with derision. "She wants to reconcile with my bank balance."

Parker strummed his fingers on Ryan's massive mahogany desk. "You're probably right. Either way, she wants half of everything you have."

Ryan spun around. "I've already offered her millions. I'm willing to meet some of her demands just to be rid of her, but I won't give her half of the Double Crown and all its holdings."

Parker kept his gaze trained on Ryan, but Ryan turned to look out the window. Technically, it was the weekend. The hundred head of cattle in the distance didn't care that it was Saturday. Neither did the ranch hands on horseback who were moving them to greener pastures. The ranch was vast, but it was so much more than dirt and grass and cattle and outbuildings. Lily was in the stables right now, checking on the filly that had been born a few weeks ago. Rosita, his housekeeper, had predicted the filly's birth right down to the day and the lily-shaped mark on its narrow head. She'd always had metaphorical dreams, but lately they'd been coming to pass with astounding accuracy. He took the birth of that filly as a good sign. Anything that kept Lily close to him was good, as far as he was concerned. He wanted his divorce behind him, so he and Lily could go forward with their lives.

Continuing to stare out the window, Ryan said, "My father would roll over in his grave if he knew anyone was trying to get half of his empire, but that isn't the reason I won't agree to Sophia's terms. He'd be angry, but he wouldn't overlook his own mistakes. God knows, he made his share of them over the years. Kingston Fortune loved this ranch. He loved my mother first and foremost. The original tract of land on which the entire Fortune empire was founded belonged to her. Together, they built this ranch acre by acre, investment by investment. Selena Fortune saw her family through loss and hardships, sometimes with little more than her own blood, sweat and tears to carry us all through. This ranch is a legacy to her, and I will not split it up for a woman like Sophia.''

Parker's eyes had narrowed, but the rest of his features remained unchanged. If Ryan's tirade had been an act, it would have warranted a standing ovation. But it wasn't an act. The man was passionate, adamant about his holdings and his stand. Parker dealt with passionate, adamant husbands or wives every day. It wasn't his job to judge. It was his job to reason, wheedle, finagle and negotiate on their behalf. Parker Malone, of Malone, Malone & Associates *always* cut the best deal, insuring that his client retained as big a cut, as large a percentage of his or her assets as was humanly possible.

Tensions normally ran high during divorce proceedings. It had been his experience that couples whose passion had been banned from the bedroom found a new outlet through vindictiveness, anger and blame. It was Parker's job to remain focused, sharp, and assessing. It was his job to protect his clients's best interests.

''Sophia won't get half of the Double Crown, Ryan.'' Parker motioned toward the packet of papers lying nearby. ''This is merely a delay tactic. She wants to see you suffer. I believe she would like to see you squirm. This would have been eliminated if you had insisted she sign a prenuptial agreement prior to your marriage to her.''

Backing his words up with carefully calculated actions, Parker reached into his briefcase and pulled out the prenuptial agreement he'd advised Ryan to have Lily sign.

Out of the blue, Ryan said, ''How old are you, son?''

Parker's eyes narrowed. Dammit, the question interrupted the point he was trying to make.

''I don't mean to sound condescending.''

Parker conceded with a slight nod. After all, Ryan couldn't have gotten where he was today without being astute. If he had something to say, Parker would be stupid not to listen.

He met Ryan's level look with one of his own. "I'm thirty-one."

"Have you ever been in love?"

Parker's surprise infiltrated his carefully schooled expression. His eyebrows drew down, not in consideration of the question, but in his attempt to understand where the question had come from and where it was leading.

"I didn't think so," Ryan said. "I've loved two women. My first wife, Janine, and Lily. I've wasted enough years on Sophia. Too many. I have the utmost faith in your capabilities, but the sooner you secure her signature on the divorce papers the better. Lily Redgrove Cassidy is my second chance at happiness. I don't intend to waste a moment of it."

Parker began gathering his papers, his reason for paying Ryan a visit at the ranch nearly complete. Placing a legal document on Ryan's desk, Parker said, "Look over this prenuptial agreement, Ryan. As your attorney, I can't advise you strongly enough to think long and hard and then refrain from tossing it into the wastebasket."

Ryan took one step toward his desk. Rather than looking long and hard at the document as Parker had advised, he looked long and hard at Parker. Parker reached for his briefcase, then met Ryan's gaze. "You might as well say what's on your mind."

Ryan continued to look at Parker, breaking the silence only when he was good and ready. "You have the reputation for being the best and most shrewd divorce attorney in all of San Antonio. I can't help but wonder if you would be as shrewd and as cunning if you were to fall in love."

"Don't worry. I'm immune."

Ryan settled his hands on his hips. "You shouldn't

worry that you might fall in love. You should worry that you might not.''

Parker didn't know how to respond to that.

Ryan didn't seem to expect a reply. ''I sensed you'd taken a fancy to Lily's daughter.''

''You sensed that?''

Ryan dismissed Parker's arched look with a quick shrug. ''I happened to see the two of you in a private moment out in my garden.''

The sound Parker made involved releasing his breath through his nose at the same time he muttered a one-syllable expletive. Had everyone seen them on that garden path?

''I was interested in Hannah Cassidy.'' He remembered the slam of her door. ''It turns out it was a passing fancy.''

He motioned to the papers lying on Ryan's desk. ''Read them carefully. There's a place for Lily's signature, and that of a notary public, at the bottom.''

Taking his briefcase in one hand, he shook Ryan's hand with the other, then strode toward the door.

The sheaf of papers made a distinctive thud in the bottom of the wastebasket about the same time Parker opened the heavy oak-paneled door.

''Wow.''

Raising the antique door knocker at the back entrance of the sprawling ranch house, Hannah glanced at Adrienne. ''I know. The Double Crown can be intimidating.''

Adrienne nudged Hannah with one sharp elbow. ''Intimidating. Are y'all crazy? My mama lives in a bigger house than this back in Atlanta. I just can't believe that somebody who runs a kitchen in a place like this wants a recipe from little, helpless ole me.''

When the door opened, Hannah was still smiling at the

notion that her best friend in the killer heels and leather miniskirt was either helpless or old. "Hi, Angie," Hannah said.

The nineteen-year-old girl who had been hired to help Rosita with the housework wrung her hands. "I tried to reach you, but you must have already been on your way here. And now you've wasted your trip."

"What is it?" Hannah asked.

"I'm afraid Rosita has taken to her pillows. She had another dream last night, and she's worried herself into a fit of exhaustion."

"A nightmare?" Hannah asked.

Angie nodded her head dramatically. "A premonition."

Hannah had heard of Rosita Perez's premonitions. In Red Rock, where Rosita had been born, she was known for her visionary dreams. Although some scoffed, Hannah's mother believed that Rosita's dreams were windows into the future. Her dreams were often metaphorical. Therefore, those windows were usually smoky and unclear.

"A premonition, really?" Adrienne asked.

Angie Sanchez eyed the strangely dressed blonde with obvious trepidation. "Do you believe in such things?" she asked suspiciously.

"Of course I do."

That was news to Hannah.

"What?" Adrienne said, her blue eyes guileless and serene. "Didn't I ever mention that my great-aunt on my father's side was clairvoyant? I have a cousin in Savannah who claims she has the power, too, only the ghost of an old woman who was killed by Sherman's soldiers chases away most of her vibes."

Angie and Hannah stared at Adrienne, speechless. Finally, Angie said, "You have a cousin who lives with a ghost?"

"A lot of old houses in the South are haunted. But don't worry. Cousin Edith's ghost is a lost soul, not a mean spirit."

"Come," Angie said. "I think you might be good for Rosita today."

Adrienne and Hannah followed the girl into a small sitting room off the kitchen where shades were drawn against the high noon sun. Looking pale and drawn, Rosita Perez pushed herself to a sitting position. "You are Señorita Adrienne?"

"The one and only."

Rosita's gaze made a careful sweep up and down Adrienne. "You wear shoes like that often?"

"I have a passion for heels."

Rosita harrumphed. "You have a penchant for bunions, I think. I am sorry to bring you all this way for nothing. I was hoping the chicken-fried steak Señor Ryan had last week at your Pink Pelican would bring him out of the dark mood that plagues him while he waits for his divorce from that evil Sophia."

"The Pink Flamingo." Adrienne arched one blond eyebrow. "I named my restaurant The Pink Flamingo, not The Pink Pelican."

"Ah. I knew it was a bird. There was a bird in my dream last night."

Adrienne, Hannah and Angie all sat, as if in one motion. "Tell them about it, Señora Rosita," Angie said. "I think they will understand."

Rosita took a shaky breath. "It was horrible. When I woke up, I could not breathe. Ruben brought me an antacid. It is his remedy for everything."

Hannah smiled to herself, and Adrienne said, "That sounds like a man."

Rosita nodded in understanding. "That husband of mine

is built like a bull and is as strong as an ox, but sometimes his brain is the size of a chicken's. My dream was not heartburn. Although it filled my heart with an ache. And with fear.''

"Can you describe your dream to us?" Hannah asked, her voice soft and comforting.

Taking a shuddering breath, Rosita began. "Ever since Señora Lily has come back into Señor Ryan's life, my dreams have centered around her. I do not understand it, nor do I understand the dreams. Strange things have happened. For a time, whenever I cracked an egg, it had two yolks. A sure sign that two babies are on the way. And then little Bryan was kidnapped, and another Fortune baby was returned in his place. One night I dreamed that Señora Lily was breast-feeding a baby. Before my eyes, the child turned into a scorpion and stung her.''

The room was suddenly very quiet. Hannah didn't necessarily see the correlation between eggs with two yolks and the tragic events surrounding the kidnapping of Matthew and Claudia Fortune's child, but Rosita's dream about the scorpion bothered Hannah, for it represented danger to her mother, and possibly death.

"Is that the dream you had last night?" she asked.

Rosita shook her head. "Last night's was worse. You see, many years ago, before Señora Janine took sick with cancer, she had a favorite horse, a beautiful Arabian mare she named Madisha. It means dream. Janine spent hours on the ranch with Madisha. When Señora Janine died, Madisha stayed in her stall for seven days. *Lamentando.*''

"In mourning," Angie translated.

Rosita nodded. "When the *bruja,* that is, witch, Sophia, became Señor Ryan's wife, she secretly ordered that Madisha be killed. My Ruben whisked Madisha away to a neighbor's ranch. This new filly of Señora Lily's is a descendent of Madisha, who died of old age three springs ago. Last night, in the guise of a dream, I saw Madisha again.''

Hannah, Adrienne and Angie all leaned forward in their seats, intent upon Rosita's tale. ''The new filly and Madisha were grazing peacefully, when another horse, beautiful but fierce and mean, approached at a gallop. The horse reared up as if in a rage, kicking Madisha and the filly, biting them, inflicting terrible pain. Madisha and the filly tried to get away, but the evil horse was more cunning and swift. Suddenly a horrible screech split the air. A huge bird of prey, part condor, part monster, I think, descended upon all three horses. There was a terrible scream, and then only silence. The meadow was empty. All three horses were gone, a single trail of blood the only evidence that they had been there at all.''

Adrienne uttered the Lord's name, which prompted Rosita to make the sign of the cross.

''Sorry. I think I prefer my cousin's ghost.''

''What do you think it means?'' Angie asked.

Rosita shook her head. ''I do not know, but it is not good.''

Hannah placed her hand over her racing heart. It did little to alleviate the fear and dread the dream had instilled deep in her chest.

Adrienne said, ''I'd planned to give you everything to make the chicken-fried steak wonderful, but I intended to leave out my own personal, private ingredient. Goodness gracious. After the night you had, I think I'll give you the secret ingredient, too.''

Rosita perked up considerably. ''There is a secret ingredient?''

Reaching into her bright purple purse, Adrienne pulled

out a recipe card. Rosita studied it carefully. "Batter-fried steak? How can this be good for a man's heart?"

"Who's to say what's bad for a man's heart?" Adrienne replied. "I guarantee this is good for a man's soul. Y'all serve a mixed-green salad the size of an ice-cream scoop with it and people will think they're eating healthy."

Rosita nodded knowingly. Adrienne and Hannah rose to leave. "*Gracias,*" Rosita said, her color returning. "And the secret ingredient?"

Hannah smiled, and Adrienne strolled across the room and whispered something in Rosita's ear. Rosita's eyes widened.

Adrienne said, "If that doesn't do the trick, I'll ask Gerard to come here and prepare his own tureen of duck for Ryan. It's to die for. He does a mean stuffed lobster, too."

"You make this for your man and then you make wedding plans," Rosita exclaimed.

"I don't have a man. Besides, Hannah's the wedding planner," Adrienne answered. "She's also the one who's recently been thoroughly kissed."

"Ah, yes, I saw Hannah and Señor Malone on the garden path."

Suddenly, Hannah felt like a deer trapped in headlights. Releasing a long, audible breath, she didn't see any reason to explain that whatever might have been between her and Parker was over. Besides, after that fiasco with him in her apartment a few days ago, she doubted she would ever see him again.

"Actually," Rosita said, "I see romance in the near future for both of you."

Hannah was even with the doorway, Adrienne close behind. "You see a prince charming for little ole me?" Adrienne said, laughing.

"Not charming, and not young, I think. Cunning like a fox, with teeth as sharp as a wolf's."

"What do you mean, not young? How 'not young'?" Adrienne asked.

"You will see."

"You're telling me I'm going to fall in love with a cunning, *older* man with sharp teeth?"

"*Sí*, and a sharp mind. Similar to Hannah's suitor. A pair. A matched set."

Adrienne gasped. Hannah couldn't even do that. She was too busy stopping in her tracks as she came face-to-face with Parker Malone.

Five

The sound of that prenuptial agreement hitting the bottom of the wastebasket was still ringing in Parker's ears as he walked into the foyer. At the same time, Hannah entered the room from the opposite side. Both froze in stunned tableau.

Parker was the first to recover. Ryan squeezed past him with little trouble, but there seemed to be a bottleneck in the doorway behind Hannah. Adrienne Blakely, Rosita Perez and another young woman Parker hadn't met ran into Hannah from behind, shoving her unceremoniously forward.

Toward him.

Her chin came up a fraction, her shoulders a good deal more. She took a quick, sharp breath, maintaining a cool reserve even in her obvious surprise. She was angry at him. Fine. Parker had intended to remain aloof anyway. After all, he was the one who'd had the door slammed in his face. As far as he was concerned, that gave him a hell of a lot more right to be angry than her. He stared at her boldly, challenging her to make something of it.

There was a slight scuffle behind her, and then a sultry voice with a distinctly Southern drawl filled the foyer. "If y'all are right, and there really is romance in my immediate future, I could use some of that antacid you mentioned earlier, Rosita."

Rosita smiled, looking much better than she had when

Parker had arrived an hour ago. Adrienne's smile slid away the instant she noticed him. Evidently, Hannah had told her friend about the way his date with Hannah had ended.

Turning his attention back to Hannah, he was beginning to question his timing. How often could one man run into one woman? And how long could the strained silence stretch between them?

"Hannah, my dear, there you are." Ryan strode to the center of the foyer and took one of Hannah's hands. "Your mother is in the stables with the new filly."

"That's nice, Ryan."

Parker thought she seemed distracted, which proved that she wasn't as unaware of him as she wanted him to believe. It didn't, however, change her cool reserve.

"I know she would love to see you," Ryan was saying. "Why don't you go out and say hello?"

Parker gave everyone in the room a quick glance. Rosita was speaking in hushed undertones to a young woman wearing an apron. Adrienne seemed to have recovered from her initial surprise and was watching *him* closely. As far as he knew, Hannah hadn't looked at him since that first moment when she'd entered the foyer. She was giving him the old cold shoulder.

He could handle that. In fact, he could top it. After all, he was...

Intrigued.

The hell he was.

An unwelcome tension settled over him. Intrigue such as that could only lead to complications. And complications such as that would be confusing. And there was no place in his life for confusion. He told himself he wasn't intrigued. And he meant it. He was...

Attracted.

Damn. That was worse. His mouth set in annoyance at his sudden change in body temperature.

Ryan was still talking. Raking a hand through his hair, Parker admitted that it was a good thing nobody had left the responsibility of carrying the conversation up to *him*.

"Why don't you go out to the stables and say hello?" Ryan said to Hannah.

"In these shoes?"

Although she cleared her throat and pretended not to be affected, Parker would bet the law practice that she recognized the excuse as the serious mistake that it was, because it drew attention to her feet. He would have to be a fool not to take advantage of the golden opportunity she'd given him.

No fool, Parker let his gaze take a slow dip down her body. She was wearing a simple short-sleeved shirt tucked into camel-colored slacks. Lightweight and pleated, the material draped elegantly over her legs, delineating the shape of one thigh, the narrow little ridge of her knee, and the slender bones in her ankles. She was right about the shoes. Smooth leather numbers with open toes and clunky heels weren't exactly the kinds of footwear suited for trudging through barnyards.

He wondered if she ever wore jeans and tennis shoes. He rarely did. Chinos or khakis and last year's loafers were his casual attire. Still, he wondered what Hannah wore for fun. Fleetingly, he wondered what she did for fun.

Obviously she didn't get into casual sex. His mouth set in annoyance all over again.

"I'd love to, Ryan, really I would," she said. "But I'm afraid I can't. I rode out here with Adrienne."

Ryan's attention swung to the eccentric blonde. Parker followed suit. Noting her attire for the first time, he nearly did a double take. A leather skirt in July?

She tucked her chin-length blond hair behind her ear and chewed on one bright pink fingernail. "Hannah's right," she said. "As much as we would love to stay and visit with y'all's new horse, my chef is expecting me back at the restaurant shortly."

Ryan smiled disarmingly. Adrienne stopped chewing on her fingernail and began twirling a lock of hair, her blue eyes going wide. Parker wondered if he was the only one who knew it was an act.

"Parker," Ryan said, "you're going straight back to the city, aren't you?"

Parker felt his eyes narrow. "I'd planned to, yes."

"Perfect," Ryan said, turning his attention back to Adrienne. "You can return to your restaurant immediately, and Hannah can ride back to San Antonio with Parker after she's said hello to Lily."

Adrienne glanced from Ryan to Hannah then back to Ryan.

Ryan had the audacity to wink at her. "Don't worry," he said. "Hannah will be in good hands."

"So I've heard."

It was Ryan's turn to grin. Turning to Hannah, he said, "Do you trust Parker, my dear?"

She looked at Parker grudgingly. "I suppose."

Ryan slapped his hands together, as if it was all settled. The next thing Parker knew, Rosita was seeing Adrienne out through the kitchen. He and Hannah had little choice but to follow Ryan out another door, around the beautifully kept courtyard on the opposite side of the house, to the driveway where Parker's car was parked.

The sun was hot, the air heavy with humidity. Cattle lowed far in the distance. Other than the low buzz of a bee nearby, the only sound Hannah heard was the soft scuffle of three pairs of shoes on the flagstone walkway. The barns were nearly half a mile away, the stables only slightly closer. Wondering how she'd gotten herself into this, she glanced at Parker. He was stone-faced.

Waving as Adrienne drove past her on her way down the long, curving driveway, Hannah was sure Ryan noticed his divorce attorney's discomfiture. Instead of commenting on it, Ryan stopped at the edge of the driveway and said, "This is where I will bid you goodbye."

"You aren't coming?" she asked.

"I'm afraid I can't," Ryan explained. "I'm expecting an important phone call. You two go ahead. Take this driveway to the stables. Oh, and Hannah? Your mother spoke with Maria over the telephone last night. I'm sure she would like to tell you about it."

He turned on his heel and disappeared inside the house. And Hannah and Parker were alone. They stared at each other for several seconds. Crossing her arms and tapping one foot, she said, "We've just been effectively manipulated."

Parker made a derisive snort.

"I don't mind the fact that Ryan's shrewd," she said. "It's the conniving part that gets to me."

Parker knew the feeling. Damn, he felt the way he did when an opposing attorney produced an incriminating slip of evidence on a case Parker had believed was open and shut. Shaking his head, he said, "Ryan Fortune didn't acquire his billions playing the lottery."

He strode to the passenger door of his dusty red car. "You might as well get in. Like you said, it would be a hell of a walk in those shoes."

She clamped her mouth shut and got in.

Hannah remained aloof during the short drive to the stables. She was a reasonable woman, and she had good reason for her cool reserve. She spoke when spoken to, answering Parker's questions with a word or two, but she added nothing to his attempt at conversation. Her stoicism brought back her sense of control.

She'd done a lot of thinking after he'd left her apartment the other night...okay, after she'd pushed him from it. Parker Malone elicited strong feelings, some good, some bad. The fact was, she reacted to him. He brought out the best and the worst in her. Take his smiles, for instance. They warmed her, and made her smile in return. Then there was his intelligence. She didn't always agree with the things he said, but when it came right down to it, he made her think. And his kisses. What they did to her was pretty incredible. Whoa. She decided then and there that she wouldn't think about Parker's kisses. Instead, she concentrated on his opinions. He was very stubborn about his views. He saw the world as black and white, marriage and divorce, a beginning and an end. She doubted forever was even in his vocabulary. That was the bottom line. That was why she couldn't give in to all the positive things about him, all the favorable reactions she had to those positive things. That was why she opened the door and got out of the car before Parker had shut off the engine. Sadly, Parker Malone was too big a risk to her heart.

A couple of the cowboys who worked for Ryan tipped their hats as she strode past them in the stable. "You must be Lily's daughter," one of them said.

A genuine smile, the first in several minutes, lit her face. "Do you know where my mother is?" she asked.

The cowboy motioned to a doorway on the far wall. "She's in the east corral with the new horse."

Hannah thanked the young hired hand. Being careful where she walked, she went in search of her mother.

As it turned out, she wouldn't have needed directions. All she had to do was follow the sound of Lily's voice.

"There, there. That's it," Lily murmured to the baby horse. "You're a dainty little thing, aren't you?"

Hannah raised her eyebrows at that. Dainty? The tip of the black filly's head already reached Lily's shoulder, which she bunted in a way that most definitely was not dainty.

"Hi, Mom."

Lily's face shone when she turned. "Hannah. Hello. Where's Adrienne?"

"She already left for town."

Her mother raised her exotically arched eyebrows. "How will you get back to San Antonio?"

"Parker has agreed to drive me."

"Parker?"

"It was Ryan's idea."

Lily chuckled. "That sounds like Ryan. What do you think of my new baby?"

"She's very...energetic."

"She just hasn't learned her manners, yet. I'm glad you're here. It's time I came up with a name for her. Any ideas?"

Hannah cocked her head to one side, strolling out into the corral. The horse was dark black, like the mare hovering nearby. Her coat was shiny, her legs long and thin. Hannah knew there was a huge segment of the population who had a passion for horses. Her mother was one of them. For a time, Maria had been wild about the creatures, but as with so many of Maria's hobbies, it had been a passing phase.

Hannah studied the foal. The only names she could think of were names she'd heard on the news or in the movies. Flicka, Black Beauty, High Stepper, Possum, Morning

Glory. Since this particular filly was black, Midnight seemed fitting, although more than a little trite. "What have you considered and discarded so far?" she asked.

Lily rubbed the filly's knobby head. "With that white mark in the middle of her forehead, an obvious name would be Lily. But I simply can't name her after me. I've considered Lilith, it means 'of the night,' and Leila, which means 'dark as night,' and Lisha, 'darkness before midnight.' But she's too pretty to be named after darkness."

Hannah shrugged one shoulder, and cautiously held out a hand to stroke the animal's short mane. "Linda is the Spanish word for pretty."

"A horse named Linda?" Lily asked.

Hannah grinned. "You'll come up with something, Mom. In the meantime, she's lucky to have so much love and attention."

Mother and daughter both paused. Their gazes met, and they both grinned. "Lucky," Lily said. "Why, that's perfect, especially since lately I feel like the luckiest woman alive. Look here, Lucky. Atta girl. What do you think? Are you feeling lucky today?"

The filly batted her inch-long eye lashes flirtatiously. For a moment she reminded Hannah of Maria. "Mom? Ryan said you talked to Maria last night."

"Thank goodness I finally reached her."

"How is she?"

"She sounded good," Lily said, her fingers slipping into the back pockets of her jeans, her eyes delving into Hannah's. "Better than she has in a long time."

Lily's relief was evident in every feature. Her brown eyes shone with affection, not worry, her smile was soft-looking and serene. Hannah heaved a heartfelt sigh. Maria had always been plagued with dark moods. She was easily bored and easily angered. Lily used to say her youngest child was like the girl in the nursery rhyme who had a little curl in the middle of her forehead. When she was good, she was really very good, but when she was bad, she was horrid. Hannah smiled at the memory. On her good days, Maria had been such fun. And on her bad days...well. Hannah had spent more time worrying about her younger sister than about everyone else in the family combined.

"Is Maria seeing anyone?" she asked her mother.

For a while now Hannah had suspected that her sister was involved with a married man. What other explanation could there be for her obsessive desire for privacy and seclusion?

"I don't know, dear, but she's agreed to come to the ranch for a visit. Ryan suggested we make it a celebration. We're both hoping it will allay Maria's fears and reservations about him."

"I think that's a good idea, Mom."

"You'll come, won't you?"

"You know I will."

Lily beamed at her daughter, and laughed out loud when the filly nudged her in an obvious ploy for attention. "See? Didn't I tell you I'm the luckiest woman in the world?"

Hugging her mother goodbye, Hannah remembered the dream Rosita had described. A shiver crawled up her spine. Forcing the unease away, she prayed her mother would always be this happy.

Parker jiggled the change in his pocket. Never one to enjoy standing around doing nothing, he glanced at his watch. He had a meeting at three. Although he had plenty of time, he was in a hurry to be on his way.

He'd been waiting by his car. Wondering how much longer Hannah would be, he strode into the stables. The air was rife with the smell of horses and hay and manure. Several of the animals poked their heads out as he passed. Two teenage boys were pitching straw, a couple of slightly older ranch hands were cleaning out stalls. It made Parker appreciate his clean, tastefully decorated office in the city.

Through a window, he could see Lily brushing down a young horse. Hannah wasn't with her. Where had she gone? Glancing around, he caught a glimpse of her white shirt up ahead. She stopped abruptly and let out a little yelp. Listening intently, he stayed in the shadows, and crept closer.

Hannah pressed a hand to her throat. "Oh," she said, her eyes trained on a man who seemed to have appeared out of nowhere. "I didn't know anyone else was in here."

The man was large, broad-shouldered and muscular. Although she couldn't see his eyes beneath the brim of his dusty cowboy hat, she could feel them on her body. Something in that gaze made her skin crawl. If only she hadn't allowed her curiosity to get the best of her. Then she would have been safe with her mother instead of roaming the stables.

"You must be one of the Cassidy woman's daughters," he said. "The resemblance is unmistakable."

The guttural rasp in his voice prevented his observation from being a compliment. Unwilling to let him see how nervous he made her, Hannah forced her lips into a semblance of a smile. "Do you know my mother?"

The man lifted his chin, and Hannah got her first glimpse of cold, blue eyes. "I know everything that goes on around this place. I'm Ryan's right-hand man. Have been since I was practically still a kid. The Double Crown couldn't run without me."

A braggart, she thought. That didn't necessarily mean

he was dangerous. It didn't mean he wasn't, either. Keeping her distance, she said, "Watching over a ranch this size must be difficult."

His step in her direction was deliberate. His expression said he was enjoying playing cat and mouse.

He wasn't the kind of man she would want to meet in a dark alley. But it wasn't as if they were alone in the huge building, she told herself. There were ranch hands nearby, and her mother, and Parker was somewhere.

"I was born to ranching," he said. "Among other things." His gaze raked over her boldly. "I'm Clint Lockhart."

Hannah turned in a half circle, pretending that she hadn't noticed the hand he'd held out. "I should be going."

"No need to rush off," he declared. "See that horse over there? It's an Arabian mare. Worth a small fortune."

Keeping Clint Lockhart in her peripheral vision, she glanced at the animal. The horse was black, large, and beautiful. "It reminds me of the filly Ryan gave to my mother."

"Ryan has a good eye for horseflesh. Among other things."

She felt Clint Lockhart's eyes on her breasts. It required a conscious effort not to squirm.

"But then," he murmured, "so do I."

This time when he stepped toward her, she stepped away. His eyes narrowed, and she could see the lines beside them. He looked to be in his mid-forties. His hair hung down his neck in a short pony tail. Neither the style nor the fact that there was no gray in the reddish-brown tresses did anything to make him look young. Or less intimidating.

His lips lifted in a smile that didn't reach his eyes.

"Don't be shy, little darlin'. When you're the best there is, you don't have to use force."

He tipped his hat, and finally went back to his earlier task. Hannah hurried away with her heart in her throat.

"Hey."

A second mewling scream in a matter of minutes rushed out of her. She jumped back. "Parker! You scared me half to death."

Since apologizing for something that wasn't his fault evidently wasn't his style, he made no reply. Glancing over his shoulder, he said, "What do you say we get out of here?"

They bumped into each other in the center of the corridor, a direct reaction to the horses poking their heads out of the stalls lining both walls. Keeping well out of the horses' reach, they turned to face each other. Hannah's heart pounded an erratic rhythm. She took a deep, steadying breath, and wound up wrinkling up her nose. "The next time someone from the country complains about the smell of exhaust fumes and smog, I'm going to have a reply."

Parker's chuckle came as a surprise even to him. "Ryan thinks everyone loves the beasts," he said.

They both took a deep breath the instant they reached the outdoors. Ah, that was better, Hannah thought. "I take it you don't?" Hannah asked.

"I don't *dislike* them. But I prefer cars. Any make. Any year. Any day."

She eyed several chestnut-colored horses in a nearby corral. "They're beautiful creatures, but they scare me." And then, in a voice gone noticeably deeper, she said, "But not as much as Clint Lockhart."

Parker's eyes narrowed as they followed the red-haired man in the distance. He hadn't been close enough to hear the conversation between Hannah and Ryan's foreman, but he'd heard the tone in the other man's voice. Clint Lockhart wasn't a man Parker trusted.

"I asked Ryan about him once," he said. "He said two things. Number one, Lockhart knows ranching. And number two, their fathers went way back."

"Is he really Ryan's right-hand man?"

"Lockhart likes to think so."

Hannah shuddered.

"I wouldn't want to meet him in a dark alley. I'm not so sure he would take no for an answer."

"The way I did, you mean."

Hannah's silence drew Parker's attention. She was gazing into the distance as they walked, the breeze tangling her hair, ruffling the sleeves of her white shirt.

"I should have handled the other night better," she said without looking at him. "I rarely get angry."

"I rarely get turned down."

A smile started at the corners of her mouth, blooming into a full-fledged grin.

"I'm glad somebody finds this situation amusing," he said.

"This isn't a situation, Parker."

They'd reached his car. "What would you call it?" he asked over the car's roof.

She turned her head smoothly, finally meeting his gaze. It occurred to him that she was studying him as closely as he was studying her. "I'd say we're becoming friends."

"Friends?" There was disbelief in his voice.

Hannah's smile returned.

"Friends," he said again. "I'll be damned."

"So basically, you're saying that you take marriages apart, piece by piece."

Parker could feel Hannah's eyes on him, but he kept his gaze trained on the highway and the traffic. He and Hannah had been bona fide friends for more than an hour. He still couldn't believe it. "The marriage has already come apart by the time a client comes to me."

"Do you ever try to talk a client into reconciling?"

He checked the rearview mirror, changed lanes. "That's a marriage counselor's job. Most of my clients have already been through that step. I don't split up two people. I split up their assets, preferably not down the middle."

"That doesn't sound fair."

"It's all done within the limits of the law, Hannah."

He could tell by her noisily drawn breath how she felt about the laws he'd mentioned. He hid a smile. They'd been arguing about the same thing for the entire car ride. The trip back into San Antonio had never gone faster.

The traffic light on the edge of the downtown district turned red as he neared. Pulling to a stop, he glanced in her direction. She was looking out the window at a man holding a sign on the corner.

"I still say it's too easy to get a divorce these days."

Parker thought about suggesting that she tell that to Ryan the next time she saw him, but Hannah unhooked her seat belt and opened her door before he had the chance. "Where are you—"

He was too late. The door closed, and she rushed to the corner, dropping some bills into the begging man's hand. She was back in a flash, slightly winded, slightly windblown, and glowing.

"Why the hell did you do that?"

"He's hungry."

"You're enabling him to continue to beg."

"I'm enabling him to buy himself supper."

"Or booze."

"You don't know what he's been through, Parker. Maybe he used to be a hardworking citizen, and his life fell apart a little at a time. Maybe he lost his job and then his wife got sick and died and he didn't have any insurance so he lost his house and his will to go on. Maybe he's forgotten how it feels to be looked at with kindness and not derision. Maybe—"

"Maybe he's never known how it feels to put in an honest day's work."

"Maybe. But I doubt it. Even if that's true, there was probably a reason."

Shaking his head, he stared at her.

"What?" she asked.

"I was just looking for the rose-colored glasses."

She ran a hand through the air a few inches in front of her face. "Contacts."

She turned those eyes, contacts and all, on him. They were gray, soulful, the kind of eyes a man could lose himself in. Parker was losing himself right now, losing his train of thought, his sense of composure, his sense of reality. He was waiting at a busy intersection, but he was remembering another time, another place, the weight of her breast in his hand, her breath on his cheek, her soft sigh of pleasure.

A sound came from behind him. Somewhere.

"Parker?"

He grunted something that passed for, "Yes?"

"Green means go."

A horn honked in annoyance.

Jerking slightly, Parker put the car in gear and his mind back on track. Where were they? Oh, yes. He was pointing out the obvious pitfalls to feeding beggars. "People will take advantage of you if you let them."

She shrugged, totally unaffected. "I've found that if I

keep my expectations good and high, people try to live up to them.''

Parker strummed his fingers on the steering wheel. The fact that Hannah exuded a dynamic vitality didn't change the fact that her unfailing belief in people was as impractical as it was impossible.

She must have noticed his barely controlled annoyance because she said, ''What?''

He kept all expression from his voice as he said, ''I was just wondering what fairy tale you stepped out of.''

''People rarely let me down, Parker. How about you?''

''How about me?''

''Do people often let you down?'' she asked.

He didn't give people the chance to let him down. He'd learned that at his father's knee.

He supposed it was possible that there was a grain of truth to her theory. Perhaps there were people in the world who strove to live up to her expectations simply because she kept her expectations high. His gaze caught on her mouth. Maybe it was her wholesomeness. Or maybe it was because she was easy to like. Hell, he liked her, and he didn't like many people. More surprising was that she seemed to like him. Surprising and unsettling, because he wanted her to like him. And Parker Malone rarely cared. He was out to win cases, not popularity contests. He'd learned that at his father's knee, too.

''My father would have a field day with you,'' he said.

''Ah, yes, the legendary J. D. Malone. The lean, mean divorce machine.''

''Some people say I'm just like him.''

''What would you say?'' she asked.

He pulled to a stop at the curb in front of The Perfect Occasion. ''I'd say they're right.''

''I've got news for you.''

"Meaning?"

"Don't panic, but there's goodness in you, Parker. I'll bet I could find some goodness in your father, too."

That sounded like a challenge. And he liked challenges almost as much as he liked winning. "Care to put your money where your mouth is?"

Hannah turned her head slowly. There had been something lazily seductive in the tone of Parker's voice. There was something just as seductive in his eyes. "You mean, bet?" she asked.

His nod said one thing, his smile something else entirely. "Betting is illegal. Think of it as an experiment."

"What kind of stakes would this *experiment* entail?"

His gaze homed in on her mouth. She raised her eyebrows in silent expectation. "If you suggest the winner gets to take the loser to bed, I'll be forced to hit you with my purse."

Only his eyes smiled. "I like the way your mind works. Normally, I would agree to those terms. After all, I'd be a winner either way, but it would be awkward, since you're waiting for a commitment, and we're just friends."

Hannah studied him thoughtfully. No wonder women put their panties in his pockets.

No matter how sexy he was, there was more to him than dark good looks and a cunning mind. She wouldn't mind the opportunity to prove it to him. "I think we're getting off the subject. Correct me if I'm wrong, but I believe the *experiment* on the table is that I can find goodness in your father. You're on."

"We still need stakes."

"Experiments don't have stakes."

"This one will," he said. "We can decide on them after tonight."

"Tonight?" she asked.

"After we have dinner at my father's."

Dinner? she thought. "You're almost as manipulative as Ryan."

He shrugged. "You have your work cut out for you."

She studied his profile. He had a broad forehead, dark eyebrows, a straight, longish nose. The little cleft in his chin gave his chiseled features a touch of mystery.

He turned his head, and found her watching him. "Well?" he asked.

From now on she was going to have to remember that she wasn't dealing with any ordinary man here. She was dealing with a sharp and assessing divorce attorney.

"Hannah?"

"I can't tonight." The quirk of his left eyebrow prompted her to add, "I already made plans. With Adrienne."

"Set plans or so-so plans?"

"So-so, I suppose."

"Then get out of them."

"I don't ditch my friends."

"Then bring her along."

Bring Adrienne?

"It's just dinner, Hannah."

Hannah started to smile. Bring Adrienne. Of course.

Tonight was going to be a night to remember. She stuck out her hand. He took it, and shook it.

They had a deal.

Six

"Turn right at the next intersection."

Hannah did as Adrienne directed, pulling her five-year-old compact past a lavishly landscaped sign indicating the entrance into one of the most elite suburbs of San Antonio.

Adrienne sat in the passenger seat, one finger on the map in her lap, her eyes trained on street signs and markers. "Tell me again why y'all are having dinner here, and why you insisted I accompany you on your date."

"First of all, this isn't a date," Hannah said, her voice low and composed in her effort to keep the awe she felt at the sight of so many huge homes at bay. "It's an experiment. And I invited you because you're my best friend. And J. D. Malone intimidates me, and well, nobody intimidates you."

"Sugar, some people intimidate me. The trick is to never let them know it."

"How did you acquire so much backbone?"

Adrienne shrugged. "My mama taught me some of it, but most of it comes from turning the big three-O. Everything starts to fall into place after that. Women say things make even more sense after forty. Personally, I'm not ready to have things make that much sense."

Hannah smiled. For a woman so obviously at ease with herself and her place in the universe, Adrienne practically held a wake on the eve of every birthday. "Luckily," Hannah said, "you have seven years before you have to find out."

"Yes," Adrienne agreed. "And everybody knows that seven is lucky. There it is. The home of the legendary J. D. Malone."

Hannah recognized Parker's car parked in the driveway of the address he'd given her. To keep the evening in the experimental category and completely un-datelike, she'd turned down his offer to pick her up, insisting they meet here, instead. As she waited for the wrought-iron gate to open, she took advantage of the opportunity to look around. J.D.'s house sat on a hill and was surrounded by immaculately tended grounds. The house was pretentious, beautiful, and so far removed from the comfortable little house where Hannah had grown up that nerves fluttered in her stomach.

"Even Ryan's house, with all his fortune, is less formidable than this."

"Shoot, sugar. This is nothing. I once dated a basketball player who owns a house in The Dominion. Several of the Spurs players live there, and let me tell you, they make these houses look like shacks. Come on. Let's go pound on this shack's door and get this experiment of yours under way. Hello, Parker. Nice tie."

Hannah hadn't realized she'd reached the front door until she found herself face-to-face with Parker. His tie was blue. It matched his eyes. Leave it to Adrienne to notice.

"Hello, Parker," she said. "You remember Adrienne."

He nodded, greeted both women, then ushered them inside. Adrienne's three-inch heels clicked over the marble floor of the foyer, Hannah's lower heels thudding more quietly. The plush carpet in the next room muted their footsteps altogether.

Hannah was vaguely aware of gleaming chandeliers and

gold-framed paintings. Although there was an aroma of cooking in the air, it was difficult to imagine anyone growing up in a house like this.

"Where's your father?" she asked.

"He's taking a business call in his office. Clara has just put the steaks on. Would either of you care for something to drink?"

Adrienne and Hannah both agreed that a tall iced tea would taste good. While Parker disappeared to get them, Adrienne wandered to a wall completely dominated by artwork. Joining her there, Hannah rubbed her arms against the cold. After a long stretch of companionable silence, Hannah said, "We should have asked for a steaming pot of herbal tea."

"How silly of us to wear summer clothes."

Hannah smiled. "I wonder why men like it so cold."

"Good question. If I would have known the air-conditioning would be set at fifty-three degrees, I would have worn a sweater. And a bra."

They turned at the sound of ice cubes clinking in glasses on the far side of the room. The two Malones stood near the doorway. Both men were immaculately dressed in business suits and ties, both were dark-haired and intense. Both happened to wear the look of a man whose thoughts had recently taken a slow dip into the forbidden. J.D. couldn't seem to take his eyes off Adrienne. As for Parker, well... Hannah's breath caught in her throat at the sight of the dark-blue eyes that were trained slightly below *her* shoulders.

"You asked why men like a cold house," Adrienne said under her breath. "There's your answer."

Before meeting Adrienne, Hannah would have blushed and stammered her way through this type of situation.

Shaking her head at her friend, she had to fight the urge to laugh.

Without a word, J.D. went to the hall where the thermostat was located and turned up the temperature a few degrees. Parker handed Hannah and Adrienne their glasses of tea and indicated that they take a seat. "Father," he said, standing near a wing chair, "you remember Hannah. This is her friend, Adrienne Blakely."

Although J.D. had already met Hannah briefly, he shook her hand again. He lingered slightly longer over Adrienne's handshake, then took a seat in a nearby chair.

At first glance Parker had thought that Hannah and Adrienne were an unlikely pair. Since then, he'd sensed a deep friendship, a mutual respect. Hell, the women liked each other, accepted each other, had a lot of fun together. Adrienne was five or six years older, and the epitome of a modern-day Southern belle. Her dress was flowered, the skirt full. It was the kind of dress women in Georgia probably wore hats with. Parker was more interested in Hannah's clothes. She was wearing a skirt. Not quite tight, not short, not brown. Her blouse was scoop-necked and sleeveless, the fabric made up of softly muted flowers in beige, yellow and blue.

"I see you like Monet." Adrienne gestured to the artwork on the wall.

J.D. said, "I have a keen appreciation for beautiful things, yes."

Hannah glanced sharply at Parker. He half expected her to roll her eyes. He could only shrug. After all, she was the one who'd insisted she could find goodness in everyone. When she pulled a face, Parker felt an unaccustomed urge to chuckle. From the beginning, this had all the makings of an interesting evening. It was getting more interesting by the minute.

Settling herself more comfortably in the chair, Hannah crossed her legs and made careful note of her surroundings. The main purpose of her visit was to get to know Parker's father, thereby discovering his good qualities. A year ago she'd read that he'd turned fifty. Other than a little gray in the hair at his temples, he didn't look it. Parker had mentioned a slightly older sister. That meant that J.D. had become a father at a very young age. She had a difficult time imagining J.D. attending soccer games or tossing a baseball. He wasn't cold, exactly. He just wasn't very "fatherly."

The room was tastefully decorated, but it held very little of anything personal, certainly nothing feminine. There were no photographs of either of his children, no mementos of vacations, no hints into his past or his personality. J.D. was a talented conversationalist, a conscientious host. He was civil to his help. When a gray-haired woman announced that dinner was ready, he even went so far as to tell her it smelled wonderful.

They ate on real china, drank from genuine crystal, and used expensive silver. J.D. asked Hannah about her mother, and Parker about a case he was working on, but it became increasingly obvious, to Hannah at least, that he was the most interested in Adrienne. Hannah was rather enjoying watching her friend in action.

"I understand you own a restaurant downtown."

Adrienne toyed with her watercress, smiling blandly. "The Pink Flamingo."

"I'll have to try it sometime."

As far as Hannah was concerned, Adrienne's failure to invite him to do just that spoke volumes. J.D. didn't seem to mind. "Your accent is delightful."

This time Adrienne's smile was slightly more genuine, but still, no personal information was forthcoming.

"It's Georgian, isn't it?"

"Yes."

"San Antonio is a long way from Georgia. Most people have a reason for venturing so far from their roots."

Obviously, J. D. Malone hadn't made a name for himself as the most feared attorney in his field by honoring people's privacy. Hannah half expected Adrienne to tell J.D. to mind his own business. Instead she batted her eyelashes, smiled coquettishly, and said, "My secret's out. How on earth did y'all get so smart?"

Parker and Hannah exchanged yet another telling look.

"You might say it's a honed skill. *Is* the reason you left Atlanta a secret?" J.D. asked.

"I don't recall mentioning that I'm from Atlanta."

Hannah glanced at her friend. Adrienne's tone had been uncustomarily sharp.

"Parker must have mentioned it," J.D. said, completely nonplussed. "Was it supposed to be a secret?"

Hannah couldn't have mastered Adrienne's small smile no matter how hard she tried. It was a Southern smile, pretty, all for show, giving nothing away. "It's hardly a secret. You see, I came this close to winning a beauty contest."

"What happened?"

She batted her eyelashes again, and poured on the honey-coated Southern accent. "Oh, those silly old contests are so picky. A girl gets accused, privately, of course, of sleeping with a judge, and the best she can do is first runner-up."

The room was completely quiet. Nobody moved, not to chew, not even to breathe. Hannah had a feeling she was witnessing history in the making. J. D. Malone didn't seem to know how to proceed.

Adrienne beamed around the table. Spearing a small

piece of steak, she finally said, "This is wonderful, done to perfection. It's neither Texas style—black on the outside and gray on the inside, nor cowboy style—with the tail and horns still attached."

Parker answered. "Clara was a real find. Isn't that right, J.D.?"

J.D. recovered instantaneously and the conversation turned away from cuts of meat and beauty contests. Parker asked Hannah about a wedding she was planning. He even told a joke about three attorneys who were waiting at the pearly gates. Even funnier than the punch line was the quip he made when he was finished.

"Some people might contend that there are no attorneys in heaven," he said, looking directly into Hannah's eyes.

It was Adrienne who said, "Not Hannah. She finds goodness in everyone." There was a slight pause. "Or almost everyone."

Parker was the first to laugh. Shortly after Clara served dessert, the telephone rang. "There's a phone call for you," Clara said to Adrienne. "He said it's important."

Adrienne excused herself. Moments later she was back. "I'm afraid I have to go."

Hannah rose to her feet instantly. Parker and J.D. a few seconds behind. "Is everything okay?" Hannah asked.

Adrienne nodded reassuringly. "The stove went out in the restaurant. Gerard says it's a madhouse."

After saying their goodbyes and thanking J.D. for the delicious meal, Hannah and Adrienne hurried out to the car. J.D. and Parker returned to the table and finished their desserts in silence.

J.D. didn't speak until he'd taken his last sip of coffee and had dropped his linen napkin onto the table. "Did she really do it?"

Parker had always been intrigued by the way his father's

mind worked. It had been at least a half hour since Adrienne had mentioned the beauty pageant, and yet he knew exactly what J.D. was talking about. Shrugging, he said, "I could probably find out."

J.D. shook his head. "You have enough to worry about with this Fortune case. Are there any new developments, by the way?"

Parker had barely finished filling his father in when the telephone rang again. J.D. took the call. Shortly thereafter, Parker took his leave.

The light was still on in Hannah's boutique when Parker pulled to a stop at the curb later that night. She didn't jump when he rapped on the window. She was probably accustomed to having friends drop in on her at all hours.

The idea that he and Hannah were friends gave Parker a moment's pause. He was friendly with the receptionist at the office, and he maintained business relationships with several women in his field. But his *friends* were former college roommates he kept in touch with a few times a year, or associates, or men he played racquetball with or met for a round of golf. It wasn't impossible that he and Hannah were becoming friends…

She smiled at him as she unlocked the door, and a zing went through him. "Parker, what are you doing here?"

…No, it wasn't impossible.

A dozen thoughts scrambled through his mind, but only one sensation took hold deep in his body. That didn't happen when any of his other friends graced him with a smile.

"I went for a drive to unwind and wound up here. I wanted to hear what you thought of the legendary J. D. Malone. Are you ready to concede defeat?"

She practically pulled him inside, locking the door behind him. "Why on earth would I do that?"

"Are you saying you found the goodness you were looking for in my father?"

"I might have found some. If you have major issues with your father, Parker, I think you should read books on the subject, or perhaps talk to a family counselor."

Parker almost laughed. Although J.D. would never make father of the year, Parker knew his father loved him in his own way. He accepted his father exactly as he was, and vice versa. He hadn't suggested this little experiment to find fault with the man who had raised him. He'd done it to better understand this woman with the sunny disposition and glowing outlook on life.

The fact that she'd refused to see him otherwise had been a factor, but only in the beginning. The truth was, Hannah Cassidy was a breath of fresh air.

"I don't have issues with my father, Hannah. I'm just trying to get a glimpse of how he looks through your eyes. You can tell me what you really think of him. I can take the truth."

Hannah gave the matter a great deal of thought. J. D. Malone hadn't put on airs tonight, nor had he gushed in an effort to put her and Adrienne at ease. Whether it had been precalculated or not, his no-nonsense attitude had made her feel surprisingly comfortable. But being comfortable around a man and finding goodness in him were two entirely different things.

"It isn't that J.D. is a hard man to like," she said, placing a bridal veil that had arrived late that afternoon on a high shelf. "He's a hard man to get to know." His manners were certainly impeccable. She thought of the way he'd turned the air-conditioning off, the way he shook her hand, and the delicious meal he'd invited her to share. "To tell you the truth, I felt a little sorry for him."

"You're kidding."

The sheer surprise in Parker's voice drew Hannah around. He was still wearing his business suit, but he'd removed his tie and opened the top button on his light blue dress shirt. He was tall and lean, and although he had a tan, there were shadows under his eyes, and an edginess in his movements. There was a ranginess about Parker, a kind of pent-up energy that needed to be worked off.

"I was planning to take a walk as soon as I took care of a few details for a wedding I'm planning. Care to join me?" she asked.

He nodded, but she could tell his mind was still on her last comment. She wondered how long he would wait to ask her to explain herself.

Her store was on the edge of the downtown district. She and Parker had strolled the business area the last time they'd taken a walk. Tonight they ducked through the alley and came out in a residential neighborhood. The sun had set an hour ago and the moon was a sliver low in the sky. There were streetlights on the corners, and mercury lights on most garages. The houses in this section were old and in a continuous state of repair. It seemed that every summer, somebody on the block was scraping peeling paint or shoring up a porch or replanting a trampled yard. The people who lived in this neighborhood carried their lunches, and made their living driving buses, working in factories, on pipelines or in grocery stores. These houses weren't nearly as grand as the house she'd been in tonight. The people who lived in them rarely had any money left at the end of a month, let alone enough to worry about losing in investments. They had problems. Everyone did, but for the most part, the people in this neighborhood weren't lonely. She'd sensed that J. D. Malone was. And so was his son.

She doubted Parker would welcome the notion or the comparison. Matching her stride to his longer one, she said, "I got the feeling your father was interested in Adrienne."

"You're very astute."

So she was right, about that at least. "That's why I felt a little sorry for him."

"Go on."

"It's just that he's all alone, and she shut him down cold."

"That's what you think."

Hannah's head came up, her gaze finding Parker's. He had the grace to shrug. "I doubt Adrienne has seen the last of my father."

"You don't know Adrienne like I do."

"I know how my father's mind works. He asked about the beauty pageant after she left. Did she do it?"

Rather than crossing the street, Hannah and Parker strode around the block, heading back the way they'd come. "Are you asking if Adrienne slept with that contest judge?"

Parker's nod was followed closely by a brief shake of Hannah's head.

"Are you saying she lost fair and square?"

"Let's just say somebody had some incriminating evidence."

Parker was beginning to get the picture. "The girl who won had possession of this evidence. Am I correct?"

"It was pretty incriminating," Hannah said, "but nonconclusive."

They'd reached the street in front of The Perfect Occasion. Parker's car was sitting at the curb. Striding to it, they leaned against the front fender, facing the store.

"How nonconclusive was it?" Parker asked.

She turned slightly, her body straining forward, as if she were completely intent upon clearing her friend's name.

"Adrienne was in love with the judge of that contest. He was older. Her first serious relationship. No matter what the tape recording indicated, she didn't sleep with him. It turned out the girl who won did that. Adrienne *says* she was shattered because she lost. But really, she was shattered because she'd been *used* by a man she'd loved."

"I thought judges weren't allowed access to contestants, and vice versa."

"Usually, they aren't. National pageants have nearly impenetrable systems to make sure judges and contestants don't mix, but it's harder to enforce at the local level. Where there's a will, there's a way, I guess."

A horn honked at the corner, the bump of a teenager's bass pulsating through the night air. A breeze stirred Hannah's hair, raising goosebumps on her arms. Parker shook his head at the idea that anybody could be cold when it was still so warm outside. He shrugged out of his suit coat, and slipped it over her shoulders.

"What happened to the judge?"

"He and his tiara queen went on to make a fortune in the music industry in Nashville."

Lowering his voice so nobody else could hear him, he said, "If my instincts are correct, J.D. is going to look into the matter. When J.D. looks into a matter, the perpetrators usually get what's coming to them."

She blinked, obviously dismayed. Keeping her voice as low as his had been, she said, "The other man won't find himself trapped beneath something heavy, will he?"

Parker smiled at her wry humor. "Don't worry. My father won't break the law. But that former contest judge might find himself in the throes of a string of bad luck."

She stared at him for a long time, so long, he wondered what she saw. Finally she said, "You've found goodness in your father all by yourself."

"I've always known there was goodness in my father, Hannah."

"Then why the experiment?"

"I told you. I wanted the opportunity to see things from your perspective. It's possible that I wanted to spend time with you, as well."

Hannah didn't know what to say. Parker's voice had been like the wind after midnight, a deep sigh, a gentle mooning, a slow sweep across her senses. Gripping a lapel in each fist, she crossed her hands over her heart. Her brother Cole swore she was the only woman on the planet who could be cold when it was seventy-eight degrees out. She was warm now, but this heat had more to do with what was happening inside her than with the jacket Parker had draped over her shoulders.

She could have been angered by his confession. Instead she felt honored. She doubted he spent many evenings taking walks or leaning against his car, talking. He wouldn't have had to tell her he'd wanted to spend time with her. He was a man of few words, after all. It gave what he *did* say more depth, a truer meaning.

Feeling strangely weightless, she went up on tiptoe and whispered, "J.D. isn't the only Malone who has a grain of goodness running through him."

"A rumor like that could ruin us."

His humor felt like a perfect end to an enchanting night. "Your secret's safe with me." Smiling, she kissed his cheek. "Good night, Parker."

Floating on a hazy cloud of contentment, she strode to her door and disappeared inside.

Parker didn't remember replying. And yet he couldn't seem to forget the way her breasts had brushed against his arm, ever so softly, far too fleetingly.

The type of woman he normally saw didn't end an evening with a kiss on the cheek. Hannah wasn't his type. Hell, he'd known that from the beginning. Problem was, he'd never met a woman who drew him more. He didn't know where that kiss left them. And he didn't know where it would lead.

Pulling into his driveway twenty minutes later, he only knew he was looking forward to finding out.

"Ready?" Hannah asked the pretty, petite woman who was standing in front of the full-length baroque mirror in the back of The Perfect Occasion.

"Ready? I'm so excited I think I'm going to be sick," Starr Weston exclaimed, a slender hand going to her abdomen.

"Don't y'all dare," Adrienne said from an overstuffed love seat a few feet away.

"Take a deep breath," Hannah said. "And close your eyes." With utmost care, she placed a multitiered wedding veil, its layers trimmed with thousands of tiny, iridescent pearls, on Starr's head. Adjusting the satin and bead-covered headpiece so that it sat on her client's head like a crown, Hannah said, "Now open your eyes."

Starr's brown eyes opened, darkened, then glazed with tears. All three women stared in reverence and in silence.

"Moonie isn't going to know what hit him," Starr finally said in a whisper one used in church. Giddiness bubbled up inside her, spilling over. "Oh, Adrienne, you were so right. Hannah is the best wedding planner in the world. I thought it was going to be hard, and she's making it easy. It's just so important. I mean, I've been imagining my wedding day since I was twelve years old."

"Haven't we all, sugar."

Hannah's vision blurred, her thoughts turning hazy. It had been happening all morning, more specifically, since she'd taken a walk with Parker last night and kissed his cheek. Like Starr and Adrienne, she'd been dreaming of her wedding day for as long as she could remember, too. Until last night her dreams had been misty affairs, with images of flowing white dresses and candlelight and flowers and gleaming silver. In every other dream, her groom had been charming, debonair, faceless. Last night the groom in her dream had had dark hair and a familiar little cleft in his chin.

She'd lain awake for a long time after, waiting for the sun to come up, thinking about Parker. She knew he was the kind of man who could keep her on her toes, and keep her warm at night. He was the kind of man who would give as much to a relationship as he took. But he wasn't the kind of man who believed in forever.

"What do you think, Hannah?"

"Hannah?"

"Earth to Hannah."

She came to her senses, only to find Starr and Adrienne watching her closely. "I do believe Hannah has a man on her mind, Adrienne. Love is in the air, I can feel it."

Hannah doubted she'd ever seen more stars in any other woman's eyes than in Starr Weston's right now. She loved hearing the stories of how her clients met and fell in love. Starr's tale was as unusual and romantic as she was. Standing five feet tall in her stocking feet and weighing ninety-seven pounds at the ripe old age of twenty-five, she claimed she'd always believed she would know instinctively the instant she met the man of her dreams. Two years ago a businessman named Harrison "Moonie" Leight walked into The Pink Flamingo where Starr waitressed, and whispered her name, even though he'd never seen her before. Moonie, who had made a name for himself in the oil business, literally whisked Starr away. He proposed later that very night at the stroke of midnight, saying it was written in the stars that the two of them should be known as Moonie and Star Leight. Two years to the day, they were to be wed during a midnight ceremony at the very restaurant where they'd met.

"Here, Adrienne," Starr said, reaching for the veil. "You try it on."

The former Southern belle was shaking her head before Starr had plucked the veil from her own tresses. "Oh, no, y'all don't. There must be some sort of superstition associated with wearing another bride's veil before the wedding, and frankly, I don't need any more bad omens."

"You've had a bad omen?" Starr asked, eyes that tended to look too large for her narrow face at first glance widening dramatically.

Hannah took the delicate veil from the soon-to-be bride's hands, saying, "Adrienne's been a little out of sorts ever since she met J. D. Malone."

"Where have I heard that name?"

"It doesn't matter. He's playing dirty," Adrienne exclaimed. "Sending me roses, pink roses, one bouquet every hour on the hour. There ought to be a law."

"How romantic. How long has this been going on?" Starr asked.

"Since last night. I hardly got any sleep at all. Either he owns a florist shop, or he paid someone to deliver flowers all night."

So, Hannah thought, Parker had been right. J.D. was pursuing Adrienne.

"Why didn't you just send them back?" Hannah asked.

"I did. He obviously doesn't understand the concept of no."

Starr shook her head slowly. "You can run, Adrienne, but you can't hide from fate."

"I'm not hiding from it, sugar, I'm avoiding it like the plague. From now on there is just no way on God's green earth that I'm going to agree to have dinner with any man over the age of thirty...say, two."

"Moonie's fifteen years older than I am. And we're perfect for each other."

Adrienne shrugged. "I don't have anything against May-December romances. I'm from the South, remember? Back home, women have been marrying older men for centuries. If there is indeed a May-December romance in my future, I'm going to be December, that's all."

After stretching like a cat in a patch of sunshine, Adrienne slid her feet into lime-green high-heels and strolled out the door. Starr left soon after.

Alone, Hannah wandered through her boutique, her thoughts swirling from one thing to the next. Starr's wedding was going to be truly magnificent. She had to remember to talk to the florist about the final number of flowers for the tables. And then she should put in a call to Starr's mother, who was having a little temper tantrum about the dress the groom's mother was wearing. Tensions were always so high before weddings. Secretly, Hannah agreed that the dress was ghastly, but there was only so much she could do.

She glided her fingers over the outer edge of her desk, then moved on to the suit jacket hanging over the back of her chair. On impulse, she brought the jacket to her nose. She took one breath, and then a second deeper one. Mmm. It smelled like Parker, faintly of soap, aftershave, and fine wool.

She wondered if he'd realized he was missing his jacket. Surely, he would have noticed it when he undressed last night. Opening her desk drawer, she rummaged through notes and receipts until she found the business card she'd tucked inside weeks ago. She slipped the card into her purse. Without stopping to analyze her actions, she put a Closed sign in the window, and hurried out the back door to her car.

She arrived at the offices of Malone, Malone & Associates shortly before one o'clock. The office was exactly what she'd expected. Lots of glass, gleaming wood, and polished brass. Quiet, posh, very upper-crust. The reception area was filled with a vast array of flower arrangements, but the receptionist's chair was empty. The nameplate on the desk read Adalaide Smith. Wondering if Adalaide had gone to lunch, Hannah decided to surprise Parker. She skirted the desk, and opened a heavy glass door at the end of a wide hallway.

"What the hell kind of woman refuses flowers?"

"It's not as uncommon as you think, J.D."

She paused at the sound of the voices carrying to her ears.

"You're going to have to try another approach."

She recognized one of the voices as Parker's. Obviously the other baritone belonged to J.D.

"Or perhaps face the fact that she isn't interested," Parker said.

"Oh, she wants me. She just doesn't know it yet."

Hannah moved to take the first step into the hall just as J.D. said, "At least one of us is getting on well with the opposite sex. You seem to be making headway with the Cassidy woman."

Hannah froze.

"Headway?" It was Parker's voice again.

"Don't be obtuse, Parker. Have you gotten close enough to her to convince her to work with us in obtaining a signature on that prenuptial agreement between her mother and Ryan?"

Realization sliced through Hannah. She didn't know whether to storm forward or retreat.

"May I help you?"

She glanced over her shoulder as a gray-haired woman slid behind her desk. Closing the door quietly, Hannah shook her head. She smoothed a hand over the suit jacket on her arm, and forced words past the lump in her throat. "This belongs to Parker."

The woman's expression gave little away. "I'll see if he's left for lunch yet."

"He hasn't left." Hannah handed the coat to the woman on her way by.

"Are you a client of Mr. Malone's?"

"What?" Oh. Hannah shook her head.

"A friend then?"

"Apparently not."

Rather than stick around to explain, Hannah rushed out into the midday heat. She didn't stop until she'd reached her car. Even then, she didn't look back.

"A delivery for you, Mr. Malone."

Parker, J.D., and Dale Minskie, an intense junior partner, all turned their heads at ninety-degree angles, but it was J.D. who spoke to Adalaide.

"Not another returned floral arrangement."

She shook her head, leveling her gaze at Parker. "I believe this is yours."

Parker took the jacket from Adalaide's outstretched hand. "Is Hannah Cassidy here?"

"Hannah Cassidy? Is that who she was?"

Was? Parker rushed out into the reception area. "She left?"

"Yes. In quite a hurry."

"Why—"

"It's hard to say," Adalaide quipped. "Perhaps she had another appointment. Or perhaps it was something she overheard."

Parker didn't like the sound of that. Adalaide Smith had worked for the law firm of Malone, Malone & Associates for ten years, and ran the office the way a captain ran a tight ship. Practically old enough to be his grandmother, Adalaide was normally pleasant. Right now, she was looking at him as if he were something stuck to the bottom of her shoe.

He could well imagine what Hannah had overheard. A judge would have ruled it hearsay, circumstantial evidence at best. Parker happened to know hearsay could be very incriminating.

All four of them looked up when the outer door opened. When a delivery man carried in yet another flower arrangement, it was J.D. who sputtered, "Oh, hell."

Eyeing the jacket folded neatly over Adalaide's arm, Parker ran a hand through his hair, trying to think. He had a business lunch with a very rich client in twenty-five minutes. Setting things right with Hannah was going to have to wait.

He started for the door, only to pause and call over his shoulder. "Adalaide, call Everett Krizanski and ask him to meet me at The Pink Flamingo instead of at the Hillcrest. You can reach me on my cellular phone if necessary."

"The Pink Flamingo?"

"Yes, it's on Smith Street."

The door swung shut on Adalaide's, "Yes, sir."

Seven

With her pencil poised over her notebook, Hannah punched the proper buttons, then raised the telephone to her ear. She listened to the recorded spiel and pressed the appropriate buttons, only to listen to the music playing on the other end for a few seconds. In no mood to be left on hold indefinitely, she hung up.

She'd only been back in the boutique for fifteen minutes, and already she'd conferred with a caterer, double-checked a cake order, reserved a hall for an anniversary party, and booked a clown for a four-year-old's birthday party. At this rate she was going to get out of work on time today. There was nothing like disappointment threaded with hurt and dashed with self-recriminations to increase a person's productivity.

She didn't jump when the door opened, but she paused for a moment when her gaze met Parker's. It wasn't that she hadn't been expecting him. She just hadn't expected him so soon.

"I understand you stopped by my office."

He took the attorney's approach, walking in as if he owned the place. Fine. That didn't mean she had to play the witness. She could have come back with a snippy reply, but snideness wasn't her style. Sometimes, she wished it was. Suddenly tired, she said, "You don't need me to produce Exhibit A or Exhibit B. If you didn't know I stopped by your office, you wouldn't be here now, would you?"

He made no reply.

Taking a deep breath, she asked, "What are you doing here, Parker?"

"Everybody deserves a fair trial, Hannah."

She was a little surprised by the anger in his voice. Two lines formed between his eyes as he watched her. For a long moment she simply looked back at him.

He strode closer, stopping near the corner of her desk. "I'm keeping a very rich client waiting."

And yet he made no move to hurry, or to leave. Keeping a tight rein on her senses just in case she felt compelled to give in and allow herself to actually feel honored that he was gracing her with his presence, she said, "I heard what your father said, Parker."

"And what did you hear me say?"

She didn't want to repeat what she'd heard. Taking a deep breath, she said, "Let's just say I overheard your reference to prenuptial agreements, and leave it at that."

"The voices you're referring to belonged to J.D. and Dale Minskie." He let her mull it over for a few seconds. And then he said, "Dale is young and intense. He reminds me of me a few years ago. As far as J.D. goes, well, maybe this proves that a lot of people are right about him. But it doesn't prove anything else."

Had there been three separate voices? She tried to recall the inflection and tone of each. She opened her desk drawer and dropped a pen inside. It gave her something to do with her hands. Unfortunately, it wasn't enough to occupy her mind. She'd jumped to conclusions in Parker's office. That alone proved that she cared about him more than she wanted to admit.

"Are you saying my mother's relationship with Ryan

has nothing to do with you, or me? Or more specifically, you and me?''

''That's one way to put it. Have I mentioned Ryan's prenuptial agreement lately?'' he asked. She looked up at him, but he didn't give her a chance to answer. ''And have I done anything which could be construed as coercing you, or convincing you to side with me when it comes to your mother's relationship with Ryan?''

''Well, I can't—''

Again he interrupted her. ''What do you see when you look at me?''

This time she made no move to answer immediately. She studied him unhurriedly. He was sitting on the corner of her desk, the fabric of his dress slacks stretched over one muscled thigh. What did she see?

She saw a man whose ruggedness couldn't be hidden behind expensive suits, a man whose intelligence couldn't be masked in a blank stare, a man whose gaze kept straying to her lips, as if he was enthralled by what he saw.

If it was a ploy to soften her resolve, it was working. Tracing a paper clip with one finger, she said, ''I see a very cunning divorce attorney.''

''That's what I do. Not who I am.''

She borrowed his technique, and continued as if he hadn't spoken. ''I see a man who scares me.''

''I don't mean to scare you, Hannah.''

''I see a man who elicits emotions from me, and reactions, and feelings I don't want to feel.''

''Then we're even.''

''I honestly doubt that, Parker.''

''Do you think you have the market cornered on honesty? I'm not dishonest, Hannah. Okay, I'm not saying I never lie. But there's only one thing I've ever lied about to you.''

''You've lied to me?''

He found his feet, and circled her desk, his eyes on her all the while. "If I've lied, it's been a lie of omission."

She had the presence of mind to remain quiet, when her every impulse screamed for her to parrot his last three words.

"It has to do with our relationship."

"In what way?" She watched him closely.

"What did you call it? Oh, yes. Friendship."

In a movement so quick and precise it left her no time to resist, he slipped his hands around her, pulling her to her feet, and in the process, firmly against him.

"Parker, what are—"

His mouth covered hers. As far as answers went, it was extremely direct.

She felt a fast little jolt of excitement, followed by a rousing dose of desire. She'd dreamed of kissing Parker last night. Real life was so much better than dreams, for the man in her dream had been hazy. The man with his arms wrapped around her was solid, hard, real.

Her arms found their way around his back; her lips moved beneath his. Noses bumped, chins rasped, breaths mingled. It was a far cry from the carefully choreographed kisses in the movies. This kiss was hungry, demanding, explosive.

Parker was a hard man. It was what she'd expected. Steel. And heat. His softness surprised her, tricked her, into softening in return. Her mouth opened, her lips clung. All the while, he was sliding his hands down her back. Spreading his fingers wide, he seemed to be memorizing the feel of her, the texture of muscles covered by soft flesh.

Her thoughts went spinning, the moment fast burning out of control. She was melting, one cell at a time. The softness in his lips cajoled, the warmth in his fingertips made her swoon. Suddenly he brought her hips hard against him. Oh, yes, it was a surprise, and a trick. And she reveled in it, all of it.

With an agonized moan, he dragged his mouth from hers, kissing her cheek, her chin, the hollow below her ear. "Do you still think it's prudent to consider us just friends?"

Her eyes opened, focusing on a satin bow lying on a chest of drawers near the back of the boutique. She thought it was interesting that he'd used the word prudent, because there had been nothing prudent about that kiss.

"I'll rephrase the question. Do you kiss all your male friends the way you just kissed me?"

His voice was a deep rasp in her ear. It tickled, but it wasn't the reason for her small smile. She could have told him that *she* hadn't kissed him; he'd kissed her. He *had* started it. But that was just semantics. No matter who'd started it, she'd returned his kisses, willingly and eagerly. If he hadn't stopped, she would be kissing him still.

"Well?" he asked.

She straightened slightly, putting a few inches between them. Even in remembrance, she felt the intimacy of his kiss. "I can't think of any off the top of my head. Friends that I've kissed like that, that is."

She'd almost taken an entire step away from him when he graced her with his smile. Her gaze caught on his mouth, and her backward retreat came to an end.

"Then you agree that there's potentially more between us than friendship."

She could think of no response.

With a maddening, even tone of voice, he said, "What do you propose to do about it?"

"Do?"

He nodded.

"I don't know. I haven't had time to think about it."

"This isn't a thinking situation. It requires action, and reaction. And time spent together. You. And me. What are you doing right now?"

"Now?" Her thoughts spun all over again. Shaking her head to clear it, she said, "I have an appointment with a bride at two. And you have a rich client waiting for you."

Accustomed to having people wait for him, he made no move to hurry. "What about tonight? Are you free then?"

She nodded, and he backed from the room.

"I'll call you. Until tonight, Hannah."

Yes, Hannah thought, watching him go. Until tonight. But what then?

Hannah rummaged through her oversize leather bag, hurriedly searching for a clasp or an elastic band to use to secure her hair away from her face, and out of the wind streaming over the windshield of Parker's car. He'd offered to put the top up, but she didn't want him to. Riding in a convertible was exhilarating.

True to his word, he'd called her in the middle of the afternoon. Asking pointed questions about her likes and dislikes, they'd discovered that they both enjoyed the symphony. Unfortunately, it was too late to obtain tickets for this evening's performance. There were several tourist attractions in San Antonio, from water parks to roller coasters to comedy clubs. They'd decided on a quiet stroll through the Botanical Gardens. She'd already changed into an airy summer dress when he arrived. He, on the other hand, had just come from a meeting with a private investigator, and had insisted that it would only take him a few minutes to shower and change back at his place.

For all practical intents and purposes, they were just two people enjoying a ride in an expensive car on a warm July evening. Why, then, did it feel so extraordinary?

Parker turned his head in her direction, his eyes hidden from her view by a pair of dark sunglasses. He was good-looking, but there was nothing unusual about the cut of his dark hair or the angle of his chin. It wasn't surprising to see tanned skin in the middle of summer, and his expensive suit and imported tie weren't much different than a thousand other affluent men's clothing. Still, there was something unique about Parker, something as elusive as it was inviting.

Hannah had always believed that people's houses said a lot about the people who lived in them. She was curious to see what Parker's house said about him. They were heading north on Highway 281. The suburbs here had names that ended with Hills or Heights. Less prestigious and expensive than the houses and estates in The Dominion and Hollywood Park, the homes in this area were still pricey.

Parker turned right, and then left, and then left again onto Ridgewood Drive. "Here we are," he said, pulling into a concrete driveway beside a large, two-story house.

She got out of the car on her side, and preceded him along a sidewalk and through the door he held for her. She turned in a half circle in the high-ceilinged foyer. "It's...beautiful."

"But?"

"I mean it. It truly is beautiful."

He riffled through the mail on an ornate hall table, then led the way into the adjoining living room. "I bought it for its resalability factor."

Some of Hannah's fondest memories were of growing up in her parents' cozy, comfortable old house in the nearby small town of Leather Bucket. Her apartment over the store was small, too, but it was charming, and certainly convenient to work. When she could afford a house, she wouldn't buy it for its resalability factor.

Folding her arms close to her body, she strolled to the other side of the room where a collection of sculptures was displayed on a marble table. She suspected Parker had used the same interior decorator his father had used. She wouldn't go so far as to call either house cozy, but Parker's held hints into his personality. There were photographs, an antique law book, a golf trophy, magazines, and a fica plant that had dropped several leaves.

She picked up a framed photo of Parker's father. Setting it down again, she said, "At least J.D. finally stopped sending Adrienne flowers."

"He had little choice."

She hadn't realized Parker was standing directly behind her until he'd spoken. "What do you mean?" she asked, looking over her shoulder.

"The office was beginning to look like a funeral parlor. She won't accept his flowers, and she won't take his calls."

Hannah nodded. She'd been in Adrienne's office the first time J.D. had called this morning. Adrienne had answered, then promptly hung up. After that, she'd had the help screen her calls. "Everyone at The Pink Flamingo is talking about it, wondering what the legendary J. D. Malone will try next."

"I don't remember the last time J.D. openly pursued a woman. Lately, I can't seem to remember the last time I did, either."

She turned to face him, the look in his eyes as warm as his voice. "Is that what you're doing?"

"You and I both know what I'm doing."

Hannah was pretty sure her heart had risen to her throat. That would explain the fluttering sensation she felt there.

Parker could turn her inside out with a look, but when he turned that directness on her, and unleashed his "barely there" smile, her knees went weak and her resistance turned to mush.

Parker veered a little to the right, slowly moving closer. Attraction flared inside him. He'd always had a good imagination, but it was nothing compared to the memory of how Hannah had felt in his arms earlier. It had wreaked havoc with his concentration all day. Her body had fit his so perfectly. He would have liked to lower her to the carpet, to roll her underneath him, and finish what they'd started. But he wouldn't, at least not yet.

"Is this where you offer to show me your etchings?" she whispered.

"I don't etch."

"Are you telling me I'm safe with you?"

As one moment stretched to two, his gaze traveled over her. "Are you flirting with me, Hannah?"

Flirting? Her? Hannah didn't know what was coming over her, but she wasn't flirting. Although she was enjoying the bantering very much.

She should have been nervous, and yet she felt safe with Parker. Not from his advances. He had bedroom eyes if she'd ever seen any, and yet with him, she felt safe in a different way. With him, she could talk, and laugh, and be herself.

A telephone rang in another area of the house. Moments later, a dark-haired young woman who was probably in her early twenties appeared in the doorway. Hannah reeled backward. She hadn't thought to ask if she and Parker were alone.

"An urgent call for you, Mr. Malone."

"Thanks, Lissett." To Hannah he said, "Will you excuse me?"

"Of course."

"I'll be as brief as possible."

He spoke to Lissett on his way through the doorway. The other woman nodded, then strode stiffly into the room. "Can I bring you something to drink?"

Hannah shook her head. When the younger woman turned to leave the room, Hannah said, "Lissett. What a beautiful name."

Lissett's large brown eyes warmed instantly. "My mother promised my grandmother she would name her first daughter after her. After giving birth to four boys, she was finally able to keep her promise. I'm just glad my grandmother's name wasn't Bathsheba."

Hannah smiled. "Dating with one older brother looking out for me was difficult enough. I can't imagine finding a boy who could pass four brothers' inspections."

Without warning, Lissett burst into tears.

Parker hung up the phone. Trying to knead a kink out of his neck, he left his study and went in search of Hannah. The business call had taken longer than he'd anticipated, much longer than he'd realized. He had an apology all ready. Certainly, one was called for.

He found her sitting on the end of his leather sectional, her bare feet curled beneath her. She had a half-empty glass of lemonade in one hand, a magazine in the other. He couldn't tell for sure, but she didn't *look* angry. He knew better than anyone that looks could be deceiving.

"I'm sorry that took so long, Hannah."

She looked up at him, her gray eyes large and serene. "Was it important?"

He nodded, waiting for some sort of scathing comment or sarcastic remark.

"That's what I thought."

That was it. No reproach, no fault-finding, just a calm acceptance, as if she knew there had to be a good reason for the delay.

She uncurled her legs, slid her feet to the floor, and stood, stretching like a cat in the sun. Her movements shouldn't have been lust arousing, and yet a restless tension stirred inside him.

"Did Lissett leave?" he asked.

"She went home a little while ago." Wandering to the glass topped table behind the sofa, Hannah said, "She's sweet, but if her four older brothers don't stop trying to control her and force her not to see the man she's in love with, I have a feeling they're going to see a different side of her."

His housekeeper had four older brothers? Parker had known her for two years, and yet it was news to him. Hannah had known her for less than an hour and she seemed to know the intimate details of Lissett's life.

Hannah was a people person. But it went beyond that. She wasn't like other women he knew. She certainly wasn't like *him*. He was still in need of that shower and change of clothes. Reluctant to leave Hannah alone again, he took a moment to study her. She'd removed the clasp from her hair, but hadn't bothered to slip into her shoes. She picked up a family photograph that had been taken when he and Beth had been small children.

"Happier times?" she asked.

He took the photo from her hand, studied it for a few seconds, then returned it to the table. "Looks can be deceiving."

"Your parents must have been in love once."

"Define love."

Her head came up. "You can't define love. It's a feeling, and feelings are indefinable."

"I don't know if they were ever in love. Frankly, I never asked. By the time I was old enough to talk, they were fighting like cats and dogs."

"They must have been very young."

"They were seventeen when they met. My grandfather forbade J.D. to see her. So naturally, they snuck around behind their parents' backs. She got pregnant. So he married her."

"That's exactly what I told Lissett would happen if she doesn't stand up to her brothers. Sorry. Go on."

"Six months after the wedding, my sister, Beth was born. Eighteen years later, she made the same mistake our parents made."

"Babies aren't mistakes, Parker." He shrugged, and she said, "Sometimes they're surprises, but not mistakes. Your sister has a child?"

He pointed to a silver-framed picture of a dark-haired boy in his early teens. "His name is Reed Harrison Malone Wilder. That's a lot of name to live down."

Hannah had been thinking it was a lot of name to live up to. "How old is he?" she asked.

"He's fourteen. He's smart, but he doesn't work to his potential. He went through a pudgy stage a few years ago, but the last time I saw him, he could practically look me in the eye. He's snide, manipulative and, when he isn't paying attention, charming."

He sounded like somebody else she knew.

"He's the spitting image of my father, inside and out."

Hannah had been thinking of somebody else.

"It drives Beth crazy."

"What about Beth?"

"She looks more like our mother."

Hannah shook her head. "I meant, what is she like?"

"She's stubborn."

Like the other Malones she knew, she thought. "What does she do?"

"She runs a little diner on the outskirts of San Antonio."

"Is she married?"

"She was. Lord, what a whiner. Stan is the only man I've ever met who could beat his breast with both hands tied behind his back. If she would have let me handle the divorce, she wouldn't be in this predicament, trying to make ends meet, coming up short every month, and so exhausted at the end of the day she can't see straight, let alone keep track of a kid like Reed. It's one of the reasons he gets in trouble. He needs a firm hand."

"Do you believe in disciplining children?"

"Damn right I do. But then, I also believe in a lot of issues politicians like to skirt."

Hannah could well imagine what those issues were. It drove home the fact that they were nothing alike. She was forgive and forget. He was an eye for an eye. She believed in the sanctity of marriage. He believed in ending such a union by obtaining the proper signatures on the dotted line.

Still, he cared deeply for his sister. Hannah didn't know why it mattered to her, but it did. He seemed lonely just now. And tired, and in need of a warm smile.

Wandering to the other wall, she said, "Are you still planning to go to the Botanical Gardens?"

"I'd have to shower and change first."

She didn't see that as a problem.

"Care to join me?"

She shook her head and rolled her eyes.

"Scared?"

Her *harumph* spoke volumes. "You don't scare me, Malone."

"Why don't you come over here and say that?"

"Do I look stupid?"

"You look beautiful."

Just like that, her knees went weak. She'd bet her eyeteeth his step in her direction was deliberate. Still, she was pretty sure the compliment had been as genuine as the intensity in his eyes.

She held up one hand in a halting gesture. Taking the hint, he didn't come any closer. "We don't have to go out. I could fix us something to eat here."

It was getting late, and she was hungry, as well as intrigued. "Can you cook?" She didn't even apologize for the incredulity in her voice.

He slid a hand into his pocket and rolled his shoulders. "I wouldn't starve if I was marooned on a tropical island."

"Well, what do you know. We have something in common."

He picked up her glass of lemonade on his way into the kitchen. While he gathered all the ingredients he needed to prepare western omelettes, she said, "I planned a wedding for a couple who met when they became stranded together on a remote island. The bride wore mangoes on her head, and the groom carried a spear. It was one of the more unusual weddings I've attended."

She sipped her lemonade, and watched Parker crack eggs, add a pinch of salt and a little Tabasco sauce before beating the mixture with a wire whisk. The kitchen was well stocked, but it wasn't what she would call cozy. The coziness came from the easy camaraderie between her and Parker. He was really a very good conversationalist. She supposed it went with the territory.

He told her about a few of the more bizarre divorce cases he'd handled, and she told him about some of the people she'd planned parties and weddings for. "I'd say the most unusual couple, other than the mango and spear-toting pair, is one I'm working with right now. Their names are Starr and Moonie.''

He listened intently the entire time she described Moonie Leight and Starr Weston. "He whispered her name, although they'd never met, and she fell in love at first sight. She's convinced it was written in the stars. Moonie calls it fate."

There was a long stretch of silence after she finished. The omelettes sizzled, and Parker finally said, "Don't the waiters and waitresses at The Pink Flamingo wear name tags?"

"You're missing the point."

"What point?"

He smiled, and it occurred to her that he was teasing her. Something had shifted in their relationship. Mesmerized by his smile, so stark and white and mysterious, so uniquely his own and so different from her openness, something shifted in her, something a lot like hope and a little like desire. Or was it the other way around?

"I like what you're thinking, Hannah."

Was she that transparent? "I'm thinking that we're complete opposites."

"Which just proves that opposites attract."

"Attraction isn't enough. I'm not looking for a wild, passionate fling."

"Don't knock it until you've tried it."

"There's the commitment factor."

"You mean forever. An impossible notion."

She could have argued, but what was the point? He believed in passion. She believed in forever. Which left them in limbo, between the proverbial rock and a hard place.

"I want you. You want me. The question seems to be, what are we going to do about it?"

Hannah carried two place settings to the bar. Adrienne

always said that if she ever found a man who could challenge her way of thinking and who didn't turn her stomach at breakfast, she would marry him. Hannah was beginning to understand that type of reasoning. Parker certainly fit the criteria. Oh, sure, there was the bothersome little fact that they were complete opposites. Or were they?

They shared common interests, common ground. Hannah loved her family. Parker loved his. She was a fair cook. So was he. They liked the same kind of omelettes, the same music, the top down on the convertible. They both liked living in the city, and they both enjoyed easy bantering and thought-provoking conversation. And she doubted she would ever tire of looking at him across any table, morning, noon or night.

He was a man she could fall deeply in love with. A part of her was on the brink of doing just that. For his part, he'd made no secret of the fact that he wanted her. No matter what he said, or what he claimed, she believed there was more to his feelings than that. He'd had an unhappy childhood, poor role models. To make matters worse, he saw the negative side of marriages every day in his work. As a result, he saw marriage as a risk. Given time, she wondered if he might come to realize that there were some risks worth taking.

Doling out silverware, she said, "Ryan's having another dinner party this weekend."

"Yes?"

"My sister is going to be there."

"I'm not interested in your sister, Hannah."

Parker watched Hannah's expression change with her changing thoughts. He wasn't certain she appreciated his brand of humor, but he certainly enjoyed baiting her. "You were saying?"

"Would you like to go?" she asked.

"You mean, as your date?"

She didn't look up, but he noticed the tremble in her fingertips where she toyed with the edge of a pot holder. Something told him she was having a difficult time restraining the impulse to throw something at him.

"Hannah?"

"Yes," she finally said. "As my date."

"This weekend?"

She nodded. "Friday. Why, is that a problem?"

"Not really. I was just wondering how I was going to learn to etch by Friday."

The pot holder she'd been holding bounced off his chest. Or maybe that was desire.

Eight

Parker stood with a small group of men in the living room in Ryan's sprawling ranch home. He contributed to the conversation from time to time, but his attention rarely strayed far from Hannah.

Her head was bent close to Lily's, the overhead lights glinting off hair nearly the same rich, dark shade of brown. It had been a festive gathering, relaxed and informal from the beginning. Ryan and Lily had greeted their guests at the front door. "Is she here yet?" Hannah had asked before she'd even said hello. As it turned out, Maria had been the last to arrive. Hannah and Lily welcomed her and fussed over her like the prodigal son of Bible notoriety.

The party was small, consisting of Ryan and Lily, and eleven guests, some family, some long-time friends. The atmosphere was easy, the conversation flowing as freely as the champagne Ryan had poured before toasting to the future. After the toast, everyone had wafted outside to the courtyard where Ryan himself had manned the grill, insisting that Rosita and her husband Ruben were his guests along with the others.

Ryan was an astute businessman, but only a mediocre cook. He'd taken a lot of ribbing about the height of the flames shooting out of the grill. No one had really minded eating blackened hamburgers, including Parker. Tonight, Parker couldn't even bring himself to mind the fact that Ryan and Lily were so open in their affection and commitment to one another despite the fact that it was making obtaining a divorce for his client much more complicated than it already was.

The outdoor lights had come on automatically without anyone's notice. When the mosquitoes had invaded the party, the guests had retreated inside. Parker spent part of the evening with Hannah, but more often than not, he found himself separated from her while she talked with her mother and sister. Parker didn't mind. He could be patient when he wanted to be. He laughed and joked along with everyone else, but his gaze repeatedly returned to Hannah.

A need had been building in him all day, hovering beneath the surface, waiting. This desire was nothing new. It had been in the foreground since the first time they'd met. Studies indicated that first impressions were strong. And his first impression of her had been sexual in nature.

Since then he'd come to realize that Hannah was much more wholesome than his earlier impression had indicated. She was fresh, her expressions honest, her smiles genuine. A man knew where he stood with her. Parker liked that about her.

Their gazes met across the room, her smile sliding away, only to be replaced by a sultry expression he liked even better. She wanted him. It didn't matter that they were opposites, that she believed in forever, and he believed in tonight. She wanted him. And being wanted by Hannah Cassidy was a heady sensation.

"Hannah's a lovely girl," Ryan said.

Hannah was a lovely *woman.* Since Ryan wasn't being condescending, Parker simply nodded.

"My children are a mixture of both their parents, but all three of Lily's children take after her."

Again, Parker nodded. Although Cole hadn't been able to get away from his law practice in Denver on such short notice, Parker had met Hannah's brother at Ryan and Lily's party. He had no idea what Chester Cassidy had looked like, but Ryan was right. The Cassidy offspring all shared the Spanish-Apache characteristics that were so evident in Lily. All of the surviving Cassidys had dark hair, and long, lean builds. Maria, although thin to the point of being gaunt, looked the most like Lily. Maybe it was their brown eyes. Hannah's were gray. Or maybe it was the brightly colored clothes they'd chosen. As usual, Hannah's clothes were neither brightly colored nor revealing. Unlike Maria, Hannah seemed to realize that she didn't need to broadcast her femininity in neon lights. Her white blouse was simple yet elegant, her black slacks draping over her hips and thighs in such a way that drew a man's eyes and toyed with his imagination.

There was something different about her tonight, and it wasn't simply the fact that she wasn't wearing brown. It was a difference that came from the inside, like a warm glow, a slow smile, a secret look. All those things combined in the most intriguing way. As most men, Parker knew what they meant. She wanted him. And she was thinking about that, and what she was going to do about it. She was going to have him. Perhaps not tonight. Perhaps not even tomorrow night. But soon.

"Look at her." Ryan gestured toward Lily with his right hand, the ice cubes in his glass clinking at the sudden movement. "She's like a mother hen, clucking over her long-lost chick. There isn't anything I wouldn't do to ensure that she is always this happy. If there's one thing I've learned in this life, it's that there's no insurance for happiness. Which is why we should all live life to the fullest, savoring the good times."

Ryan's nephew, Logan, caught Parker's eye from the other side of the small group of men who were standing in a semicircle near the fireplace. Winking broadly, the younger Fortune said, "Does anyone else hear harp music?"

After making a hollow threat to cut Logan out of the will, Ryan handed his nephew his empty glass, then sauntered toward his intended.

"Girls," he said, snagging Lily's hand. "Mind if I borrow your mother for a few minutes?"

Hannah smiled warmly at Ryan, and beamed at Maria. It was so good to see Maria, to spend time with her, to connect with her baby sister. Although she was a little thinner than she'd been the last time Hannah had seen her, Maria looked good. She'd always loved bold, bright colors. Her red dress was cut low in the front, and there was a slit up the skirt. Her lipstick was bright red, too. It gave her an exotic look, and made her appear older than twenty-three. The same inner excitement she'd had as a child was bright in Maria's brown eyes. Hannah had been worried about her younger sister, but seeing her tonight had eased her mind and held the worries at bay.

While Ryan spoke in hushed undertones to Lily, Hannah said, "Mom seems happy, doesn't she?"

Maria glanced at the couple who had paused in the center of the room. "Yes," she said quietly. "He must be good in bed."

Hannah gasped, and Maria laughed.

"Oh, don't be a prude, Hannah. And don't knock it unless you've tried it."

Hannah couldn't help smiling. Reveling in the feeling of closeness with her sister, she whispered, "Now you sound like Parker."

"Ah, yes," Maria said. "Mother said you and Parker arrived together. That must mean you're a couple. Lucky you. After all, if a man looks as good as Parker in a suit, he must look out of this world in the buff.''

"Maria, for heaven's sake.''

"Well?'' she asked wryly, grinning. "Does he?''

Hannah's gaze strayed to Parker. The room took on a dreamy quality, her voice dipping low as she said, "I wouldn't know.''

Maria turned pensive, but she didn't say any more because Ryan was calling for attention. "Everyone,'' he said loudly over the din of the other voices. When all eyes had turned to him, he smiled around the room. "I'd like to thank everyone for coming tonight.'' His gaze homed in on Maria. "I'd especially like to thank you, Maria. Your presence here tonight has made your mother and I both very happy.''

Lily nodded at her youngest child, her eyes artful and serene. Maria nodded in return, smiling for everyone. For a moment Hannah felt the way she had before her father had died, when they were all together and all was right with the world.

While everyone else watched Ryan reach for Lily's hand, Hannah looked beyond them, where three men stood in companionable silence. Parker chose that moment to look her way, his gaze meeting hers from the other side of the room. One of the other men said something. Parker nodded, but his gaze didn't leave hers. Something intense flared through Hannah, something she wasn't sure she'd felt in exactly this way. It wasn't just a simple case of a woman wanting a man. There was more to it than that.

"Lily won't wear my engagement ring until I'm a free man,'' Ryan said loud enough for everyone to hear. He reached into his pocket. Bringing out a thin box, he lowered his voice, and spoke to Lily, alone. "Not only do I understand, but I love you even more for your goodness, your honor, and your conviction. But you'll have to forgive a smitten man for wanting to inundate you with gifts.''

Lily slipped her finger beneath a row of clear tape, deftly opening the package. Eyes bright with emotion, she lifted a delicate tennis bracelet from the folds of expensive silk. ''Oh, Ryan.''

He took the bracelet and painstakingly fastened it around Lily's slender wrist. ''I had your name inscribed on the charm near the clasp. I look forward to the day when you wear my engagement ring, my dear. There are some who say I went a little overboard with diamonds, rubies and sapphires in that ring. This bracelet is bright and yet less flashy. Perhaps it's more your style.''

''Ryan, the ring is beautiful. You don't have to give me another gift.''

Ryan's nephew, Logan, made light of the moment, jokingly calling, ''You heard the woman, Uncle Ryan. Might as well take it back.''

Logan's new wife Emily elbowed him in the ribs. It gave the men a chance to clear their throats and the women the opportunity to blink the moisture from their eyes.

Maria Cassidy's eyes had narrowed slightly, but they were as dry as the desert.

Ryan went to a tall cupboard and brought out a tray containing several more wrapped packages, which he proceeded to hand to each of the women present. Maria played along, opening her gift, pretending to be thrilled at the sight of the ruby earrings. Hannah's earrings were blue sapphires, Logan's wife's were studded with emeralds.

Maria was as gracious as the other women, but inside she seethed. Perhaps it was fitting that hers were made of rubies, because she saw red. A man of Ryan's wealth could well afford to give expensive gifts. As far as Maria was concerned, the earrings were nothing but a token, a mere pittance of what the Cassidys deserved.

Maria allowed herself to be pulled into the excitement as her mother and Ryan both took her hand, pulling her to her feet. She loved being the life of the party, the belle of the ball, and she truly basked in the warm glow of adoration and attention. It brought back her cloud of euphoria. Nobody guessed that she'd gotten her dress at a secondhand store. Maria forced the thought away, lest it should gather other dark thoughts. She didn't want the darkness to descend upon her, not tonight.

Bonnie Schumaker, the grandmotherly woman who lived in the trailer next to Maria's in the small, dried-up town of Leather Bucket, had offered to keep the baby overnight. That meant Maria was free. For one entire night. She could stay up until dawn and sleep until noon. The only thing that would make the night more perfect was a man to share it with, a man who told her things she wanted to hear in return for the opportunity to touch her lithe, supple body.

Her mother had told her the gathering would be low-key and informal. Maria wouldn't have agreed to attend if all the Fortune men had been invited. After all, she'd seduced half of the younger generation and had tried to seduce the other half. All because Hannah and her mother had refused to listen when she'd insisted that Cole's birthmark was proof that he was a Fortune. If they had taken her seriously, she never would have had to take matters into her own hands. She never would have been forced to concoct a plan to produce a Fortune heir to get the Cassidys what was rightfully theirs. She wouldn't have had to try so hard, so long, to get pregnant. She certainly wouldn't have been forced to visit a sperm bank in order to conceive.

If only Lily, Cole and Hannah would have listened.

The darkness hovered, closer. Maria pushed it away. What was done was done. It had been a good plan. It wasn't her fault it had gone awry, just as it wasn't her fault that she had Matthew and Claudia's baby, and they had hers. She would find a way to make things right. But she didn't have to do it tonight. Tonight, she was free. Tonight, she looked more like her old self. Hadn't Lily and Hannah and Ryan all told her she was beautiful? She felt more like her old self, too. Oh, yes, she felt beautiful and lithe and sexy.

If only she had a man to appreciate it.

Unfortunately, the majority of the men present tonight were married. She happened to glance at Hannah. It was all she could do not to scowl at the moisture in boring old Hannah's eyes.

Maria cast a covert glance at Parker. It wasn't fair that Hannah was here with a man so obviously virile. A man such as Parker deserved a woman who knew how to take care of his every need. Hannah had as much as admitted that she didn't know how he was in bed. Good old boring Hannah was probably still waiting for a commitment.

The poor guy. Maybe Maria should do him a favor and tell him he's barking up the wrong tree.

"Isn't that right, Maria?" Lily asked.

"Hmm?" she murmured, bringing her attention to the matter at hand. She answered her mother's questions and smiled at Ryan. Underneath, she was bored to tears. Of course, nobody knew. God, she should have been an actress.

She was aware of the soft murmur of voices all around her, just as she'd always been. Her teachers used to say she lacked concentration and failed to work up to her potential. They were wrong. She was smart. In many ways,

she was smarter than they were. She always knew where
everybody was in a given room. She remembered the most
minute details of people's appearances, their houses, their
very lives. Every detail was bright and indelibly imprinted
in her mind. Every noise was compounded. She'd bored
easily in school, but that was because there were so many
more interesting things to think about than math or English
or geography.

There were boys. And later, men. Certain men, that is,
who knew how to hold a woman's attention. A delicious
tingle washed over her. She wet her lips and crossed her
legs. Yes, it was too bad all the men here were taken.

A movement near the doorway drew her attention. She
glanced up just as Parker left the room. Oh, my, but he
was a virile man. Couldn't he see that he was far too virile,
far too exciting for her dowdy older sister? It wasn't that
Hannah was ugly. She wasn't. She was just so ungodly
plain. Her makeup was practically nonexistent, her choice
of clothing nondescript and boring. Poor Parker.

No one saw Maria's eyes narrow slightly. No one
thought anything was amiss when she excused herself a
few minutes later, not even Rosita, who watched her like
a hawk. While everyone else was oohing over the way the
light caught on the rich gems in the tennis bracelet encircling her mother's wrist and the earrings the other woman
had received, Maria slipped through another door. Heart
beating excitedly, she crept stealthily in the direction Parker had taken.

Parker dried his hands on the most luxurious towel
money could buy. He'd been raised with opulence and was
neither in awe of it, nor oblivious to it. He wasn't oblivious
to the slow burn deep inside him tonight, either. In fact,

there had been times throughout the evening when it had been difficult to think about anything else.

He slid his hand into his pocket. Normally, his fingers would have come into contact with his keys. Since his car was in the shop, Hannah had picked him up tonight. He wondered how much longer she would want to stay. Far be it from him to rush her. Oh, no, tonight, she was setting the pace.

He was so lost in his thoughts that he didn't hear the voice calling to him until he'd passed a doorway. Backtracking, he poked his head inside the den. Hannah's sister, Maria, took a few steps toward him, replacing the pout on her face with a small smile.

"Fancy meeting you here. I was just taking a little breather. Care to join me?"

He removed his hand from his pocket, and slowly nodded.

"I understand you're handling Ryan's divorce." She sidled closer. Wetting her lips, she practically purred. "I'm so glad you're on our side. Why, I'll bet you're the best there is."

He regarded her somberly, wondering if it was possible that he was misreading her intent. "I've earned my reputation. I should be getting back."

Her hand glided to his arm before he'd taken one backward step. "Can't you stay and talk for a minute?"

"Talk?"

She spun around, leaving behind the bold scent of her perfume. "You're not afraid of Hannah's baby sister, are you?"

"Why would I be afraid of you?"

She laughed out loud. "My point exactly. Besides, I wouldn't dream of hurting a man. Quite the contrary. I love to make a man feel glorious."

All the while she was talking, she was circling him, moving closer and closer. Parker held perfectly still, poised and ready to leave.

She shifted toward him, turning slightly, so that the outer swell of her breast brushed his arm. His fingers flexed, and a muscle worked in his jaw. He hadn't misread anything.

She looked up at him, and pressed her little body closer to his. She was like a cat, quiet and sleek, curling around a man, all rub and purr. He knew her type. She was the kind of woman who could make a man yowl.

"I'm staying in San Antonio tonight." The invitation was crystal clear.

He grasped both her wrists, holding her away from him. "No thanks," he said, his voice ominously low. "I already have plans."

She practically meowed. Straining closer, she whispered, "So change them."

He used his strength to hold her away from him, but he didn't try to keep the derision out of his voice. "There was a time when I would have gone for your type. I've upped my standards, and frankly, I don't want what you're selling."

He protected himself from the knee that came up swift and hard, but not from the foot that stomped on his.

"How dare you make a pass at me," she said. "When you're dating my big sister."

What the hell was she talking—

"Hannah," Maria said. "You're going to have to keep this man on a shorter leash."

Hannah? Parker swung around, and came face-to-face with the quieter, gentler Cassidy sister.

All the blood had drained out of her face, leaving her cheeks pale. She brought her hand up, as if in slow motion, covering her gaping mouth. Parker took a step toward her. "Hannah—"

"There you three are!"

Hannah, Maria and Parker all turned as Logan and Emily entered the small den. "Ryan's about ready to send out a search party," Logan exclaimed.

Emily nodded. "He's passing out more gifts. Honestly, since he found Lily again, every day is like Christmas."

Parker didn't know what Hannah was thinking. Although her back remained ramrod straight, she allowed Maria to loop her arm through hers. She answered when Emily spoke to her. She even laughed at something Logan said. Limping slightly, Parker wondered if he was the only one who noticed that her voice had changed, and that her laughter rang hollow.

Forcing a sense of calm she didn't feel, Hannah quietly returned to the living room. Tears stung the backs of her eyes. Her lungs ached from lack of oxygen. Her heart ached the most of all.

A deep breath made her lungs feel better. She didn't know what it would take to soothe the ache in her heart. Everything had seemed so perfect before. The subdued shades of light in the room had changed to a blinding whiteness. Where there had been warmth, there was starkness, where there had been hues of gold and honey, there was now a cool veneer.

Hannah and Parker left the party together. Parker waited to speak until after she started her car's engine. "Hannah, I can explain."

She gripped the steering wheel so tightly her knuckles turned white. "No. Don't. It's going to require everything

I have to hold myself together. I won't be able to drive if we talk.''

"Then let me drive, dammit.''

She shook her head. And bit her lip. Pulling out of the Double Crown's curving driveway, she pointed her car toward the city.

Parker abided by her wishes. Neither of them said another word until after she'd pulled into her usual parking space in the alley behind her boutique, until after they got out of the car and climbed the back stairs. He wasn't sure if she'd brought him to her place because she was so distraught she'd forgotten to take him home, or if she'd done it because she wanted an explanation. And he didn't ask.

She unlocked the heavy door and preceded him into her apartment just as she'd done a few nights ago when they'd taken a walk. She turned on a lamp, but tonight, she didn't open a window. The air was stuffy. Sweat broke out on his brow. Wiping it away, he whispered, "I can explain.''

She twirled around so suddenly he didn't know what to expect. She faced him, her eyes delving into his in the semi-darkness. What he saw in their depths sent dread all the way through him. It wasn't the first time she'd *thought* she'd overheard a damning conversation. It had happened a few short days ago when she'd returned his suit coat to the office.

"Hannah,'' he said again.

She shook her head. "You don't have to explain.''

"Well, I'm going to, dammit. And you had damn well better listen.''

The hurt in her eyes drained the anger out of him. He raked a hand through his hair. "Look,'' he said quietly. "How long were you standing in the doorway?''

"Long enough to hear you, and to see you with Maria.''

He wanted to grasp her by the shoulders and yell that

he hadn't been *with* Maria, dammit. "I don't know what you heard, Hannah."

"I heard it all."

"It wasn't—"

"Yes, it was. I heard her, Parker. I heard what she said to you. I saw what she did. Why?"

There was no accusation in her voice, or in her eyes. She wasn't angry at him. And she wasn't blaming him. The realization was dredged from a place deep inside of Parker, a place beyond logic or reason. She wasn't asking why *he* had done anything despicable. She was asking why the sister she loved so dearly would do something so callous, so crass, so hurtful.

Hannah not only believed him, but she believed *in* him. A bruise was already forming on his foot where Maria had stomped on it. The pain in Hannah's eyes was a lot worse. Parker Malone was known for his sharp tongue, for his wide command of the English language. Yet now he struggled to find the right words to explain something unexplainable, to help Hannah understand something he didn't understand himself.

"You know Maria better than I do. You know what she's capable of. Has she ever done anything like this before?"

Hannah blinked, trying to clear her mind. Did she really know Maria at all?

She thought of all the times they'd spent together when they were kids. They'd grown apart these past few years, the way all grown siblings did. But Hannah had believed the love had remained. She would have done anything for Maria. She would have given her the shirt off her back, a port in a storm, a kidney, for God's sake. She'd assumed Maria would do the same for her. The realization of how wrong she'd been was shattering.

"I just don't understand." It was all she could think to say.

Parker said, "Younger sisters are often jealous of older sisters, aren't they?" He swore to himself at the feebleness of the question. After all, trying to seduce your sister's boyfriend took sibling rivalry around the bend. Way around the bend.

"Jealous! What does she have to be jealous of?"

Parker could think of several things.

"Look at her," Hannah said. "She's beautiful."

Parker decided not to tell her she was wrong. Oh, Maria had all the right parts in all the right places. But it took more than large breasts and long hair and the right shade of lipstick to make a woman truly beautiful.

"I'm just so gosh darn mad at her I can't think straight."

Parker very nearly groaned out loud. Leave it to Hannah to refrain from swearing even now. He might have made light of it, if he hadn't seen the tear trail slowly down her cheek.

He raised his hand to her face. Sliding his fingers into the hair covering her ear, he said, "Maybe Maria has an emotional problem. But it isn't your fault. And no matter what you think, she's not as beautiful as you are. She doesn't even come close."

She started to protest, but he glided his thumb over her cheekbone and continued. "Everything about you is soft and understated. I'm coming to realize it isn't a conscious choice. It's who and what you are. There are so many layers to you. Even your scent has subtle layers, some sweet, some musky, all unforgettable. Yours is a gentle blend, your shampoo, your perfume, even the breath mints you chew. Nothing is blatant. Instead, you're all warm shades, soft hues. You're not weak. Far from it. You're strong, but your strength comes from within.''

She'd gone very still. Her eyes had lost some of their sadness, her face some of its paleness. She turned her head, bringing her cheek more fully into his hand, as if seeking his warmth.

''Your beauty is the same way, Hannah. It comes from inside you.''

He saw her, felt her, take a shuddering breath. ''Next thing you know you're going to tell me I have a nice personality. Isn't that what guys say when they describe a girl they know isn't pretty?''

He shook his head. He damn near sputtered. That wasn't what he'd meant at all. His thoughts raced. In the end, he knew she had good reason to be insecure. The sister she loved dearly had flaunted herself at *him*.

He would have to try again.

His voice, when it came, sounded deeper, raspier in his own ears. ''I could tell you how beautiful you are, Hannah. I've been told I have an uncanny way with words. But even better, I could show you how lovely I find you, how serene your eyes are right now, how full and warm and sweet your lips taste, how lithe and supple your body is, how perfectly it fits mine. Oh, yes, I could tell you, but I could show you so much better.''

She was looking up at him, her pupils so large her irises were merely a gray ring beneath the shadow of her lashes. There was such warmth in her gaze, such feeling in her sigh. ''Parker?'' she whispered.

He leaned closer, because she'd spoken so softly he almost couldn't hear.

''Yes, Hannah?''

She swayed slightly. It reminded him of a willow switch swaying in a heavy wind. Placing a steadying hand on his chest, she brought her lips close to his ear.

"Show me."

Nine

Her tiny living room was completely silent but for the sound of Parker's sharply drawn breath. If Hannah breathed, she wasn't aware of it. All her attention was trained on him.

She knew what she was asking of him, and she knew why. But she didn't want to think about that now. She didn't want to think about anything. She only wanted to feel.

He cupped her cheek in his palm, tipping her face up. He came closer, his chin lowering, his lips mere inches from hers. He'd been like this in her dreams, but those had been fantasies. The breath on her cheek was real, the fingers splaying wide through her hair were warm. Her eyes fluttered closed, only to open again, her gaze trained on the shadow in the center of his chin. Unable to help herself, she touched the indentation with her fingertip, the beginnings of whisker stubble coarse beneath her sensitive skin.

"You're beautiful," he whispered, his lips grazing first one eyelid, and in turn, the other.

She didn't speak, wanting only to yield to the sweet warmth that was hovering all around her, slowly encircling her, and him.

"Here." He murmured the word against her cheekbone, across the bridge of her nose.

Her breath came in a long, shuddering sigh.

"And here," he whispered along her jaw and at the edge

of her lips. "And here." His lips trailed down her throat, his hand spreading wide along the base of her neck, coming to rest where her heart beat an erratic rhythm. "You're beautiful everywhere, Hannah." His voice was a deep rasp in the summer night. "But you're the most beautiful here, inside."

She whimpered. When he slid a hand along either side of her face and finally covered her mouth with his own, she swooned.

If she lived to be a hundred, she would always remember this moment in time as the instant she fell in love. She'd been hovering, floating on the surface of love for days. It made the gentle lap and subsequent slip into full submersion all the more incredible.

The kiss ended as sweetly as it had begun. Feeling as if she was coming to life, she took his hand in both of hers, kissing his palm. With tears brimming in her eyes, she led him into the adjoining room. There was no hesitancy in her movements, no qualms or self-doubts. With a sureness she hadn't known in a long time, she switched on the overhead fan and turned on a lava lamp one of her clients had given her months ago.

The lamp barely penetrated the darkness, the fan moving warm, humid air in circular currents. It was exotic, erotic, but nothing compared to the look in Parker's eyes, the heat in the fingertips slowly doing away with the buttons down the back of her blouse.

He kissed her cheek, the sound of his breath mingling with the quiet swish of the thin garment landing on the floor. "Look at me, Hannah."

She hadn't realized she'd closed her eyes, but she did as he asked, opening them. And there was Parker, his dark brown hair moving slightly in the fan-induced breeze, a tiny vein in his forehead beating a steady rhythm. When she gazed into his eyes, she couldn't look away from the heat and intensity there. She held perfectly still for a moment, then swayed toward him.

As if it was all the invitation he needed, his arms shot around her, dragging her against him. He made short work of removing her slacks. She helped with his tie, and then his shirt. The clasp on his dress pants took two hands; the breath he sucked in as she undid the button and slowly lowered his zipper made her feel bold, wanton almost.

Desire kicked through Parker. He toed out of his shoes and peeled off his pants and socks. He wanted to press her hand over the part of him throbbing for attention. But this wasn't for him. It was for her. And for her sake, he took a steadying breath and forced himself to slow down.

Feather-light tresses of coffee-colored hair clung to her forehead, skimming her eyebrows. There were shadows beneath her eyes, a soft glow on her cheeks, a sultry curve on her lips.

He lifted her long hair away from her neck. Her throat and shoulders were tanned and smooth, her bra, beige lace, a shade darker than the skin it covered. He slid a strap down each shoulder, unfastened the back clasp. With a sensual, luxuriant movement, she let the garment fall to the floor.

"So beautiful," he whispered, covering her breast with his hand.

He'd glimpsed her body through clothes, but he savored the reality of flesh against flesh. Her groan of pleasure lowered his own eyelids. He kissed, kneaded and caressed until her head lolled back. When she arched against him, he did it all over again.

She slipped out of his arms long enough to open a drawer in her nightstand. When she took out a handful of the pastel-colored packages she'd dropped on the floor the first time they'd met, he nuzzled her neck, then turned her into his arms once again.

Hannah wasn't sure how they ended up in her bed, but suddenly her back was being pressed into her white quilt, and her legs were tangling with his. He did away with his briefs and her panties, then kissed her mouth, her neck, her breasts, the edge of one hip, the length of her thigh, her stomach. In that order, and in every other order.

This was what she needed. Wanted. This moment, this rapture, this man.

The things he did to her made her gasp, writhe, and yearn for more. And more is what he gave her. She touched him, too, and kissed him, her hands molding, memorizing, seeking and giving. It was exhilarating, awe-inspiring. Until now, she hadn't known how love sounded, tasted, felt. And knowing was the most amazing thing.

Her breath caught in her throat as he pulled her to him, breast to chest, skin to skin, man to woman.

Parker had always considered himself a skilled lover, but he wasn't relying on skill tonight. He relied on instinct, and on the sounds Hannah made deep in her throat, and the way she moaned and moved, returning his kisses, his caresses, touch for touch, pleasure for pleasure.

She smelled of woman, and soap, and flowery perfume, her touch strong and brazen one moment, gentle and inquisitive the next, arousing always. She learned his secrets as he learned hers, sometimes patient, often not.

Neither of them spoke. But when she opened her eyes and found him looking at her, she smiled. It was nearly his undoing. Before he lost the last shred of control, he reached onto the bedside table.

Someplace far away, on the other side of a haze of a desire so strong he couldn't think, he was aware that she was whispering his name as she pressed herself closer to him. When he couldn't stand another moment, another touch, he rolled her to her back, poised over her, and made them one.

They began to move again in a slow dance of two bodies, one desire. The overhead fan stirred the warm air, its whirr a backdrop for lustier cries, throatier sighs, and needs that built in strength and intensity. He took her to the brink of completion. Waiting a moment until she went over the edge, he followed, the hot, heavy desire rolling from one to the other.

Hannah opened her eyes when she was able, but it was a long time before she thought of moving again. A deep feeling of peace had enveloped her. She'd come to life tonight in a way she never had before. As a woman, as a lover, as a woman in love.

She shuddered when he shifted to his side, missing him already. She would have liked to murmur her feelings out loud, but her instincts warned her to keep quiet.

She hadn't made love in a long time, had never made love like this. Actually, she'd only had one other lover. She knew it was ghastly to compare lovers, but she couldn't help it. Next to Parker, her boyfriend in college had been exactly that: A boy. She knew, even then, that she wasn't the type to sleep around. The day she and Alan broke up, she'd vowed to wait for the right man.

She'd known of a strong passion within her, but she'd never been so brazen, so consumed with need. She was relieved when he slid an arm around her, pulling her to him, as if he wasn't ready for the closeness to end, either.

They stayed that way for an immeasurable stretch of time, chests rising and falling, heart rates lowering, breathing returning to normal. She groaned when the phone rang, but she made no move to get up.

"Don't you want to get that?" he asked.

His voice sounded husky, and as spent as she was. "I'm not sure I ever want to move again."

She felt more than saw him smile just as the answering machine clicked on in the next room. Her brother's voice carried to her ears. "Hannah? It's me, Cole. I just talked to Mom. She said you seemed preoccupied when you left the ranch tonight. Is everything okay?"

Some things were wonderful, she thought to herself. Some things might never be right again.

"Mom said Maria seemed great," Cole continued in the background. "Call me when you get the chance, okay?"

The answering machine clicked off. And Parker said, "Sounds like Maria fooled your mother. I, for one, am glad Cole didn't call any earlier."

The concern in Cole's voice had reminded Hannah of her troubles, but she smiled in spite of herself. "Cole has great timing."

"It's an inherent characteristic," Parker murmured, "present in the best attorneys."

She glanced up at him and slowly shook her head. The smoke had cleared from his eyes, his face still hard and beautiful and intense. "At least success hasn't gone to your head."

"In case you hadn't noticed, success isn't what went to my head tonight." He moved slightly, as if to get up.

Hannah wasn't experienced enough in these situations to know what to do or say. Secretly terrified that tonight had been a once in a lifetime experience, she reached for a silk robe lying on her side of the bed.

The mattress creaked on the other side, but Parker's voice was still warm and deep as he said, "A client gave me tickets to the symphony."

She glanced over her shoulder. His back was to her, his movements graceful, his body sleek, all sinew and muscle.

"Care to go with me?" he asked.

Happiness washed over her. "Tomorrow night?"

He nodded. "I know it's short notice."

Doing her best not to sound completely breathless, she said, "I would love to go, Parker."

She didn't know what came over her, but before another second went by, she scooted across the bed. Going up on one elbow, she reached a hand to his shoulder, and let it slowly glide down his spine. He sucked in a quick, sharp breath. And held very still.

Her hand slipped around his waist, spreading wide across his abdomen, flexing over ridges, inching lower. He made a sound deep in his throat, part groan, part hum, all male.

"If you're not careful," he said, his voice raw with need, "we're going to have to do that all over again."

Hannah would have liked to hear words of love, but she wasn't altogether disappointed when none were forthcoming. "Define careful." Pressing her lips to the back of his shoulder, she let her left hand spread wide over his chest, while her other hand continued an exploration of its own.

"And to think I even considered the notion that you didn't know your way around a man."

She couldn't help smiling wryly. She knew Parker was referring to the argument they'd had concerning her declaration that she was waiting for a commitment before taking a man to her bed. Tonight, he'd proved her wrong. It was so like him to try to get the last word, even weeks later.

"There was a boy I thought I loved in college," she said, moving against him, "but I don't want to think about him. I'd rather think about this."

Parker sucked in a ragged breath when her hand closed around him. There was a roaring din in his ears. In some far corner of his mind, he knew there was more to the danger signals going off inside his skull than desire. He was trying to think clearly, to identify the problem, but passion closed in on him and he didn't see any reason to think when he could be kissing Hannah again.

Shadows played over the bed. In a movement so quick she gasped, he had her on her back, right where he wanted her.

"Oh, my," she whispered.

He grinned wickedly, and decided then and there that there would be time to analyze later.

"Hannah? Are you home?"

"I'm in here, Adrienne," Hannah called from her bedroom.

It was Saturday night. The carpet muted Adrienne's footsteps, but it didn't quiet the whistle she let loose at the sight of Hannah. Glancing at the doorway Hannah said, "Does that mean I look okay?"

Adrienne sauntered closer. "You look gorgeous, and you know it."

Hannah studied her reflection. She'd been on the receiving end of a lot of compliments these past few days. She had to admit she looked better than she had when Adrienne had seen her this morning. Then, tears had brimmed in her eyes as she'd recounted what she'd seen and overheard at the Double Crown last night. Adrienne had asked a few questions, but for the most part she'd listened. When Hannah had finished, Adrienne had shaken her head and said, "When I was small I used to beg my mother for a baby sister. Times like these make me glad I'm an only child. What are you going to do about Maria?"

Hannah thought she should confront Maria, but how? When? She didn't know how she felt about her sister. Oh, there was still love, but there were other emotions now, as well. Sadness, disappointment, anger, disbelief. It was all so confusing. She was hurt, bewildered, incensed. She didn't know whether she had the right to confront Maria, or an obligation to. It seemed she'd spent half the day worrying about that, and the other half thinking about Parker. He'd called a cab, then crept out of her apartment in the wee hours of the morning, and she already missed him. She would have liked him to spend the night. She told herself the fact that he didn't was no cause for alarm. After all, he had an early meeting. And she had clients to see and parties to plan.

He'd been ardent, passionate, wonderful. And so caring it took her breath away even in memory. Just because he'd been silent and pensive afterward was no reason to worry. He wanted to see her again. He wouldn't have said so if he hadn't meant it. Surely her disappointment over Maria was affecting her self-confidence.

"Do you have those earrings I asked to borrow?" she asked.

"What? Oh." Adrienne came to with a start. Flipping her deep purple boa over one shoulder, she took a pair of amber earrings from her pocket. "I still don't understand why you want to borrow these when Ryan gave you those gorgeous sapphire earrings."

"I'm saving those for a special occasion. Besides, blue sapphires with this dress?" Hannah put the borrowed jewelry on. "What do you think?"

Again, Adrienne was so preoccupied she didn't answer.

Eyeing her friend, Hannah said, "Is everything okay, Adrienne?"

"What? Oh, of course. Why wouldn't it be?"

Hannah returned the lip gloss to the vanity. "You were miles away just now."

"Maybe I was. I called my mother a little while ago, right after she sent me an interesting fax. It seems that a former beauty contest judge and his wife who now reside in Nashville are being investigated for tax evasion."

Hannah knew that Adrienne's mother had been waiting for this day for years, which was how long she'd been planning her retaliation for the wrong that had been done to her daughter. "Your mother must be pleased."

"Shoot, sugar, she's ecstatic. Says she wishes she would have thought to have them investigated."

"It wasn't her?" Hannah turned at her makeup table so she could look directly at Adrienne.

"Nope. Who else could it be?"

"Fate?"

Adrienne shrugged.

"My mother always says what goes around comes around."

Adrienne shrugged again. "Something doesn't add up."

"That's probably what the IRS thought," Hannah agreed.

Adrienne was quiet. Shaking her head as if to clear it, she said, "That dress is going to knock Parker's socks off. And you're right. The earrings are perfect. While you're enjoying a cultural evening, I'm going to be trying to balance my accounts."

"If Parker shows up."

Hannah had Adrienne's full attention. "Why wouldn't he show up?"

Hannah couldn't say why. It was just a feeling she'd had all day. It had to do with the way Parker had looked when he'd crawled out of her bed that last time. He'd kissed her goodbye, but he'd seemed distant, aloof, as if his mind had already been on something else by then.

"He'll show up," Adrienne insisted. "Or else."

"Or else what?"

"Or else he'll hear an earful from you. Besides, some-how I have a feeling that last night was more than a one-night stand. If all Parker had wanted was a fast, hard romp, he could have gotten it with Maria. And he turned her down, remember?"

Hannah pulled a face. Adrienne was, among other things, painfully blunt. She was also usually right.

"I'd better get back to my accounting," she said. "I'll talk to you tomorrow. In the meantime, don't worry. Remember, whatever happens, you have control."

Listening to the click of her own front door, Hannah wanted to believe Adrienne was right. But when Parker hadn't shown up an hour later, she couldn't help wondering whether he was simply late or if he had decided not to come at all.

By the time another hour had crept by, she faced the fact that he was more than fashionably late. A flash of grief ripped through her. First Maria. And now Parker.

Staring at her reflection, she remembered Adrienne's words. Repeating them to herself, she whispered, "I am in control."

Keeping her shoulders up and her upper lip stiff, she reached for her purse. Maybe there was no explanation for what Maria had done. But Parker had darn well better have a good excuse for standing her up tonight.

Adrienne punched a couple of numbers on the old adding machine, double-checked her figures, then punched a few more. She was penciling in the total when a sound filtered through her concentration. She turned her head slightly. Listening. Was someone at the back door?

"Hannah," she called. "Is that you?"

There was only silence. It was Saturday night and the

restaurant was officially closed until Monday. The high school boys she'd hired to wash dishes had left an hour ago. Which meant that she was alone in the building. Just her and her shadow.

There were people who told Adrienne she worked too hard, spent too many Saturday nights balancing books. She didn't mind. The Pink Flamingo was her favorite place to be. Just a few short hours ago her mother had asked how long she was going to wait before thinking about starting a family. Hannah was the only one who seemed to understand that Adrienne didn't necessarily want to have children. It wasn't that she wasn't drawn to a baby's smile, a preschooler's prattle, a teenager's humor. She loved children of all ages. She just didn't feel the need to have any of her own.

The Pink Flamingo was her baby, a mix and match of soft lights and strong flavors. Everything about it was her creation, from the stained-glass window decor, to the pink flamingo on every table. She chose the menu, and she decided who she wanted to hire. Her instructors in culinary school had said she'd never be successful. Not because she couldn't cook, but because she refused to be chained to the norm. What was wrong with putting whimsy with bright colors? Of course she watched the flavor pallet. Nobody would taste bread pudding after eating three-siren chili. That required something cold and rich and soothing, like ice cream, or cheesecake, or four kinds of chocolate. She knew her wine, but she preferred Scotch. As soon as she finished these books, she was going to treat herself to a sip or two out of her most expensive bottle, which she kept in the small kitchen in the apartment upstairs.

A quiet thud carried to her ears. It sounded like footsteps, and reminded her of the special effects in the horror show she'd watched a few nights ago. Of course, in the movie a machete had come crashing through the door inches from a poor victim's head.

Heart in her throat, Adrienne cursed her overactive imagination. She wasn't imagining the fall of footsteps outside her office door. An alarm went off in her head.

Think, Adrienne. And whatever you do, remain calm.

She'd been working by the light of the green lamp on her desk. The rest of the office was in shadow. Rising blithely to her feet, she pressed her back against the wall, and waited. She took a deep, silent breath, and caught a whiff of aftershave. A heartbeat later a hand reached for the light switch a few inches from her elbow.

She let loose a blood-curdling scream. For once she wished she'd have chosen flat shoes. Her three-inch heels were going to make running impossible. Not about to be a victim, she dove into action. Keeping the element of surprise on her side, she swung around.

She saw the shape of a man materialize in the doorway. Everything happened quickly after that. She planted her feet solidly at the same time she grabbed the man's arm. She tugged with all her might to throw him off balance, then stuck her foot out before he could right himself.

He toppled to the floor like a felled oak.

"What the hell—"

The voice sounded deep, surprised and angry.

Adrienne flipped on the light. Squinting beneath the sudden glare, she gasped. She knew her mouth was gaping, but she couldn't help it.

She and the intruder both froze. Adrienne, where she stood near the door, and J. D. Malone, on his back in the middle of her office floor.

Ten

"What the hell are you trying to do, kill me?"

Adrienne stared at J.D. Even flat on his back, the man was formidable. And it really ticked her off. "Don't yell at me!"

He groaned, and she felt compelled to defend herself. That ticked her off, too. "You scared me half to death! What are you doing here, anyway?"

"I'm lying on your floor." He groaned again. "Call 9-1-1."

She uttered the same expletive that had gotten her kicked out of charm school more than twenty years ago. He simply looked up at her, his features stark, his mouth pinched, his face drawn. Although it seemed highly unlikely that they taught young girls how to handle themselves in situations even remotely similar to this one, she found herself wishing she would have paid a little closer attention to what her charm school teacher, Miss Prichart, had said back then. Any help or insight would have been welcome.

"Do you really need an ambulance?" Adrienne asked.

He moaned gruffly, and pushed himself to a sitting position. Adrienne had always heard it wasn't wise to move an injured person. She figured the notorious J. D. Malone knew what he was doing. What she didn't know was what he was doing in her restaurant after closing.

"How did you get in here?"

If he heard the distrust in her voice, he didn't mention it. "I came—" he grimaced as he rose to his knees "—through the back door."

She continued to eye him warily, even after he'd climbed stiffly to his feet. "I locked that door myself."

He met her stare. "The lock is faulty. Anybody could have gotten in."

"Anybody did."

"You're lucky it was me, and not an ax murderer."

She shot him a withering stare. Roughly translated, it meant drop dead.

He lumbered closer. She noticed he gave her a wide berth. She figured she'd given him good reason.

"That was one hell of a self-defense technique," he said.

She nodded. "It was one of three I learned at a class sponsored by and held at the women's center when I first moved to Texas. One involves applying pressure to an assailant's eyeball. Another is the old knee in the groin maneuver."

She thought she saw him wince.

"I had never put any of them to the test. Until now."

He ran a hand through his hair, another down the front of his starched shirt. "I'd say I received the lesser of three evils."

Adrienne really did not want to smile. And yet she felt one hovering dangerously close to her lips. Keeping a tight rein on her expression, she raised her chin a notch and asked, "What are you doing here, Mr. Malone?"

He stared into her eyes, his gaze hypnotic, no doubt a tactic he used to his full advantage in court. He lowered his voice, and she wasn't sure, but she thought he'd eased slightly closer. "I can't seem to stop thinking about you."

Refusing to let him get to her, she gestured to her untidy desk. "As you can see, I'm busy."

He glanced at the account books and ledgers and receipts spread out on the cluttered surface. "You do your own bookkeeping?"

She nodded. "I try. Now if you'll excuse me, I'd better try to keep Uncle Sam happy." When he made no move to leave, she said, "Or did you want to watch?"

"Our accountant hates quarterly taxes. Since the IRS frowns when you miss a payment, they're a necessary evil."

"The IRS?" Adrienne asked.

"Did you say watch?" he said at the same time.

They regarded each other somberly. J.D. was the first to speak. "I normally prefer to participate."

He took a step closer and then, more cautiously, another. She hid a smile. "Why did you stop by, J.D.?"

He held her gaze. "Since all my earlier efforts have failed, I'd hoped to have better luck face-to-face."

"Better luck with what?"

He didn't answer her. Leave it to an attorney, she thought, to take the fifth. They'd reached a standstill, a stalemate, an impasse. She could send him on his way. And she would. But his mention of the IRS seemed a little too coincidental to be, well, a coincidence. She glanced at the fax her mother had sent her. He followed her gaze.

"It's interesting that y'all mentioned the IRS," she said.

He made a tut-tut-tut sound. "Those audits can keep a person busy for months. Nasty things. They can strike anytime, anyone. Even the former judge of an ill-fated beauty contest."

Adrienne could count on one hand the number of times in her life she'd been struck speechless. Once when her father had died. Once when an anonymous caller had played the incriminating tape over the phone two nights before the beauty pageant. And now. She studied the man who was somehow responsible for the latest episode. She could see the resemblance to Parker, but J.D. was even more intimidating. There was a little gray in the hair at his temples, squint lines beside his eyes. As far as Adrienne was concerned, no fifty-one-year-old man had the right to look so handsome. She read the society pages, and she vaguely remembered seeing his name and photo from time to time these past few years. Reportedly, men either feared or respected him, but apparently women adored him. Now that she'd seen him in person, she didn't scoff at them. After all, J. D. Malone was a handsome, rich, powerful man. She understood why so many women succumbed to his every wish.

She reminded herself that she wasn't like a lot of women. She would tell him to leave, as soon as she satisfied her curiosity. "How did you do it?"

J.D. made a show of glancing nonchalantly around the cluttered office, but he doubted he was fooling Adrienne. She was too smart for that. Still, it never hurt to take a look around, to get a feel for a person's surroundings. The desk was large, the computer antiquated, the filing cabinets old. He wasn't certain what to make of the purple boa draped over a chair, but he knew what to make of the woman tucked so nicely into a matching miniskirt.

She was an interesting woman. Her clothes were brightly colored, her eyes a deep moss-green. Her hair was a gorgeous shade of honey-blond, styled in easy, chin-length layers. Her grip had been strong, and yet her hands, soft. Her smile, the few times he'd glimpsed it, was the softest of all.

He didn't normally go to so much trouble to see a woman. He didn't normally have to.

Smoothing a hand over his chin and down his throat, he strolled to the edge of her desk and perched on one corner. "I didn't do anything, really," he said in answer to her question. "I might have gathered a few names, dates, facts. After that, I put in a phone call to a friend of mine in Washington. A person who makes as much money as your former contest judge really should hire more qualified people to handle his money. His finances are a mess. And they're going to get messier."

She strode closer. It occurred to him that he had no idea how she would react. He prepared himself for any possibility. Anger. Disdain. Loathing. To be on the safe side, he crossed his legs.

Nothing could have prepared him for her smile.

"Hannah was right," she said. "If you wait long enough, what goes around really does come around."

"I'm not a particularly patient man, Adrienne."

His declaration brought her right eyebrow up, but she remained silent.

"I want you," he said matter-of-factly.

She started to speak, but he cut her off. "Come on, Adrienne. Admit it. You want me. You don't want to, but you do."

"If I do, it's my problem, not yours."

His smile wasn't a conscious decision. "I've decided to give you what you want, sugar."

She opened her mouth to speak, only to clamp it shut again. "Me. You." Shooting him a withering stare, she said, "Don't call me sugar."

There was plenty of smug satisfaction in hearing her stutter. "What do you want me to call you?" he asked.

Walking past him, she slid into her chair. "I don't want you to call me anything. I may seem like a challenge, but I'm not your type."

"Describe the kind of woman you perceive to be my type."

She picked up a pencil, sharpened it in the electric sharpener on one corner of her desk. "I've found that most people have more than one type. I'd say yours are probably either rich socialites or bored divorcées who show their appreciation in myriad ways."

"Such as?"

She tested the point of her pencil on her fingertip. "Hannah told me about the client who slipped her panties into Parker's pocket."

J.D. shrugged. "It comes with the territory."

"A perk of the trade, I'm sure. Like a good insurance plan or retirement benefits."

"Some consider it a benefit, others a damned nuisance. It hasn't happened to me in a long time. Care to remedy that?"

She looked up at him coquettishly. J.D. uncrossed his legs and studied her unhurriedly. She was doing that helpless dame routine, complete with fluttering fingers and batting eyelashes. She was about as helpless as a mountain lion in a flock of sheep. He had the backache to prove it.

"I can't," she said simply.

"Come on. Give it the old college try."

"I mean it. I can't. It so happens there's a good reason for that."

"Sure you…"

"I'm not wearing any."

A zing went through J.D., heading straight for his lap. He stood, hoping to ease the sudden tight fit of his pants.

He didn't know Adrienne Blakely well, but something told him she wasn't lying. The idea that she wasn't wearing underwear beneath that adorable purple skirt was potent and stimulating as hell. Since he didn't relish the idea of being on the receiving end of another of her defense maneuvers, he decided a change of subject was in order.

"Would you like to get out of here for a while?" he asked. "Have a drink with me, or dinner. Or we can fly to Rome if you'd like."

"I really have to get back to work."

He gestured to the bookkeeping on her desk. "Isn't there anything else you'd rather do tonight, Adrienne?"

She looked up at him. "Of course there is. But I have responsibilities." Her voice was amazingly free of sarcasm.

"Can any of them wait an hour or two?" he asked.

She was silently thoughtful. Suddenly she said, "There is one thing I wouldn't mind doing."

"Yes?"

She lowered her voice provocatively. "It involves an increased heart rate, a dark room, and buttery fingers."

He almost smiled. "That sounds adventurous."

"Are y'all in the mood for a dangerous adventure, J.D.?"

His senses reeled as if short-circuited. "I think I could be persuaded."

She slapped the book closed and rose to her feet. "We don't have much time."

"And why might that be?"

"The movie starts in fifteen minutes."

"Movie?"

"There's a new horror movie playing at the mall theater."

"You want to go to a horror movie?"

The Southern tart grinned. "Why, of course I do. Whatever did you think I was talking about?"

He swallowed. "Never mind."

"Do y'all want to go or not?"

He hadn't been to a horror movie in twenty-five years, and he could honestly say he hadn't missed it. Yet suddenly he found the concept extremely appealing. "You're the boss, sugar."

"Don't call me sugar. Sugar."

"Yes, ma'am."

She turned in the doorway, and slanted him a smile that went straight to his head. "I think we're going to get along just fine," she said, her voice so charmingly Southern it nearly buckled his knees.

He followed her from the room, thinking she wasn't going to get any argument from him.

For the second night in a row Hannah clutched the steering wheel so tight her knuckles turned white. She tried to ease the pressure, but the effects didn't last.

Maybe she should have done this over the phone. No, she was even less confrontational over the telephone than she was in person. Maria was the one who loved a good fight.

Don't think about Maria.

Hannah squeezed the steering wheel tighter. At this rate, it was going to disintegrate beneath her fingers.

She took a deep breath and turned onto Ridgewood Drive. She was going to drive by Parker's house. If he was there, she planned to knock on his door and ask him who he thought he was, standing her up after the night of passion they'd shared. She was going to find out if once had been enough. Technically, they'd made love three times. But it had all been in the same night, and that constituted one date.

She hoped to high heaven it didn't come down to trying to put *that* into words. Still, she'd made her decision. There was no turning back now.

She pulled into his driveway. Every light in the house was on. She thought that was strange. Even more strange were the loud voices shouting above the blaring rock music carrying to her ears through an open window.

She wondered what was going on.

Pulling the keys, she got out of her car, her heels clicking over the sidewalk. As she approached the steps, she paused.

"Where do you think you're going?"

She recognized Parker's voice, but not the somewhat younger one yelling, "Out!"

"Out where?"

"What difference does it make to you where I go? You're not my father."

She started to ring the doorbell, but knocked instead.

"We've been over this, Reed."

Reed? she thought to herself. Wasn't that Parker's nephew's name?

"I'm not going to do anything. I'm just going to Brad's house."

"Brad who?"

"None of your business."

"I'm making it my business."

"We're going to get fast food."

"You're not going anywhere, buster."

"Who's gonna stop me?"

"I am, dammit."

Hannah cringed, hoping Parker didn't use the old "as long as you're in my house you'll do as I say" spiel.

"Reed." Hannah thought Parker's voice sounded steadier. "Wait. Please."

"I don't have to wait. I go where I want when I want."

The door was yanked open and Hannah came face-to-face with a teenager who appeared hellbent on getting out of there. He was tall and lanky, his hair dark and chin-length, his shirt and jeans baggy. His scowl was a dead ringer for Parker's.

"Hello," she said. "May I come in?"

"I wouldn't recommend it."

Oh, yes, that snide sarcasm was definitely a Malone trait. She stepped over the threshold, and took it upon herself to close the door behind her. Two pairs of eyes were suddenly on her, giving her a thorough once-over. Parker's mouth went slack, his eyes narrowing with the dawn of understanding. It made the short, succinct cussword he uttered unnecessary.

His hair was unnaturally unruly, as if he'd raked his fingers through it repeatedly. The top two buttons of his shirt were open, the collar slightly askew. He looked as if he'd already been put through the wringer, which meant she probably wasn't going to have to do it again.

"God. The symphony."

"I take it you forgot," she said.

A hand went to his forehead. "You could say something came up."

Looking from one to the other, she could well imagine what that something was. "Has this argument been going on for a while?"

The boy eyed her suspiciously before nodding.

Just in case Parker was about to say something that would undoubtedly start it back up again, Hannah held the boy's gaze and said, "Did I hear you say you want to go out for fast food?"

When he nodded a second time, she said, "Does that mean you're hungry?"

Parker swore under his breath. "Oh, hell. I forgot about supper. Reed, you're hungry."

"Yeah, so?" He turned his attention back to Hannah. "Who are you?"

"Reed, your manners."

Hannah glanced from the boy to the man. Parker's lips had thinned, his eyes had narrowed, his nostrils flared slightly. "This is Hannah Cassidy."

"Is she your—"

Parker interrupted. "She's my—"

"Friend," Hannah interjected. "Your uncle Parker and I are friends." She held out her hand. The boy took it firmly, if somewhat reluctantly, in his.

"It's nice to meet you, Reed. Parker and I could probably fix something suitable."

The boy shook his head, his hair swinging into his eyes. "On Saturday night? I'm gonna have pizza at Brad's house."

"Brad who?" Parker asked.

"Is this a knock-knock joke?"

Hannah wouldn't have wanted to be on the other end of Parker's quelling glare. Reed appeared completely unaffected. He shrugged one bony shoulder, and finally answered. "Brad Taylor."

"Where does he live?"

Reed released a long-suffering sigh, but again he answered Parker's question, as well as the next three concerning whether or not Brad's parents were going to be home. "Can I go, now?"

Parker nodded. "Call when you get there, and be home by eleven."

"Yeah, right." And then, with the shock of disbelief, "You're kidding!"

"I never kid."

"Eleven o'clock? Nothing even starts to get interesting until twelve."

"Eleven o'clock, Reed. I used my influence with the judge this time. If there's a next time, it isn't going to matter if you have connections to the president of the United States. How do you plan to get there and back?"

"Ever heard of the bus?"

The Malones faced off. Hannah would have been hard-pressed to say whose glare was more withering and whose stare more frigid. As if he realized Parker wasn't going to back down, Reed turned away. He didn't say another word. He probably figured the hard slam he gave the door said enough.

Swearing under his breath, Parker aimed the remote control at the blaring television and punched the power button. The musicians disappeared through a thin line down the center of the large screen.

Hannah faced Parker in the ensuing silence.

"I prepared myself for several different scenarios," she said quietly. "This wasn't one of them."

Parker shouldn't have been surprised at the thrum of desire that went through him. The mere thought of Hannah had brought it about when he'd least expected all day long. So it stood to reason it would happen to him at the sight of her in the flesh. He swallowed, and tried to rotate a kink out of his back between his shoulder blades.

It had been a hell of a day. He'd gotten some disturbing news concerning Sophia Fortune's latest demands regarding her divorce. He'd called an emergency meeting with Dale Minskie, the sharp, young attorney who loved nothing better than going for the jugular. They were already putting a plan into action, but it was damned complicated. To top it all off, Adalaide was out with the flu, and nobody else in the office could find a damn thing. The visions that had been filtering through his mind of Hannah's kiss-swollen mouth and lush breasts, and the memory of her husky sighs and moans of pleasure hadn't helped his concentration in the least.

And then Beth had called. She was in trouble, she'd said. More specifically, Reed was. He'd been caught with a group of boys who had been accused of shoplifting. Although Reed didn't have any of the stolen items on him, his was a guilt by association. He'd said he didn't take anything, and Parker wanted to believe him. But he just didn't know. The owner of the store had agreed not to press charges this time, but Beth was frantic with worry. She said he needed a firm hand. A man's firm hand. Which left either Parker or J.D. Since she hadn't spoken with their father in years, she'd called Parker. The kid had only been here for three hours and already Parker wanted to throttle him.

Beth had said Reed was going through a difficult phase. Impossible was more like it. The kid could go from sullen to argumentative in the blink of an eye. For the past three hours, he'd exposed Parker to a huge dose of the latter. Hannah had waltzed in and diffused the situation. In the wake of so much noise, the house seemed strangely silent. Blessedly silent. Parker hoped he hadn't made a mistake by letting Reed go out tonight. But a time limit had been set, and peace had been restored, at least temporarily.

"Hear that?" he asked.

She listened intently, then shook her head.

"Silence. How did you do that?" he asked.

She shrugged, and looked up at him as if soft-touched thoughts were shaping her smile for him alone. "Some people are just natural born peacemakers."

A rush of sexual desire flooded into him. Keeping the peace wasn't all that came naturally to her. "You should be angry with me," he declared.

She sauntered closer. "What makes you think I'm not?"

Her smile shimmered over him. It was soft and sweet, the kind of smile that could light up a dark corner. The kind of smile that made a man yearn to come home. The kind of smile that made him decidedly ill at ease.

"If you're angry," he said, keeping a tight rein on his senses, "you're doing an impressive job of covering it up."

"You had good reason to forget our date, Parker. If you'd like me to punish you for it, I could probably think of something."

His thoughts took a slow dive into a wave of desire that made itself known in extremely telling ways. He'd noticed that she was dressed up the moment she set foot in his house. Now, he took the time to appreciate her appearance. Her dress was the color of dark mahogany, the fabric some sort of knit that fit her to perfection without being tight. The skirt was full enough to swirl around her legs, the hem scalloped slightly around her ankles. Her only jewelry was a pair of amber earrings. Her eyelids were tinted, her lips colored with shiny gloss, her hair fastened high on the back of her head with an amber-colored clip.

"Well?" she asked.

"Did you say 'punish'?"

She sauntered closer. "I was thinking that there might be some sort of torture I could inflict on you. Water torture comes to mind. Or perhaps you have a ticklish spot."

Withstanding that provocative smile of hers was torture in itself, the sultry heat in her eyes nearly his undoing. Something restless and unwelcome stirred inside him. Extenuating circumstances aside, Parker had stood Hannah up. Okay, he'd had good reasons. A damn good excuse. Truth be told, he wasn't certain he wouldn't have come up with an excuse to cancel their date anyway. All because of something she'd said last night. She'd mentioned a boy she'd loved in college. It wasn't that Parker cared that she'd been in love. It was just that her mention of the sentiment drove home the fact that she believed in love, in happily ever after. In forever.

He didn't want to hurt her, didn't want her to set her sights on him. He didn't want to be held accountable for anybody's broken heart.

"Are you sorry, Parker?"

He sucked in a sharp breath when her hand glided to his arm. He didn't follow the question. Was he sorry he'd stood her up? Or sorry she was here? He made a noise deep in his throat, part groan, pure frustration. His nerves were shot. Hell, he had kinks in his neck he'd never had before.

"Reed's only been here for three hours, and I've already turned into my father."

She smiled, moving her hand up his arm. "How old is he?"

"Almost fifteen. But he acts five one minute, thirty the next."

Hannah wondered if Parker was aware that he was staring deep into her eyes, mesmerized, it seemed. She also wondered if the hand gliding to her shoulder stemmed from a conscious decision on his part, or from a need to touch her. At this point, it didn't matter. She reveled in the heat in his palm either way.

"He sounds normal for a boy his age," she whispered.

His eyelids lowered, along with his voice as he said, "He was born hardheaded and stubborn. Cried for the first six months of his life. Beth says he went straight from colic to the terrible twos. He hit puberty on a run. Which is pretty much the M.O. for all Malones."

Was he trying to warn her, or scare her? She thought about suggesting that if he wanted to do either of those things in the future, he shouldn't attempt to do it while skimming a thumb over her nipple, which had puckered noticeably through the thin fabric of her dress.

"Do you think he'll be home at eleven?" she asked.

"I haven't a clue."

"What will you do if he isn't?"

"I'll blow up that bridge when I get there." His voice was husky, his eyes glazed with need.

"Kiss me, Parker."

"I shouldn't."

"Then allow me."

She went up on tiptoe, her mouth covering his in a deep, searing kiss that made the room spin, and her in it. Parker took it from there. He slanted his mouth at an angle to gain better access. She gave herself up to the kiss, welcoming, accepting the thrust of his tongue. The moment the kiss ended, he hauled her against him, as if he couldn't go another moment without full body contact.

"You look beautiful in that dress." He whispered the words between kisses placed along her shoulder, the little hollowed curve where her shoulder met her neck.

"Parker?" she whispered.

"Yes?" His voice was at one with the rasp her zipper made as he lowered it slowly down her back.

"I was just wondering..."

His fingers spread wide across the skin he'd bared on her lower back.

"...If you think I'm beautiful in this dress, why are you removing it?"

He looked into her eyes, holding her gaze as he slipped first one and then the other strap from her shoulders. The top of the dress glided gracefully to her waist. He didn't answer her question. At least not with words. His answer was in the heat in his eyes as his gaze trailed along her chin, her neck, her bare breasts.

When his hands covered her breasts, she gave in to the need swirling around her, through her. Starting a slow exploration of her own, she found that she didn't need words. Her eyes closed, her head tipped back, and she sighed. Words were highly overrated, but touch, and feel, and smell, and taste, those were heady sensations. And she needed those very much.

It seemed that Parker needed them, too.

She didn't let on, but she'd seen his expression when she'd first walked through the door. She wasn't so sure he would have shown up for their date even if Reed hadn't suddenly needed Parker's help. It wasn't because Parker didn't care for her. The warmth and tenderness in his hands, in his eyes, in his sighs, was too spontaneous to be anything but honest. Oh, he wanted her. She had a feeling he didn't like that very well, but he couldn't seem to help himself. Parker Malone was accustomed to being in control. A man like him wouldn't take kindly to losing all control to love. A man like him would fight it. But he wasn't fighting this.

"Parker?" she whispered, strolling a half step behind him as he led her, hand in hand, to his bedroom.

"Yes?" he whispered in the doorway.

"How long is Reed going to be staying with you?"

He reached up with deft fingers, plucking the clasp from her hair. "Two or three weeks," he said as her heavy hair cascaded down her neck. "A month at the most."

"Oh," she said, slipping out of her shoes.

"Why?" His shirt was open, his belt unfastened.

She decided they'd talked enough. Pressing her body against his, she whispered, "I was just wondering."

She'd fallen in love last night before she'd taken him to

her bed. In the process, she'd discovered that he was worth the risk to her heart. It was up to her to prove to him that she was worth the risk to his.

He was going to need help with his nephew, there was no doubt about that. Ah-hh. Her head lolled back at the delicious things he was doing to her body. It looked as if she was going to have two or three weeks, a month at the most, to show Parker, over and over again, if necessary, that when two people were in love, forever was possible. When two people were in love, everything was possible.

Together, they strode the remaining distance to the bed. While every light in the rest of the house was on, Parker's bedroom was wonderfully dark. Hannah liked the dark. She liked relying on taste and smell and touch and sound. Two or three weeks of this, she thought, would be heaven. But it was only the beginning of what their lives could be.

Once he realized he loved her.

"You're awfully quiet," Parker said, his breath ruffling Hannah's hair. He'd drawn a blanket over them a while ago. Their breathing had slowed to normal, but it had been so long since she'd said anything he wondered if she was asleep. "Hannah? Are you awake?"

She made a sound that meant yes.

"Are you all right?" he asked.

She snuggled closer. "I'm so all right I doubt I'll ever be able to move again."

Parker felt the effects of her teasing in all the usual places, and in a few more unique places, as well. He was concerned about the direction their relationship had taken. Hell, he hadn't planned to take it all the way to the relationship stage, period. But she'd looked up at him with those big gray eyes tonight, and he'd been lost.

He wasn't accustomed to being lost. He was a man who

thrived when in control. And yet he could have easily slid a hand to her waist, over the curve of her hip, down the soft, supple length of her thigh right now. He was losing a semblance of control just thinking about it.

His traitorous hand glided down her smooth body. He couldn't help smiling at the sound of Hannah's long, drawn-out sigh. "What time is it?" she whispered.

He glanced at the clock on the bedside table. "A quarter past ten."

"Reed will be home soon. I'd be happy to stop over after work tomorrow to help you fix dinner for him, but I don't want to be in bed when he gets back tonight."

Parker thought she had a valid point, and was prepared to agree with her when her hand inched down his abdomen.

"Hannah? What are you doing?"

Her laugh was deep and throaty. "If we want to be out of bed by eleven, we'd better hurry."

He sucked in a ragged breath, and then another. He knew that somewhere along the way he'd lost control again. He'd have to find it. Later. Right now, there were lips to kiss, murmurs to hear, sighs to moan. And a woman who knew her own mind to drive wild all over again.

Eleven

Once again, rock music greeted Hannah as she pulled into Parker's driveway. Today, it wasn't accompanied by raised voices. A bubble floated on the hot air, iridescent in the sun's rays. A few feet away, Reed Harrison Malone Wilder turned the hose on the soapsuds he'd just slathered on the hood of his uncle's car.

The boy's hair was hidden under a backward baseball cap, his upper torso, thin and wiry in youth, exposed to the burning high noon sun. Hannah couldn't help wondering if the chore was a peace offering from Reed, or a punishment from Parker. Reaching across her seat for the items she'd picked up at the supermarket minutes ago, she closed the door with her hip, smiling at the attention Reed was paying to his chore. Evidently, tall, lean and fastidiousness were dominant traits in the Malone family.

"Hello," she called over the throbbing bass coming from a nearby radio.

Reed glanced at her, but said only, "Hey."

"When did Parker get his car back?" she asked conversationally.

The boy reached for the soapy sponge. "Picked it up first thing this morning. Should have heard the riot act he read the mechanic because it wasn't clean."

"Parker has extremely high standards."

Reed made a sound that reminded Hannah of his uncle.

"The mechanic got even when he wrote up the bill. Uncle Parker didn't say a word all the way home."

"Where is he now?"

Reed gestured to the house. Leaving the boy to his task, Hannah hefted the bags higher into her arms and went in search of Parker. She found him in the kitchen, stirring something in a big pot. She paused in the doorway, taking a moment to watch him, undetected. She wondered if he always dressed this way on Sundays. His feet were bare, as if he'd just changed his clothes and hadn't gotten to his shoes. Navy chinos were slung low on his hips, a burgundy shirt clinging to his chest and shoulders. She doubted she would ever tire of looking at him. Or spending time with him. Or loving him.

He'd invited her to dinner before she'd left last night. Although that was hours away, she'd called on her cell phone while she was running errands, offering her assistance, and asking if he needed anything. She couldn't have brought herself to repeat his suggestive response out loud, but her thoughts turned hazy at the memory alone.

He looked up and over, his gaze going directly to hers. She would never know how he knew she was there. She was holding very still, so it couldn't have been movement that drew his gaze. Something powerful passed between them, something Hannah yearned to call love. Afraid it was much too soon for that, she strolled further into the room and said, "I think I have everything you need. For the three-siren chili."

She busied herself with removing items from the sacks. It gave her someplace to look, lest Parker should see in her eyes the part of the statement she left unsaid. *I have everything you need in a woman, too. So let yourself love me, Parker.*

He went back to his task at the stove. Forbidding herself

to feel disappointed, Hannah placed the chili beans and tomato juice on the counter nearby. "What time did Reed get home last night?" she asked, rummaging through a drawer for a can opener.

"Eleven-thirty."

Spying the device, she said, "Early enough to make a point, and not late enough to get in serious trouble."

They were standing side-by-side, their shoulders close but not quite touching. She looked up at him, and felt sideswiped by his thoughtful expression. "I'm the one in serious trouble, Hannah."

Hannah held perfectly still, on pins and needles because she wasn't sure if Parker was referring to his burgeoning feelings for her, or his responsibility to his nephew. "Everything is going to work out, Parker. You'll see."

She held her breath, waiting.

The onions Parker was sautéing splattered noisily, drawing his attention. He stirred them in silence for a few seconds. When he finally spoke, he didn't look up. "It's strange, having a kid in the house. It's noisy, and he doesn't take care of anything. He loves chili, and won't eat chicken. I thought I knew him, but I never knew that."

Hannah was disappointed, but she was also intrigued by the depth of feeling in Parker's voice. This was a side of him she'd barely glimpsed. "Did you tell him to wash your car?"

Parker shook his head. "I was going to, but Reed beat me to it. I figured it would be punishment for coming in late. He used it as a negotiation tactic for more freedom."

She was smiling at the expression on Parker's face. "Did it work?"

"I came damn close to falling for it. I'm going to have to remember the technique. Someday it'll come in handy in court. In the meantime, it isn't easy winning an argument with that kid. Hannah, what are you doing?"

She'd moved away from him, and had taken the other bag in her hand. "I picked up some potting soil and fertilizer for your poor fica plant. I can't stay long. I promised my mother I'd meet her at the Double Crown at two. She says she's always wanted to teach me to ride a horse, but really, after the other night, I think she's worried about me. I want to talk to her about Maria. Now that I think about it, she and Maria used to have plenty of arguments. The next time Reed tries to pick a fight, I suggest you try something more constructive than arguing. Something he sees as an even match."

Parker stopped stirring the chili. He'd been feeling uneasy for days. He didn't want to be evenly matched with that kid. He was the adult, dammit. There was more to his unease than Reed. He just wasn't sure what it was.

Hannah disappeared from the room, only to return moments later, his sickly fica plant in tow. She spread newspaper on the floor, placed the potted plant in the center of it, and proceeded to open bags and packages.

She chose that moment to look his way, her gaze meeting his from the other side of the room. She smiled. Parker felt as if the wind had been knocked out of him. Although he tried, he couldn't return her smile.

"Hannah."

"Hmm?"

Her voice was whisper-soft, her eyes, deep and dewy. He saw the symptoms, and he recognized the look of a woman who believed she was falling in love. He had to warn her, and stop her, at all costs. "I can have Lissett do that next week," he said. "I've taken advantage of you enough already."

Her gaze remained steady, but her smile drained away.

He knew from her expression that she understood what he was trying to tell her.

"You don't have to worry about me, Parker. I know exactly what I'm doing."

"And what are you doing?"

She finally broke eye contact. "I'm saving this plant's life. Consider it my contribution to the cause."

He stared at her for several tension-filled seconds. "I can't be your cause, Hannah."

"Have I asked for promises, Parker?" He shook his head slowly. "Would you stop worrying? I'm a big girl. And I'm not complaining. In case you haven't noticed, I've had a good time these past few weeks."

Parker continued to watch her for several seconds. Not entirely satisfied that she wasn't expecting forever from a man like him, he returned to Reed's chili.

Hannah went back to her task, doing everything in her power to keep the tremble in her fingers from showing. She'd heard the conviction in Parker's voice, saw it in his eyes. And she wasn't at all certain that she wouldn't end up with a broken heart.

She lifted the root-bound plant from the small pot. Replanting it in the larger container filled with new soil, she knew it was too late to turn back. She was in love with Parker. That meant her heart was already involved. All she could do now was follow it and see where it might lead.

"That's it, Hannah," Lily told her daughter later that day. "The bridle goes like this. As soon as you get it fastened, I'll show you how to cinch the saddle nice and tight. Once you've mounted this docile creature, all you'll have to do is follow my lead."

Keeping one eye on the horse, Hannah said, "Are you sure she's the most docile animal on the planet?"

"I'm sure."

Hannah looked on as her mother fastened this, tightened that. The barn smelled of horses and hay. Dust particles twinkled in the sunbeams slanting from a high window, rays of light catching on the diamond tennis bracelet peeking from the cuff of Lily's shirt. The bracelet was precious to Lily, and until Ryan's divorce was final and she could wear his engagement ring, she would wear the bracelet day and night.

Her mother was happier than Hannah had seen her in a long time, and Ryan was a big part of the reason. Hannah dreaded doing or saying anything that would mar that happiness.

"I'm just about finished," Lily said, straightening with an ease and agility that was somehow even more lovely in a woman of fifty-three. "We'll take it slow. Once you're feeling comfortable on old Ginnie here, you can tell me what's bothering you."

There was no use wondering how her mother had known. Hannah knew Cole hadn't said anything. She'd returned her brother's call, but she hadn't given him any details, deciding instead that she should talk to Maria first. Unfortunately, Maria wasn't answering her phone or returning her calls.

"Are you sure we shouldn't be taking a walk instead?" Hannah quipped, looking the huge—okay, the docile— creature up and down. "Now that Rosita's had another dream, maybe we shouldn't tempt fate by taking any unnecessary risks."

Lily shuddered. "That wasn't a dream. It was a nightmare."

Hannah accepted the reins her mother placed in her hand. Following Lily's lead, she walked out into the corral. Lily was right. Rosita's dream was more nightmare than anything else. It had been similar to the dream she'd shared with her and Adrienne weeks ago. Along with the three horses in Rosita's dream last night, she'd seen a faceless man in a cowboy hat and leather gloves. The dream had been hazy and unclear. The fear that had roused Rosita from sleep with a piercing scream had been real. Rosita was convinced it was a sign of a violent death, for lying next to the trail of blood had been a pair of leather gloves.

"We'll be careful," Lily told Hannah. "But we can't stop living altogether because Rosita's had a metaphorical dream. The trails are groomed and safe. Now, reach up for the saddle horn…"

Hannah listened intently to her mother's instructions. Placing her foot in the stirrup, she swung herself onto the horse's back. Her movements were a little jerky, but she made it onto the saddle on her first try.

"Well? What do you think?" Lily asked, looking up.

"I think it's a good thing I'm not afraid of heights," Hannah replied.

Lily's laughter rang out over the quiet afternoon. Moments later she mounted her favorite horse. Mother and daughter started toward a grassy lane.

From around the corner, in the shadows just inside the barn, Clint Lockhart flexed his gloved hands at his side. Shaking his head, he scowled. Dreams, premonitions. Hell, it was nothing but superstition, and he didn't believe in any of it. He believed in action, and planning, and thinking ahead. After all, a man never knew when something he saw or heard today would come in handy.

Besides, Clint hadn't had a dream in years. But he thought all the time. He was forty-three years old, and he'd spent years as a hired hand on the Fortune ranch, oversee-

ing thousands of acres of land and an operation that should
have been his. His, dammit.

His old man never should have sold out to Kingston
Fortune. Clint had hated his father for doing that. He hated
the Fortunes even more. He seethed whenever he thought
of the way both his older sisters had betrayed him by marrying into the Fortune family. He spit. Seducing Sophia,
Ryan's second wife, right here in this very barn had been
gratifying for a while, but it wasn't nearly enough.

Clint wanted more than a romp in the hay with Sophia,
the woman Ryan Fortune no longer wanted. He was sick
to death of seconds. He wanted what was rightfully his.
Clint had come to terms with the fact that the ranch would
never be his. He could live with that, so long as he was
compensated with money. Lots of it. Along with the
money, he wanted revenge. He wanted to be revered. Most
of all, he wanted the satisfaction that would come with
knowing that all these years he'd spent planning had finally paid off.

Things had gone awry in his scheme to kidnap the Fortune baby to make Ryan pay in money, and in worry. So
he'd been forced to relay information to Sophia. In the
end, he would receive a hefty portion of her divorce settlement, as well.

In the end, he thought. The end of all his planning was
so near he could practically taste it.

Stepping out of the shadows, he spit again. He could
see Lily Cassidy and her daughter as they meandered toward the north lane. Clint shook his head. Hannah couldn't
ride a horse worth a damn. She needed to loosen up a little.
He knew of one surefire way to accomplish that. It would
be a pleasure to show her how to wrap her long legs
around him for the ride of her life.

The gathering tightness of his jeans reminded him of

how long it had been since he'd been able to get away to
the city to meet Sophia and partake in that particular brand
of pleasure. He bent his knee slightly, and pushed up the
brim of his hat. Squinting into the sun, he watched the
Cassidy women ride over the hill and out of sight.

His dusty boots creaked as he strode into the center of
the corral and looked around. He wouldn't have minded a
good, hard romp with either one of them. These days Lily
had eyes only for Ryan. And he'd seen the daughter with
that arrogant attorney who was trying to bilk Sophia out
of her share of Ryan's fortune. It was just like a Fortune
to assume they deserved the lion's share while everyone
else got peanuts.

Clint hated Ryan, but even he couldn't blame the man
for wanting to be rid of Sophia. Sophia was a world-class
bitch. But she certainly knew what a man needed in bed.
She could buck like a bronco and scratch like a barn cat.

He glanced all around. The Cassidy women were out of
sight. And none of the ranch hands was around. Not that
he would have cared if one of them could see the fit of
his jeans. He was a man, and men had urges. Nothing
wrong with that. Oh, he might fantasize about sex, but
Clint Lockhart didn't have to use force to get it when he
needed it. As soon as he had a night free, he was going to
pay Sophia a visit at her room in the Austin Arms. Chances
were she was as hard up for it as he was.

Meanwhile, he had to be patient.

Casting another glance over land that should have been
his, he turned to leave. The glare of sunlight reflected off
an object lying in the tall grass just outside the corral. He
strode to the fence, slipped through two boards. Going
down on his haunches, he eyed the delicate gold bracelet
and intricately cut rubies glinting in the sun.

He recognized the bracelet as one he'd seen on Lily's

wrist earlier. Must have fallen off when she closed the gate. Fairly certain that no one was looking, he removed one glove with his teeth, and picked up the bracelet, as well as a small stone. He pitched the stone into the distance, and discreetly dropped the bracelet into the front pocket of his jeans.

He'd been told he had a hard, cold-eyed smile. One corner of his lip twisted upward as he ran his hand over the pocket now housing Lily's bracelet. Ah, yes, a man never knew when something he saw or heard today was going to come in handy.

"Mom?"

Lily glanced sideways at Hannah. She'd heard the uncertainty in her older daughter's voice, saw it in the way she bit her lip. Hannah was worried, and there was more to it than her fear of riding.

"What is it, Hannah?"

"Do you think Maria is healthy?"

Keeping her voice quiet, Lily said, "She looked thin the other night, but I thought she seemed well, didn't you?"

Hannah took a deep breath, her eyes straight ahead. "I don't mean physically healthy, Mom."

"What then? Hannah, for heaven's sake. What's going on?" Lily reached a hand to Hannah, taking her reins. "Whoa," she murmured to both horses.

Finally, Hannah met her mother's gaze. "I don't want to do anything to hurt Maria, but do you remember all the times we used to say she was in one of her black moods? Looking back, I wonder if that was normal. She always wanted to be the center of attention. She was always upset about something, always scheming or ranting and raving."

"What are you saying?"

Hannah took another deep breath and mentally kicked

herself. She wasn't saying anything very well. In the process, she was scaring her mother to death. "Maria said something to Parker the other night, and frankly, I don't know what to think. I've tried to reach her. She won't return my calls. I can't help but wonder why she does and says the things she does. And why doesn't she ever let us come to see her? Or come to see us? Why is she so secretive? What could she be hiding?"

Lily's eyes were round now, her face pale, the fingers of one hand circling her wrist. She froze for a moment, her gaze finally going to her hand.

"Mom, what's wrong?"

"My bracelet."

Hannah glanced at her mother's wrist where the bracelet had been when she'd first arrived at the ranch. "I saw it on your wrist in the barn. It must have come off on the trail. Let's retrace our steps and look for it."

"Honey, wait."

Hannah turned her head to look at her mother.

"I cherish that bracelet, but I love my children more than anything in this world. If any of you are in trouble, I want to help."

A smile trembled on Lily's lips, warming Hannah more surely than the hot afternoon sun. Hannah didn't want to mar her mother's happiness. And she wasn't sure she was right about Maria. Maybe Maria was fine. Maybe she'd made a pass at Parker because she had unresolved issues with her older sister. The thought felt like a knife in Hannah's chest. But she and Maria were both grown up now. It wasn't fair to burden their mother with their problems.

"I know you want to help, Mom. But I'm not sure you can. I'm not even sure you should try. This is between Maria and me."

Hannah decided then and there that she would find a

way to get in touch with her only sister, even if she had to drive out to Leather Bucket and wait. Right now, she wanted to help her mother search for the bracelet that was an affirmation of Ryan's love. Hannah knew how it felt to be in love. If Parker ever presented her with such a gift, she would never want to lose it.

"Come on," she told her mother, taking back her reins. "We haven't come that far. The bracelet has to be here somewhere."

They returned to the ranch two hours later, tired and forlorn. Although they'd combed every inch of the trail, their search for the bracelet had been unsuccessful.

Lily had remained strong throughout the search, but a tear trailed down her face when she told Ryan.

"I'll buy you another bracelet, my dear," he said, taking her face in both his hands. "One more beautiful than the first."

Lily sniffled, and shook her head. "I don't need a bracelet as proof of your love, Ryan. As beautiful as the bracelet was, I would rather lose it than you."

Pitching hay in a nearby stall, Clint Lockhart slid his hand into his pocket, his blunt, work-roughened fingertips catching on the delicate gold chain and rich gemstones. He turned his back on the stall door, lest anybody see his twisted smile.

Music blasted Parker as he passed the bedroom at the top of the stairs. It wouldn't have been so bad if Reed was inside. But no, the kid was dogging Parker's every step. Arguing. Badgering.

"You can't keep me here. I'm not your prisoner."

The house still smelled of the pizza Reed had ordered for supper. As far as Parker could tell, his nephew lived on fast food and chili. For a kid so wiry, he ate like a horse. And he argued better than any divorce attorney Parker had ever met. Whoever said what we need is not a clear plan but a clear intent, must have had a kid like Reed.

It was only Monday. It was going to be a long week. After the yelling match two nights ago, things had been relatively quiet. Reed hadn't exactly been communicative, but until now he hadn't refused to take no for an answer, either.

"I washed and waxed your car. And today I mowed the lawn. That's gotta be good for something."

Yelling would have been easier to dismiss. This rationalizing required serious thinking and careful responses. Parker felt a headache coming on. Strange, he usually *caused* migraines.

"Reed, I appreciate the fact that you washed my car and mowed the lawn. I'm not your warden. I'm your uncle. And this isn't a prison. For the next few weeks, it's your home."

"I haven't seen my friends in two days. There's nothing wrong with hanging out with the guys."

"I didn't say you couldn't see your friends, Reed. I simply said you have to be home by eleven."

"You're my uncle, not my legal guardian. You don't have any right to tell me what to do."

The kid was smart. Too smart. He was also partially right. Parker didn't have a legal right, but he had a moral one. The boy's ego was smarting from his father's desertion. Just in case he considered his mother's quest for Parker's help as another low blow, Parker decided not to mention the fact that she'd given him the right to set limits for her son. How in the hell did he go about doing that without damaging the kid?

Parker needed help. Arguing wasn't working.

What was it Hannah had said the other day? Find something more constructive than arguing. What in the hell was more constructive than arguing? He'd boxed in college. Now that he thought about it, punching a wall would feel pretty good right now. Wait. Parker had a better idea.

"What do you say we take this into the kitchen?"

Reed eyed him suspiciously. "I'm not hungry."

Parker was, but that was beside the point. "Good. Because there's no food left in the house. I think I know how to settle this."

He had the boy's undivided attention.

"You want to stay out past eleven. I don't think it's necessary. Why not make it a contest? A match of wills, so to speak."

"What kind of match?"

"You ever arm wrestle?"

Parker wasn't altogether certain he liked the smug look of satisfaction settling across Reed's face. The boy rubbed his upper arm, flexed his muscle. And led the way to the kitchen table.

They took a seat at ninety-degree angles. While Reed was busy positioning his elbow and shoulders, Parker said, "Before we begin, let's make our stakes perfectly clear."

Reed nodded. "If I win, I get to stay out until two." He must have read the look in Parker's eyes, because he amended his stand with, "Okay, until one."

Parker didn't like that at all, but since he planned to win, he nodded. "And if I win, you will be home by eleven. Or before if you choose to be. Every night. From now on. With no argument."

Reed's eyes narrowed, and his jaw tightened.

Parker removed his suit jacket and loosened his tie.

Reed flipped his hat around so the bill was out of his

way. Elbows were planted, grips checked and locked. The contest began.

Parker was a little surprised to discover that Reed's hand was as large as his. But he wasn't surprised by Reed's daunting determination. The boy was stronger than he looked. Parker was strong, too. It was a good thing, because Reed meant business. He was a good thirty-five pounds lighter than his uncle, but it was obvious he intended to win every bit as much as Parker did.

The occasional bump of bass wafted through the house from the second floor. The only other sound was that of Parker's and Reed's carefully drawn breaths. Thirty seconds into the match, Reed's arm shook slightly. Out of the blue, he said, "What time's Hannah coming over?"

"Any minute now."

"She's nice."

"Yes, she is," Parker agreed.

The boy's face was stern, his jaw set in consternation. "So are ya doing it with her?"

"I don't kiss and tell, Reed."

"Me, neither."

If Reed had intended his simple statement as a surprise tactic, it backfired. The insinuation brought on an adrenaline rush that resulted in a hard and fast victory for Parker.

Reed pulled a face only a boy of nearly fifteen could manage, but he didn't call for a rematch. He rose sullenly to his feet. Mumbling under his breath, he headed for the back door.

"Hey, Reed?"

The boy turned at the door.

"Are there going to be girls at Brad's house?"

"Yeah."

"Somebody you like?"

"What if I do?"

Translated, Parker knew that meant yes. He tried to remember how it felt to be almost fifteen. He could feel himself going pale. Oh, boy, he was in big trouble.

"You know about germs and diseases and protect—"

Reed interrupted. "Don't worry, Uncle Parker. I've got it under control."

A movement in the doorway drew both their attention. Hannah breezed in, and Reed made his escape.

She glanced from the expression on Parker's face to the place Reed had been. "What does he have under control?"

Parker rose to his feet, straightened his tie. He should have told the kid to be home by nine-thirty. "I think I'd better have a talk with Reed."

"A talk?"

"*The* talk."

"You don't think he knows?"

"He likes some girl. He's going to see her tonight."

The dawning look of understanding was evident in her slow smile. "You're right. You'd probably better talk to him."

He swore under his breath.

"There's no reason to look so bewildered. You pose arguments on your clients' behalf all the time. You're a very eloquent spokesman."

"This is different."

"In what way?"

"I'm still waiting for my father to tell me."

"I don't think you need the talk, Parker."

He caught a whiff of her perfume about the same time he heard the rustle of silk beneath her sundress. His gaze caught on the light in her eyes, the shadow on her lids, the blush on her cheeks, the pout on her lips. "You don't?"

She shook her head. "You seem to know what you're doing."

Her tone was teasing, her style purely her own, so subtle a man who wasn't paying attention could miss it. Lucky for him, he was the observant type.

A rush of sexual desire flooded into him, causing his heart to change rhythm and his voice to turn husky and deep. "I guess you could say my training has been hands-on."

Hannah kept her gaze trained on Parker's face. His hair was a deep, dark brown, his eyebrows a shade darker, still. His cheekbones were prominent, his jaw and chin roughly hewn, the shadow in the center endearingly quaint. His eyes were closed slightly, hooded with secrets she was fast learning to decipher.

He was thinking about the things he wanted to do to her, with her. He wanted her. It was that simple.

She didn't want this to be a simple case of a man wanting a woman. She was waiting for a sign that Parker felt more for her than an intense physical attraction that could one day wane into little more than a passing friendship.

There were times when she believed he was coming to love her. Times when she met his gaze across a room, or picked up the phone to the sound of his deep voice, or laughed with him across his kitchen table. She was waiting for a sign, if not words, then actions or deeds. Touching a fingertip to her mouth, she thought of all the times he'd kissed her. She had a feeling she would have her sign before the month was through.

The step he took in her direction was deliberate, the tone of his voice so low it was more like a sultry sweep across her toes. "About 'the talk,' perhaps you would like to offer a few suggestions." She lifted her hands in a gesture of innocence. He reached for one of them, giving a little tug. "Go ahead, Hannah. I'm all ears."

She was in his arms so suddenly she gasped, her body pressed intimately to his. No matter what he said, he wasn't all ears. He was all man.

Of its own volition, her face tipped up for his kiss. His mouth covered hers, his hands molding her closer, kneading, drawing a response from her body, her mind, and her heart.

"I thought you would want to have dinner," she whispered.

"Later," he rasped.

Yes, she thought, they could go to dinner later. Perhaps she would have the sign she was waiting for then, as well.

Twelve

"Look," Hannah said, pointing to the uniformed man hunkered down near The Pink Flamingo's back door. "Something's wrong. Someone must have broken in to the restaurant."

Parker snagged Hannah's hand before she could rush from the car. "If there had been a break-in, the police would be here." He pointed to the locksmith logo on the side of a nearby van. "It looks as if Adrienne's having the locks changed."

Hannah glanced from Parker's face to the hand encircling her wrist. "That's what I like about you," she said. "You see things with abrupt clarity."

"And I thought you were just after my body."

A week ago, she might have said it was the other way around; *he'd* been after *her* body. Now she wasn't sure what to think. She and Parker *had* spent the better part of the past hour and a half in bed, and while it was true that she still didn't have any concrete evidence that he was falling in love with her, she had absolutely no complaints with him as a lover. He was ardent, passionate, considerate, and extremely imaginative. She fell more deeply in love with him every time they made love. It was getting increasingly difficult to keep her feelings to herself.

She opened her door and got out. Parker met her at the back of his car. Together they strode through the gathering twilight, past the man replacing the lock, and into The Pink Flamingo.

Hannah was surprised to see J.D. hovering just inside the door. The two Malones eyed one another warily. Deciding to give the men a moment to themselves, she said, "If you'll excuse me, I'd like to say hello to Adrienne."

"Go ahead," Parker said. "I'll get us a table."

When Hannah was out of sight, he turned to J.D and asked, "Is everything all right?"

"Hell, no, everything isn't all right. That confounded woman won't listen to reason."

"Adrienne's giving you a hard time?"

J.D. glanced over his shoulder toward the kitchen. "She's trouble. Turns out she's exactly the kind of trouble I want to get into."

Parker took a frank look at his father. Was it his imagination, or was there an uncustomary excitement on J.D.'s face? "Would you care to join Hannah and me for dinner?" At the slight shake of his father's head, he said, "A drink, then?"

J.D. shrugged, then led the way to a table in a relatively quiet corner of the dining room. He picked up the plastic flamingo in the center of the table, only to put it back down immediately. "Interesting place, isn't it? Interesting woman."

Parker continued to eye his father. "I take it you're seeing Adrienne."

"I wouldn't exactly call it that."

"What would you call it?"

J.D. strummed his fingers on the table. "We went to a movie. And Adrienne's been teaching me to cook." While Parker was trying to picture that, J.D. said, "Lissett mentioned you have a houseguest."

Parker studied J.D. The glint in his eyes was unusual,

but the change in topic was an old tactic. "Reed's your grandson, J.D. Not a houseguest."

"Reed. Why in the hell do you suppose she named him that?"

Parker shrugged. "Why did you name me Parker?"

J.D. shook his head when the waiter appeared, signaling that he didn't want a drink, after all. "I was named after my father, James Donovan Malone. Since he went by James, I was assigned initials. I didn't want to do that to you."

Parker never knew that. He wondered how much else he didn't know when it came to J.D.'s feelings and motivations and what really made the man tick.

"How is he?" J.D. asked.

"He's almost fifteen, and he's half Malone. How do you think he is?"

J.D.'s grimace turned into a sympathetic smile. "Sounds like you have your work cut out for you. If you want to keep him out of trouble, you're going to have to keep him busy." Without warning, he stood. "I'd better make sure the locksmith is doing the job right."

As far as Parker knew, his father had never changed a lock in his life. Since J.D. hadn't raised any fools, Parker decided to keep the observation to himself. He settled himself more comfortably in his chair and simply watched as his father disappeared through a side door.

"Oh, Adrienne," Hannah exclaimed. "In love, really? I'm so happy for you."

Adrienne rinsed a dish. Her hands were dripping with soapsuds, so she had to settle for scratching her cheek with one shoulder. Keeping her voice low so as not to be heard by Gerard, who appeared to be immersed in the white sauce he was stirring at the stove on the other side of the kitchen, she said, "It's way too soon. I've only known him a week. I'm petrified. Surely, y'all know how I feel."

Hannah's smile lost some of its vitality. Yes, she knew how it felt to be in love, and to be scared to death about it.

Before she could say anything, J.D. appeared in the doorway. Hannah mumbled a quick goodbye then made her way into the dining room. The lights were dim, half the tables empty this time of night. The low drone of voices was barely loud enough to be heard over the soft music wafting on the air along with the mingled scents of a dozen different foods. For a moment Hannah felt lost. And then her gaze settled on Parker. Her steps slowed, and her course changed like a moth drawn to light.

She felt his gaze travel over her from her head to her toes. When it settled on her face once again, he smiled. She couldn't believe she'd once thought that his face wasn't prone to smiles. A woman just had to know where to look, and when. His smile was stark and white and full of shared secrets. She wondered if he was remembering the same things she was remembering. It was a heady sensation. And it made her want him all over again.

He wanted her, too. She could tell by the way he watched her stroll closer. He waited until she was almost upon him to rise to his feet. She was accustomed to the way he held her chair. He had impeccable manners, after all. But nothing could have prepared her for the soft kiss he brushed along her cheek.

Emotions wrapped around her like strong arms and a secret smile. She took her seat as if in slow motion. That kiss hadn't been sexual in nature. It had been an honest response to seeing her, to being with her. She'd been waiting for a sign that he was coming to care for her. How could she have known that the barest brush of his lips against her cheek could be so poignant? Joy shimmered and spread, filling her chest to nearly bursting.

Her heart swelled with so much feeling she couldn't think of a thing to say. She glanced at Parker and found him looking at her. They stared at each other, their expressions mirror images.

"Did you know J.D. is seeing—"

"Adrienne is seeing your—"

They'd spoken in unison, and they smiled the same way. Their tension drained away. They talked about their respective days, they ordered their meals from the boy who had inadvertently brought them together a month earlier. They laughed, and they dined, and they discussed major issues and trivial gossip. Parker didn't tell her he loved her, but Hannah was sure it was only a matter of time before he did. She'd always been patient, believing that anticipation was half the fun. She would be patient awhile longer. In the meantime, she would anticipate, and dream.

Lily waved at her daughter through the rear window of the limousine Ryan had insisted upon furnishing to carry her to the Austin Arms Hotel. Returning her mother's wave, Hannah wondered if all daughters were this proud of their mothers.

Lily Redgrove Cassidy had been one of six children. Her father had been an alcoholic, and her mother had worked her fingers to the bone as a housekeeper just to keep food on the table and a roof over her children's heads. Years later, Lily had worked diligently at her husband's side in their grocery store. After his death more than ten years ago, she put herself through college and had obtained a degree in management, which she put to use with a finesse that had gained her recognition in the hotel industry.

Tonight, she was attending a charity banquet at one of the most prestigious hotels in Austin.

Hannah had a feeling her mother was going to bedazzle everyone present tonight. Lily had always been beautiful, but Hannah had noticed a new glow about her mother these past few days. When she'd mentioned it, Lily had confessed that Parker had good news concerning the divorce. Sophia's attorneys were getting close to reaching an agreeable compromise. Soon, Lily and Ryan would be able to formally announce their engagement.

Hannah strolled to the back of her boutique, lost in thought. She should have been concentrating on the plans for her mother's wedding. Wedding plans *were* filling her mind. Only they weren't for her mother's; they were for her own.

She pictured herself on Cole's arm as he walked her down the aisle. Her dress would be white. Neither frilly nor Victorian, it would have simple lines, a close-fitting bodice and waist. And because Parker insisted he loved her shoulders, the dress would bare her shoulders. Her closest family and friends would be present. And there would be flowers everywhere. And candles. And white lights strewn with netting, and fluted stemware, and gleaming silver.

Hannah paused. A wedding such as that would be very expensive. She didn't need fluted stemware or polished silver. She didn't even need a long white gown.

She only needed Parker's love.

It had been two weeks since they'd had dinner at The Pink Flamingo, two incredibly fun and passion-filled weeks. Although Parker had been putting in long hours on Ryan's divorce case, he'd stolen time to be with her. It seemed they couldn't get enough of each other. Every time she saw him, her head spun. She wavered between feeling complete euphoria and spine-tingling trepidation. She knew where the euphoria was coming from. The trepidation was more difficult to pin down.

Her relationship with Parker was fantastic. Sadly, she still hadn't had any success in getting in touch with Maria. She'd waited long enough. First thing tomorrow morning, she would drive to Maria's trailer in Leather Bucket. Hannah dreaded the confrontation, but she didn't think that was at the root of her unease. Perhaps the nerves fluttering in her stomach were there because she was worried about her mother, although she couldn't for the life of her say why. Or maybe it was somebody else. But who?

Hannah told herself everything was going to work out. Reed had taken a job washing dishes at The Pink Flamingo, and was staying out of trouble. Lily had never looked more radiant. Maybe, after Hannah set foot inside Maria's house, she would better understand her sister.

That left Parker.

She smoothed her hand along the length of the veil Starr Weston was picking up later. It reminded Hannah of the silver scarf Parker had draped over a lamp in his bedroom a few nights ago. Idyllic and romantic, it had been like making love in the moonlight. She sighed in memory. Surely, no man could make love to a woman the way Parker did unless his heart was involved. Weren't actions supposed to speak louder than words?

She went back to her desk and sat. Everything was going to work out. It was. Nothing was going to go wrong. Just to be on the safe side, she repeated it ten times without stopping.

Lily clenched her hands in her lap to keep them from trembling. The Austin Arms Hotel loomed up ahead. Although it was more prestigious than the Willow Creek Hotel where she worked back in San Antonio, she'd been here before. She was nervous, and she couldn't put her finger on the reason. She yearned to be at the ranch with Ryan. If this had been anything other than a charity function, she wouldn't have come tonight.

As the driver, Roy Dickson, who worked for Ryan, pulled up in front of the ornate front doors, Lily wished Ryan could have attended the banquet with her. He'd wanted to, but Parker had advised him against it because Sophia lived at the hotel.

Was that the cause of Lily's strangled sense of unease? Was she afraid of running into Sophia?

No. She doubted their paths would cross. And if they did, Lily would simply hold her head high. She wasn't ashamed of her feelings for Ryan. If anyone should be ashamed, it was Sophia.

Why, then, were nerves clamoring up and down her spine? Was it something to do with one of her children? Was something terribly wrong with Maria? Or was it something else?

"Here you go, Ms. Cassidy," Roy said, opening her door.

Lily pasted a smile on her face. She thanked Roy, got out of the limo, and went inside the prestigious hotel, nerves clamoring all the while. She held her head high, and held her nerves at bay as best she could. But she could hardly wait for the evening to be over, so she could go home to the man she wanted, more than anything else in the world, to spend the rest of her life with.

Clint Lockhart ducked around a corner the instant he saw Lily walk through the wide double door. What the hell was she doing here?

His nerves were shot. Seeing her here wasn't helping.

He peered around the corner. A primitive warning sounded in his brain. If the Cassidy woman saw him here, she would undoubtedly finger him as the link in the information that had been leaked to Sophia this past year.

Dammit to hell. He had enough to worry about tonight. He'd felt pretty good when Sophia had summoned him to her room tonight. She'd said Ryan had agreed to her terms. He'd figured he'd pick up a check for his share of the money, and end the evening with one last, good hard roll under the covers.

He'd done a hell of a lot for that money. And he'd driven a long way for sex. His gloved hand went to his pocket, where the bracelet Ryan had bought for Lily rested. He'd planned to show it to Sophia. He'd figured she'd get angry, and after she got angry, she always got turned on.

But then he'd overheard Ryan talking to his attorney on the cell phone. Ryan had named an amount that was more than twice the figure Sophia had told Clint she was receiving.

He smelled a double cross. Sophia had some explaining to do. And Lily had better not get in the way.

Clint cast another look around the corner. Lily had been joined by several other people. When they headed for a banquet room boasting a sign for some stupid charity or other, he took his first easy breath in several minutes. She wasn't here to make trouble for him. It was just a coincidence. Maybe things would work out yet.

He got into an empty elevator and rode it up to the top floor. He was agitated. Fidgety. He needed a cigarette. Or better yet, some chew. There was only one thing that calmed his nerves as good as either of those. Patting his chest pocket where a flask of whiskey rested, he thought, make that two things. He'd taken a good, healthy swig before he'd arrived at the hotel. As soon as he and Sophia took care of business, he planned to partake in the second activity with gusto.

He stopped at the door to Sophia's suite. He scowled. He swore he could smell her expensive perfume through the thick door. Raising his gloved fist, he knocked once.

He could tell she was in a bitchy mood the instant she opened the door. "What took you so long?" she practically raged.

God, he was so sick of her whining and complaining and bitching. The things a man had to put up with for a good lay.

He hung the Do Not Disturb sign on the outside of the door, then briskly turned the lock. Deciding to see if she would admit to the larger settlement, he removed his cowboy hat, hiked up his belt slightly, and stared directly into her big blue eyes. "It looks like another Fortune of Texas is coming out ahead while the rest of us eat dirt."

She spun around, her filmy negligee a pink cloud behind her. "I just can't take the waiting any longer, Clint. I have needs. Look at my hands." She held one up for him to see. "My nails are a mess. And my wardrobe is sorely lacking. You and I both know I deserve so much more for the things I've had to endure, but what's a girl to do? Surely, I'll starve on the pittance I'm being forced to accept."

Blatant lies.

Clint wasn't surprised. He was sickened. It roiled in his gut, burning like bile. He squeezed his hands into fists at his sides, staring at the woman who both repulsed him and stirred his sexual juices.

She spent more on manicures than he did on food for a month. Once, after coming out of a rage, she'd kissed him on the mouth at the same time she'd raked her fingernails down his back. He had the scars to prove it. That was all right. Clint didn't mind pain, just so long as he got his release.

He strode closer, circling, watching, waiting. "Do you take me for a fool, Sophia?"

She spun around so fast her breasts practically spilled over the top of her nightgown, yet not a lock of her strawberry-blond hair moved out of place. Her eyes flashed dramatically. "Whatever do you mean, Clint?"

Her hand fluttered to her chest. Clint's shot out, encircling it, twisting it slightly. "I heard an interesting conversation between Ryan and his attorney this afternoon."

She paled, and for a moment he felt big and victorious. But then two patches of red stained her cheeks and her lush, pink lips thinned with derision.

"That was unfortunate. So you know. So what?"

He took an ominous step closer. "So you'd better give me half, that's what."

She spun away from him. He let her go. For now.

"I don't need you anymore. And I've decided not to give you anything. Not a bloody cent. Do you hear me?"

Fury almost choked him. This was worse than he'd thought, worse, almost, than the day his father had sold the ranch to Kingston Fortune when Clint had been but a young boy.

Hatred roiled up inside him. "Oh, yes, you will. You'll give me everything I have coming."

She laughed. "I don't owe you anything. You, with your pointy-toed cowboy boots and those idiotic leather gloves you wear even in the summer. You think you're smart. Worse, you think you're sexy. Why, you're just a big, dumb cowboy who couldn't find the john without a map. You're not even any good in bed."

Resentment roiled up inside him, pounding in his ears like the ocean surf in a raging storm. She must have seen the look in his eyes, because for the first time he saw fear in her expression.

"Get out of here. Now." She reached for the phone. "Or I'll call security."

His hand shot out, striking her, the impact knocking her backward onto the bed. It stunned Clint, but Sophia screamed. Clint's eyes grew large, her scream piercing his eardrums. He stared at the gaping black hole that was her mouth.

His head pounded, his heartbeat thundered. He had to stop her. He had to stop the noise. It hurt his ears. It hurt his head. It hurt his entire body.

He grabbed a large pillow, pressed it over her face.

She went quiet for a moment. And he started to release the pressure.

She screamed again, and started to struggle. He pressed harder, his breathing ragged, pain piercing his skull.

Sometime later, he realized the screaming had stopped. Sophia lay perfectly still, one leg on the bed, one flung over the side.

He raised the pillow. And what he saw made him recoil.

His heart thundered anew, and he began to pace. Back and forth and back and forth. Thinking.

Thinking.

He'd spent most of his life thinking. Planning.

He reached into his pocket for a packet of chewing tobacco. His fingers came into contact with the ruby and diamond tennis bracelet.

He stared at the lights reflecting off the gems. So beautiful, he thought. A lethal calmness settled over him.

No one had seen him tonight—at least, no one who would recognize him.

His gaze lowered to his gloved hands. Wearing gloves was something he'd picked up from his father. What do ya know? He'd gotten something worthwhile from his old man, after all.

Calm now, his thoughts came, one at a time, in perfect order. He knew what he had to do.

He replaced the phone in its base, straightened the room slightly, being careful to avert his eyes from the bed. His hand was empty when he let himself out of Sophia's room. If anyone had been looking, they would have seen his cold-eyed smile.

Parker looked over the documents spread neatly on his large desk. He and Dale had gone over everything with a fine-tooth comb. Sophia's attorneys had run out of loopholes, had used up every strategy they could think of to prolong the inevitable. This was it. Sophia had signed on the dotted line. As far as Parker was concerned, she was getting a hell of a lot more than she deserved. But come hell or high water, Ryan's divorce was going to be finalized very soon.

Parker ran a hand through his hair and took a deep breath. A calming breath. For the life of him, he didn't know why he needed it. Everything was working out. The case. Reed. It had been more than two weeks since they'd arm wrestled, two blessedly peaceful weeks. Parker had bit the bullet, so to speak, and had broached the subject of sex. Reed had rolled his eyes. There was no way to tell if Parker had gotten through to the kid. He ran his hand through his hair again. How did parents do this on a day in, day out basis?

His days had settled into a routine of sorts. The office was neat and tidy. His house was noisy and messy. His nights were passion-filled and pleasurable.

So why was he feeling this sense of unease? Rosita was the one who had all the damn premonitions.

A rap on the door preceded J.D.'s entry into Parker's office by about three seconds. "I'm going to lunch."

Parker glanced at his watch. "It's not even ten o'clock." Oh. Parker got it. "How is Adrienne?"

J.D. shook his head. "She's horrible. Has my family jewels in a sling."

It required careful concentration to keep Parker's mind clear of that particular image. "Then Adrienne's still giving you a hard time?"

"I'm in love for what just might be the first time in my life and the woman I'm in love with won't sleep with me."

"You're in love with Adrienne?"

J.D. didn't bother to nod. "Damn scary, isn't it, son?"

Parker went perfectly still.

J.D. eyed his son. "Don't look so surprised. I've seen you with Hannah. You know how it feels."

The unease that had been bothering the pit of Parker's stomach pitched and spread. He opened his mouth to dispute his father's observation. The phone jangled near his hand, causing him to jump.

"What is it Adalaide?" His eyebrows drew down in concentration. "Yes, of course. Put him on."

Parker glanced at his father, who had moved closer and was quietly watching him.

"Yes, Harry," Parker said to his contact at the police station. "I'm here." He listened in silence, asking only those questions necessary to piece the news together. "Murdered? How?...Yes...Good God...Yes...I'll be there as soon as possible."

He hung up the phone. "Sophia Fortune was found murdered in her hotel room this morning."

"Murdered. Do they know who did it?"

"They have Lily in custody."

Thirteen

Hannah pulled her car to the side of the pothole-riddled street in front of Maria's rundown trailer. The place looked worse than it had the last time Hannah had been here months ago. Maria had always liked nice things. The sister Hannah used to know wouldn't have been happy living in a rundown trailer on the outskirts of Leather Bucket. It drove home the fact of how little Hannah knew Maria anymore.

Weeds grew among rocks and debris. The steps leading to the front door were wobbly. Those at the back door were literally rotting away. The morning sunshine, in all its brilliance, made the trailer itself look even more dismal, unkempt.

The only car nearby was one on blocks near the back of the property. Hannah picked her way over the uneven ground, being careful not to step on broken glass and discarded beer and soda cans. She wasn't really surprised when her knock on the door went unanswered. After trying again, she circled to the back of the structure, hoping for a glimpse of Maria, or some hint that she was inside.

Torn shades covered most of the windows. Hannah spied a screen in a window in the back of the trailer. It was too high to reach.

Rummaging around for something she could use to stand on, she found an old crate in the weeds. After looking to see if anyone had noticed her presence, she hauled the crate to the trailer's high window.

Birds tweeted and a warm wind fluttered through her slacks. She was nervous. It felt wrong to be looking in Maria's windows without her permission. Hannah didn't know what else to do. What if something was seriously wrong with her sister? Heart in her throat, she positioned the crate beneath the screened window. Placing one foot on the top surface, she tested it for strength, then reached for the rotting windowsill, and rose up, balancing on the crate.

Her phone jangled inside her large purse, scaring the daylights out of her. She jumped backward. Landing on her feet, she peered nervously around.

Breathing between parted lips, she reached inside her purse, grabbing the phone before it had completed its second ring. "Hello?"

At the sound of Parker's voice, she started to smile.

The phone crackled. And the smile drained off her face. Her eyes grew round as she listened. "Murdered. Parker, no."

It got worse.

"She couldn't have done it." Her knees gave out, and she sank onto the wooden crate. "My mother isn't capable of murder."

She listened intently, the dread she'd been feeling taking the form of disbelief, and finally, gut-wrenching fear. "Mom has a gentle soul. She wouldn't hurt anyone."

She wanted to scream it, shout it, yell it. She ended up whispering it a second time.

"Yes, I'm still here... She wants Cole? That's good." A tear rolled down her face. Before it could dry in the wind, another followed its trail.

She shuddered, and swallowed a sob. "I'll be right there."

It was a nightmare, worse than all of Rosita's premonitions combined. Hannah's beautiful, kind-hearted mother had been arrested and accused of murdering Sophia Fortune.

Hannah was inside the visitor section of the local jail. Before Lily had been led away, Hannah had only been allowed to see her through glass. She'd never seen her mother this way. Lily had sat in stoic silence, her brown eyes glazed with fear and disbelief. She'd been stripped of her clothing, of her dignity, of her freedom. Hannah had wanted to sob when she saw her, but for Lily's sake she'd forced herself to remain strong.

Parker had said that the police who questioned Lily had been brutal, badgering her with accusations, suggesting possible scenarios, every one uglier than the last. Lily's tennis bracelet had been found on the floor between the bed and the wall, making her their prime suspect. When they'd produced the bracelet and asked if it belonged to her, a tear had trailed down Lily's face. Yes, it was hers, she'd said. But she'd lost it two weeks ago.

No. She hadn't reported it stolen.

It didn't look good for Lily. It didn't look good, at all.

Cole was on his way from Denver. Maria had come, too. But she'd been so distraught, she'd had to be medicated. She was sleeping at Hannah's apartment right now.

Hannah had thought things were bad a few weeks ago when she'd discovered Maria coming on to Parker. This was so much worse. In fact, she didn't see how things could get any worse than this.

News of the murder would be on the front page of the morning papers. It was already on the radio and on television. Sophia Fortune had been found murdered in her hotel room in Austin early this morning. Her husband's mistress, Lily Redgrove Cassidy, had been arrested and accused of the crime. The police were doing everything by the book. Many people were calling it an open and shut case.

Ryan, bless his heart, refused to leave the jail. He growled at the press, adamantly proclaiming Lily's innocence. "Someone murdered Sophia, but it wasn't Lily Cassidy. We'll find the person responsible, mark my words."

Lily insisted the only attorney she trusted to defend her was Cole. Ryan had calls in to important officials all the way to the supreme court. He was already putting together the best defense team money could buy to be at Cole's disposal the minute he arrived from Denver.

It had been hours since Hannah had received Parker's call. During that time, she'd pulled herself together. Now she was sitting with Ryan in the waiting area in the local jail, waiting for bail to be set. As soon as it was, Ryan would post it, and take Lily home. Parker, J.D., and some of Ryan's family members were due to return from a nearby coffeeshop any moment. Far beyond the ability to make small talk, Hannah clutched Ryan's hand in a show of support and gratitude, taking comfort in his unfailing love for her mother.

Suddenly the door opened. Cameras flashed as reporters surrounded Parker, J.D., and Ryan's son and daughter and two of his nephews who had come to do whatever they could to help. The crowd parted, allowing Hannah a clear view of Parker. She and Ryan both rose to their feet.

Yearning washed over her at the sight of Parker. She so longed to go to him, to feel his arms go around her, to rest her head for just a moment on his shoulder, to absorb his warmth and strength and conviction.

She couldn't have reached him if she'd tried. The media had surrounded him, making a nuisance of themselves.

"I understand Lily Cassidy's father was an alcoholic."

"Does she have a drinking problem, too?"

"Would you say Lily is a strong woman?"

"Strong enough to smother Sophia Fortune?"

Parker said, "Lily Cassidy does not have a drinking problem. She did not murder Sophia Fortune."

A reporter shoved a microphone in Parker's face. "You're seeing Cassidy's daughter, are you not?"

A buzz went through the room.

J.D. said, "Try to stick to the matter at hand, people."

The media did no such thing. "The divorce attorney and the wedding planner."

"They say opposites attract."

"Tell us, Mr. Malone. Is Cassidy's daughter planning more than one wedding?"

The expression that passed briefly through Parker's eyes sent dread to the pit of Hannah's stomach. Her heart was in her throat; her feet seemed to have frozen to the floor.

Parker had prepared himself for a vast array of questions, but he wasn't prepared to answer this one. His heart pounded an erratic rhythm. He'd reacted in a similar fashion when his father had mentioned the word love yesterday. He'd put the notion out of his mind, but these reporters weren't going to be easily dismissed. Get married? Him?

He cleared his throat, pretending not to be affected by the question. "Hannah Cassidy knows where I stand on the subject of marriage. As I said before, Lily Cassidy did not murder Sophia Fortune. I, along with the firm of Malone, Malone & Associates intend to do everything in my power to assist Cole Cassidy in clearing Lily Cassidy's name."

The reporters fired off more questions.

The room tilted. Hannah shivered. She'd heard Parker's entire oration. She knew she should rejoice in his delivery, in his vehement stand on her mother's behalf, but she couldn't get past his view of marriage. He'd said it before, but never with more conviction. The press, in all their usual exuberance for a story, went on to another line of questions.

Hannah allowed Ryan to lead her to a chair. She huddled there, utterly cold on such a hot August day.

Parker didn't love her. And he didn't plan to marry her. Ever. For some reason she was reminded of the day they'd buried her big, kind-hearted father. She'd stood by his grave for a long time when the service was over, her heart breaking, tears streaming down her face, wondering how she would ever go on without him.

She'd gathered strength from her family then. They'd pulled together, helping each other through that sad, bleak time. Hannah had no one to turn to now. Her mother was in jail. Her father was in the ground. Maria wasn't capable of helping anybody. And when Cole arrived, he was going to have his hands full defending Lily.

Despite all his warnings, she'd thought she had Parker. She'd been such a fool.

A tear trailed down her cheek. She'd been so sure he loved her, so sure he was worth the risk to her heart.

And she'd been so wrong.

Hannah stood at the back door of The Pink Flamingo. She didn't remember driving here. In a daze, she feared she didn't have the strength to make it all the way inside. Her chest felt like a cold tomb, empty of everything except grief. She wrapped her arms around herself and slumped against the building, slowly sinking to the ground.

Adrienne found her there, rocking back and forth, tears coursing down her cheeks. "Aw, sugar, come inside. You're shivering."

"Parker says I'm the only woman he knows who's cold when it's eighty degrees outside." Her automatic mention of Parker brought fresh tears to her eyes.

"I'd like to shoot a certain divorce attorney." Adrienne helped her up, and helped her inside. She barked out orders to the staff. In almost no time, Hannah was munching on saltines and cheese and sipping sweetened tea, which Adrienne insisted only true Southerners knew how to make.

"I take it you saw him on the news."

"I saw him," Adrienne said, an arm around Hannah's shoulders. "One of my regular customers is a bona fide Gypsy. I think I'm going to ask her to put a hex on Parker Malone."

Hannah sniffled. After taking a loud slurp of her tea, she said, "What kind of hex?"

"Oh, I don't know. Nothing fancy or complicated. Maybe something along the lines of making his member fall off."

"Don't do that."

"Give me one good reason why I shouldn't."

Hannah took a shuddering breath. "Would you use anesthetic?"

Adrienne laughed. "I've got you thinking about it, don't I? There, see? I knew you were going to be all right. That's it. Take another sip of tea. I wouldn't really have her put that particular curse on him, you know. After all, he might come to his senses. If we de-manned him, you'd really be in a fine mess."

Hannah couldn't quite pull off an honest smile. She sipped her tea in silence, deep in thought.

No matter what Adrienne said, Hannah refused to live

with delusions anymore. Parker didn't believe in marriage, in forever. He didn't love her. He never had. He'd been honest. She hadn't listened. If that wasn't bad enough, something was very wrong with Maria. And their dear mother was in jail.

Hannah was already in a fine mess.

Hannah didn't see Parker again until early that evening. He was coming out of the jail as she was going in. She had really hoped to put off a face-to-face meeting until later. Much later. It just went to show how completely off-kilter her timing was these days.

"Hannah."

She stopped several feet away, waiting for him to descend the last few steps. She thought he looked tired, and wanted to kick herself for noticing. "Are there any new developments in the case?" she asked.

He ran a hand through his hair, and eyed her in a manner that told her he'd noticed her uncharacteristic cool reserve. "Ryan's still waiting for bail to be set. As soon as it is, he'll have the funds transferred and take her home to the ranch. Hannah, about that question one of the reporters asked me."

Hope surged inside her. "Yes?"

He stared at her, as if uncertain how to proceed. Her hope drained away. "There's no need to explain," she said. "I understand. It wasn't anything I didn't already know."

He looked genuinely relieved. "Do you want to grab a bite to eat somewhere?"

"You mean, with you?"

His eyes narrowed. She half expected him to say something snide like "No, with Jack the Ripper." But he simply asked, "Do you see anyone else around, Hannah?"

She shook her head. "I'm picking Cole up from the airport in a little while. Then he, Maria and I are going to the Double Crown for a late dinner. It would probably be best if you and I didn't see each other anymore. We know where we stand. No sense confusing the public."

She gave him what she hoped passed for a smile. Leaving him a wide berth, she strode up the steps that led to the jail. Her nerves were standing on end. Feeling his eyes on her, she held her head high and opened the heavy, bullet-proof door.

Parker turned as Hannah walked stiffly past him. She didn't look back, disappearing on the other side of the door.

It was strange, but he swore he could still smell her perfume. He'd never seen her quite this way. She was beyond exhaustion. He knew he was responsible for putting at least some of the hurt in her eyes. She'd heard the reporter's question regarding marriage, and she'd heard his reply. He hadn't wanted to hurt her, but he couldn't lie. Lily needed levelheaded, rational attorneys whose minds were razor-sharp. Her very life depended upon it.

He'd been honest with Hannah from the beginning. He'd always known that they were complete opposites. He never should have taken her to bed. He could see that now. She was the type of woman who turned poetic, convincing herself that making love and being in love were the same things.

The words he'd spoken to that reporter had been cutting. Hell, he was known for his cutting remarks. He'd done her a favor. A clean break was better than a long, drawn-out one.

It was for the best. Running a hand through his hair, he straightened his tie and strode to the parking lot where he'd left his car.

* * *

"I understand you're not seeing Hannah any longer."

Parker snapped his briefcase closed and met Ryan's gaze across the large, pretentious desk in Ryan's study. "It's for the best."

Ryan steepled his fingers at his chin. "I see. Have you figured out why it feels like hell?"

Parker opened his mouth to speak, only to close it again. It wasn't like him to be at a loss for words. It had been happening a lot lately, and he didn't like it. After a long pause, during which he combed his mind for a proper reply, he said, "I'm handling it." He'd responded sharply. More sharply than he'd intended. That had been happening a lot lately, too.

Dammit to hell, he didn't like that, either. But what was he supposed to do? His life had changed this summer. He couldn't put his finger on exactly what was different. Reed went home a few days ago, just in time for his fifteenth birthday. Parker's house was quiet and orderly once again. Lissett had announced that she was getting married, but had assured him she would be staying on as his housekeeper. She could cook and clean and bake, but she was no better at growing things than he was. Consequently, his fica plant had started to droop. It probably needed water. He didn't know what he needed.

He hadn't seen Hannah, except in passing, in more than a week. Ten days, to be exact. He missed her. He told himself it was nothing he wouldn't get over.

The phone jangled. Ryan moved without haste, answering it with unhurried purpose. "This is Ryan Fortune."

Parker started to get up. Ryan gestured with a firm shake of his head.

The other man listened intently, his entire countenance

changing drastically. "A rebel uprising in Santo Bonisto, you say? I know my daughter is working in that country."

He listened, asked several pointed questions, ending the conversation with, "Keep me apprised of every facet of this operation, do you understand?"

He slammed the receiver down and sat for a moment, his forehead resting in his hand. "Victoria's in danger," he finally said.

Parker had known that one of Ryan's twin daughters was working as a nurse for a humanitarian organization on a tiny island on the other side of the world. Politics in those countries was always precarious. A rebel uprising meant that Victoria was in imminent danger.

"I have to get her out of there."

Parker said, "Do you have any idea how to do that?"

Ryan picked up the phone. "I know someone who can." He dialed a number. "Ginny," he said into the mouthpiece. "Patch me through to Sam Waterman."

Within minutes, he'd spoken to someone Parker assumed was Sam Waterman, and the first step in the process was under way. Sam was going to send in Quinn McCoy, a man evidently noted for his skill in covert actions.

Ryan was silent when he hung up the phone. He glanced across the desk at Parker, as if he'd forgotten he wasn't alone in the room. Breathing deeply, he said, "Sometimes it seems like a full-time job keeping the people I love safe."

Parker studied the other man, noting the worry lines between his eyes and the grooves slashing each cheek. "Ever ask yourself if it's worth it?"

Ryan's eyebrows rose dramatically and he steepled his fingers beneath his chin once again. "Are you asking me if I would put myself through the grief and torment and worry of marriage and a family if I had it to do over again?''

Parker gave him a brief nod.

Ryan looked Parker in the eye. "With the exception of marrying Sophia, I'd do it all again in a heartbeat. Without the love of a good woman and a family, what is there?''

The question struck a nerve somewhere in the very center of Parker. There were plenty of worthwhile things to live for besides a woman and a family. He only wished he could think of one or two of them.

Rising to leave, Parker shook Ryan's hand.

The other man's grip was strong, his gaze steady as he said, "She's out riding with Lily.''

Parker didn't have to ask who.

"They've been gone the better part of two hours," Ryan said. "I suspect they'll be back shortly. Perhaps you'd like to take a look at the new Arabian mare Clint had delivered a few days ago.''

"An Arabian mare?'' Parker asked.

Ryan nodded. "Clint Lockhart knows his horseflesh. He could have been great at anything he tried. One piece of the puzzle was missing. I've never understood which piece it was. But that's neither here nor there. It so happens that the new mare is in the stall next to Lily's favorite horse.''

Parker reached for his briefcase. "You don't say. Maybe I will take a look at that horse.''

"You do that, son.''

Parker left Ryan's office, got in his car, and drove out to the stables to take a look at a mare, when he and Ryan both knew that he didn't know the difference between a good horse and a hole in the ground.

Fourteen

The barn smelled of horses and hay and dust. Parker felt as out of place as a pimp in a confessional. He almost turned on his heel and headed back the way he'd come. Instead he spied a stable hand, and asked for directions to the stall where Lily Cassidy's favorite horse was normally kept. The whiskered cowboy pointed him in the right direction, then went about his business with little more than a nod.

There was a stack of hay outside a set of wide double doors. Somebody had unloaded twenty-five or thirty bales of something—he thought he remembered reading somewhere that the golden-colored product was straw—in the shade near the barn. He didn't see any particularly unique-looking horses. But then, he was honest enough with himself to admit that he hadn't come to look at animals, no matter how magnificent they were supposed to be.

He'd come for a glimpse of a woman he'd claimed he didn't need.

The August afternoon was quiet but for the occasional lowing of a cow, the whinny of horses. In the distance, a herd of cattle lumbered toward greener pastures.

A trail led from a gate on the far side of the corral. Parker stared at it, willing a certain dark-haired woman and her mother to appear.

Parker was much better at arguing cases in court than conjuring up a woman on a horse. Ryan had said Hannah and Lily had been gone for two hours. Surely they would be back soon.

He looked all around him for a comfortable place to wait. In the movies, cowboys perched on fences. A cowboy would have saddled up a horse and gone looking for Hannah. Parker was no cowboy. He was just a man, agitated and weary from too many nights with too little sleep.

He tried pacing. It didn't take him long to realize that pacing didn't have the same calming effect when it was done on grass instead of on carpet. He strode to the bales of straw stacked in the shade nearby. He lowered to one, and carefully leaned his back against another. It wasn't as uncomfortable as it looked. He stretched his legs out, crossed his arms at his chest, and tried to figure out what he would say to her.

"Parker, wake up."

He opened his eyes, only to find Hannah's face directly in front of him, the sun casting a golden glow all around her. At first he thought he was dreaming, but the hand on his arm was real.

"You fell asleep," she said.

"That's impossible. I can't sleep without you."

"You never slept with me."

"You know what I mean."

"Parker," she said, "you're not making any sense."

He blinked. He was sprawled out on a bed made of bales, several dry blades of straw poking through his coat and pants. Hannah was leaning over him, more beautiful than he'd ever seen her. "Nothing makes sense anymore," he said.

She made no reply.

"My fica is dying."

"What?"

"My fica plant." He sat up, wincing because his leg was asleep. "Reed moved back home. The house is quiet. And the fica is dying."

Hannah straightened slowly. She didn't know what to say. Parker was still groggy from sleep. He was probably lonely now that Reed was gone.

She knew how it felt to be lonely.

"You miss Reed. That's understandable. It'll probably take a little while to get used to living alone again."

"Reed's fine. He isn't the one I miss."

Hannah had thought she'd shed all the tears she was capable of shedding. She'd been wrong. Moisture blurred her vision. She'd never seen Parker this way, bits of straw stuck in his hair, the shadow of a five o'clock beard darkening his chin, his suit wrinkled.

"I miss you, Hannah."

Don't listen to him, she told her heart.

"I miss your smile, your scent. I miss the way you make me think. The way you shiver when it's seventy-five degrees out. The way it takes you an hour to walk around the block."

She closed her eyes. Her heart hadn't listened. He was getting to her, one word at a time.

Making one last valiant effort to remain strong, she put a little distance between them. "We can't go back to the way things were between us. I can't do that. I should have listened to you in the beginning."

"No, Hannah. You were right. I was the one who was wrong."

She stared out over the Texas hill country Ryan loved so much. Just yesterday she'd overheard two of his men talking about branding the new calves. With Parker so close, she couldn't even work up a decent amount of disgust for the archaic practice.

"I love you, Hannah."

She turned slowly at the sound of those three powerful words. Parker was standing, his body in the sun, his face in shadow. His voice had been like the wind after midnight, a deep sigh, a slow sweep across her senses. She tried to tell herself he wanted her, and wanting someone and loving them were two entirely different things. But he took a step in her direction, the action bringing him fully into the light. Her gaze delved his, and she didn't know what to think.

She'd never come across a man she understood less and who drew her more. "You love me?" she whispered.

He took another step closer. "I'm as surprised as you are."

He could turn her inside out with just a look, but when he unleashed his subtle brand of humor, her knees went weak and her mind turned to mush. She absolutely, positively, forbade herself to give in to the yearning washing over her. Still, a tiny ray of hope, like sunshine, warmed her more thoroughly than the sun.

"How romantic."

Parker had always known Hannah was strong, but until these past ten days when she'd stood quietly by her mother's side, offering her unconditional love and steadfastness, he'd never realized just how strong she was. He'd felt her resolve softening a moment ago. And he knew he could probably kiss her. And the rest would be history.

But Hannah Cassidy deserved more than a romp in the hay. He strode the remaining distance to her. She probably deserved more than he could give her, but he wasn't as unselfish as she was. "Did you know that you're the only woman who's ever struck me speechless? You did it the first day we met. Remember? I thought you were propositioning me. You have no idea how many times during the past few weeks I wished I'd have taken you up on what I thought you were offering.''

She studied him warily. Her eyes closed partway, a little line forming between them, a confused expression on her face.

A smile hovered close to his lips. ''See what you've done to me? I never used to babble.''

''Oh, Parker.''

''I love you. And I want to be with you.''

She started to shake her head. His hand shot out, cupping her cheek, holding her head still. ''You're beautiful. Your eyes, your hair, your mouth. Did I ever tell you that you have a poet's mouth? And your body, well…'' He let his voice trail away. After all, he knew better than anyone that sometimes it was the things a man didn't say that made the greatest impact.

Taking up a different tack, he lowered his voice almost to a whisper. ''It wouldn't matter if you weren't beautiful. That's the kicker. I'd want you, anyway. I guess that's what love is.''

She was looking at him, neither speaking nor moving. She didn't breathe. She didn't even blink.

''Hannah?''

Her expression changed to one of softness, of yearning. It was all the encouragement he needed. ''I want to live with you. Laugh with you. Have a family with you.''

Hannah felt her eyes go wide and her breath catch in her throat. ''Do you mean it?''

''Have I ever said anything I didn't mean?''

''You told that reporter you didn't believe in marriage.''

He conceded the point. ''Besides that. Come on, Hannah. You might as well say you'll marry me, because I'll beg, barter, and badger you until you do. We Malones tend to be a pushy lot.''

"You don't say."

"What do *you* say?"

For a moment everything went perfectly still, the cows, the horses, even the birds. It felt as if Hannah and Parker were alone in the world. They were the most quiet of all.

When she could find her voice, she whispered, "Say it again."

A look of absolute bewilderment crossed his face a moment before he sputtered, "Was there one particular part you wanted me to repeat, or did you want to hear it all again?"

She moved closer, one hand going to his face, the other to the collar of his wrinkled shirt. "For now, you can just tell me you love me. A hundred times. You can tell me everything else later."

His gaze settled on her mouth. "I love you, Hannah."

She smiled.

He lowered his chin, and she just had to touch that delightful little indentation in its center.

"I love you," he whispered again.

His lips skimmed her cheek. "I love you, I love you, I love you."

He kissed her temple, her forehead, her nose, whispering his love for her at every stop. He murmured the words along the length of her neck. She lost track of the number of times he'd said it after that. But she didn't lose track of the sentiment and feelings they evoked.

"Parker," she whispered. "You can stop now."

"Stop?" he uttered, pulling her with him around the back of the haystack. "We've just begun."

He hauled her to him and kissed her on the mouth. When the need for oxygen broke the kiss, he said, "Does this mean you'll marry me?"

She nodded.

And he smiled. "It looks as if the next wedding you plan is going to be your own."

"I have a little confession to make. *Our* wedding is all planned. And just so you know, I love you, too."

He reached for her hand. "Let's go tell your mother and Ryan."

Hannah studied his hand, then placed hers firmly in his. As his fingers curled around her palm and fingers, warmth shimmered over her. She knew the future was still uncertain. Although Maria had gone back to her trailer in Leather Bucket, Hannah believed her younger sister was hiding something from the rest of the world. She was coming to accept the fact that she and Maria might never be as close as Hannah wanted them to be. It saddened her. The thought of her mother going to trial for a crime she couldn't possibly have committed sent worry all the way through her.

There were still storms to weather.

Squeezing Parker's hand, Hannah knew she wouldn't be going through them alone.

Lily and Ryan, who had been watching through a window as Hannah and Parker drove up, met them in the courtyard. Lily was thrilled with her daughter's happiness. All four of them went inside, where Rosita insisted she'd known it all along. Everyone laughed. Looking at these people who meant the world to her, Hannah felt optimistic for the first time in weeks. There was strength in numbers.

Most importantly, she thought, meeting Parker's gaze, there was strength in love.

Epilogue

A faint sound stirred Hannah in her sleep. She sighed, for she was dreaming, and she didn't want to wake up.

The sound came again, more insistent. She opened her eyes. Laying in the drowsy warmth of her bed, she tried to figure out what had awakened her. A rattle, like pebbles on glass, brought her wide awake.

Slipping out of bed, she hurried to the window just as another pebble brushed the glass. She peered at the blonde looking up from the alley below. Opening the window, Hannah leaned out. "Adrienne, what are you doing?"

"I need you to get dressed and come down here."

It had been raining when Hannah went to bed. Now, a mist seemed to rise from the ground. "All right. Why?"

"We're eloping."

Just then Parker stepped out of the shadows. His hair was uncombed, his face unshaven. "Who?" Hannah asked. "You and Parker?"

A third party stepped from the shadows. Even in the middle of the night, J.D. looked debonair. He happened to be the only one of the bunch who was properly dressed, from his silk tie to his shined shoes. "Adrienne has decided to do me the honor of becoming my wife."

"You're really going to elope?" Hannah quipped. She'd spoken a little too loudly. One by one, every dog in the neighborhood started to bark.

"Come on Hannah," Adrienne said, her voice decidedly

warmer since J.D. had placed his arm around her waist.
"Would you be my maid of honor?"

Hannah's heart swelled with feeling. "I'll be right
down."

She pulled on the first skirt and silk tank she came to
in her closet. Sliding her feet into sandals, she grabbed a
jacket and hurried down the back stairs.

They all climbed into J.D.'s Mercedes. When they were
cruising down the rain-soaked street, Hannah said, "Where
are you going?"

Adrienne turned around. Was she wearing a fuschia-
colored peignoir complete with fake fur trim underneath
her raincoat? "I happened upon the most romantic little
justice of the peace when I went for supplies yesterday.
He's at a place called the Lone Star Chapel. It has a pink
flamingo in the yard. It's a sign, I just know it is."

J.D.'s voice rumbled from the driver's seat. "I've been
trying to talk Adrienne into marrying me for weeks. I offered her a fairy tale church wedding, and a reception complete with a six-course meal and champagne served in
fluted stemware and a seven-piece orchestra."

Adrienne wrinkled up her nose. "I want something special, something money can't buy."

Parker squeezed Hannah's hand. "Who would have
thought J.D. would find a woman who refused to marry
him for his money?" And then in a deeper voice meant
for her ears alone, he whispered, "I wish it was us."

Hannah closed her eyes and fit her shoulder even closer
to Parker's side. "I wish is was us, too." They both
sighed, because they knew they had to wait until after this
horrible mess concerning Sophia Fortune's murder was re-
solved. Hannah didn't want to think about that. The windshield wipers swished, and music played softly on the ra-

dio. The man she loved was at her side. For now, it was enough.

After making a series of sudden turns, per Adrienne's instructions, J.D. pulled to a stop in front of an adobe-style structure boasting a garish neon star over its door and a pink flamingo in its front yard.

The four of them stood in the drizzle, J.D. and Parker taking turns banging on the door. Finally, a light went on inside. Moments later a man wearing a nightshirt opened the door. "Mother," he said, "I believe we have a bride and groom. From the looks of things, the bride's father came along to give her away."

Adrienne sashayed closer. "He's not my father, your honor. This handsome devil is my groom."

A plump woman with pink curlers in her gray hair bustled into the room. Five minutes later, Adrienne, wearing a borrowed veil, stood before J.D., hands joined, repeating after the stoop-shouldered justice of the peace. The place was garish enough to rival any Las Vegas wedding chapel. And yet, as Parker's gaze held Hannah's, it felt warm and right and true.

She was beautiful, this woman he'd once mistaken for a lady of the night. She was warm and witty and smart. And she was his. God yes, she'd made that fact perfectly clear.

When the justice of the peace said, "You may kiss the bride," Parker kissed Hannah. And Hannah kissed him.

While the woman in the pink curlers, introduced only as "Mother," snapped a photo of the happy bride and groom, Parker reached for Hannah's hand. "When your mother's name is cleared, we'll have the big wedding you've always dreamed of, Hannah. Until then, I, Parker Malone, promise to love, honor and cherish you, Hannah Cassidy, today, tomorrow, and always."

A tear brimmed in Hannah's eyes, then slowly trailed down her face. Holding Parker's gaze, she whispered, "I, Hannah Cassidy, promise to love, honor and cherish you, Parker Malone, today, tomorrow and always."

A camera flashed. And the unofficial Lone Star Wedding was captured on film.

*   *   *   *   *

Here's a preview of next month's

*Mercenary Quinn McCoy rescues
a stranded Fortune heiress in*

IN THE ARMS OF A HERO
by
Beverly Barton

Victoria.

The voice that spoke her name was deep and dark and decidedly American. She whipped around and came face-to-face with the stranger. Sucking in her breath, she eased backward and lost her balance. The man reached out and grabbed her shoulders to steady her.

"How do you know my name?" Her heart drummed madly in her ears. Was this man really a mercenary hired by the Nationalists or was he working for the rebels? Did he know who she really was, that her father was Ryan Fortune? If so, perhaps he was here to kidnap her.

"Don't look so worried—" he lowered his voice to a whisper as he leaned over and placed his mouth near her ear "—Ms. Fortune."

She gasped, then tried to pull out of his captive hold. "Who are you?"

"Quinn McCoy, mercenary, pilot, bodyguard. At your service, ma'am."

Victoria clenched her teeth. She didn't like that decided twinkle in his eye, as if he were playing a game with her and enjoying himself immensely. "I don't know what you have in mind, Mr. McCoy, but I can assure you that all I have to do is scream and a dozen men will come to my aid immediately."

"By all means, don't scream." A barely concealed chuckle underlaid his words.

"Then let go of me!" The moment she renewed her struggle, he released her.

Ernesto came up beside Victoria, taking a stance as her protector. "Is something wrong, Señorita Lockhart?"

Before she could reply, Quinn McCoy said, "Using your mother's maiden name as a ruse? Not a bad idea. But even a fake name won't protect you for very long, once the rebels take over Palmira."

"How—how did you know that Lockhart... Just who are you, Mr. McCoy, and what are you doing here in Santo Bonisto?"

"I've told you who I am. And as for what I'm doing in Santo Bonisto...I was hired to come here to—"

"By whom?" Her heart lodged in her throat. She had the oddest notion that she knew who Mr. McCoy's employer was.

"Your father," he told her, locking his gaze with hers. "He sent me to get you out of the country and bring you home to Texas."

"My father! I should have known." Placing her hands on her hips, Victoria glowered at her *rescuer.* "You can leave right now—and without me. Go back to Texas and tell my father that I'm needed here."

"I'm afraid you don't understand," Quinn said. "What you want or don't want doesn't enter into this equation. You're leaving with me today, before the rebel troops take over Palmira."

"That's where you're wrong. I'm not going anywhere. These people have no doctor. I'm the only trained medical staff here at the clinic. Now, with the war raging so close and all these wounded men being brought in, I can't possibly leave."

"Look, princess—" When Quinn took a step toward her, Ernesto blocked his path. "We can do this the easy way or the hard way. It's up to you. But one way or the other, you're coming with me. Today!''

"Then it's going to be the hard way," she told him, peering at him from around Ernesto's shoulder.

"Damn," Quinn mumbled under his breath. "I was afraid of that.''

SPECIAL EDITION

Stories of love and life, these powerful novels are tales that you can identify with—romances with "something special" added in!

Fall in love with the stories of authors such as **Nora Roberts, Diana Palmer, Ginna Gray** and many more of your special favorites—as well as wonderful new voices!

Special Edition brings you entertainment for the heart!

SILHOUETTE®

Desire®

Do you want...

Dangerously handsome heroes

Evocative, everlasting love stories

Sizzling and tantalizing sensuality

Incredibly sexy miniseries like **MAN OF THE MONTH**

Red-hot romance

Enticing entertainment that can't be beat!

You'll find all of this, and much *more* each and every month in **SILHOUETTE DESIRE**. Don't miss these unforgettable love stories by some of romance's hottest authors. Silhouette Desire—where your fantasies will always come true....

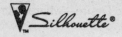

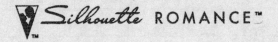

What's a single dad to do when he needs a wife by next Thursday?

Who's a confirmed bachelor to call when he finds a baby on his doorstep?

How does a plain Jane in love with her gorgeous boss get him to notice her?

From classic love stories to romantic comedies to emotional heart tuggers, **Silhouette Romance** offers six irresistible novels every month by some of your favorite authors! Such as...beloved bestsellers **Diana Palmer, Annette Broadrick, Suzanne Carey, Elizabeth August** and **Marie Ferrarella,** to name just a few—and some sure to become favorites!

Fabulous Fathers...Bundles of Joy...Miniseries... Months of blushing brides and convenient weddings... Holiday celebrations... You'll find all this and much more in **Silhouette Romance**—always emotional, always enjoyable, always about love!